Losing A Friend

by

Gary L Beer

All characters in this novel are a work of fiction,
any similarity to any persons living or dead, or yet
to be is unintentional and purely coincidental

ISBN: 9798451317334
© Copyright 2021
All Rights Reserved

Cover photo; The island of my birth showing
the white houses

Chapter One

This is a people planet,
and people can change.
The effect of that change can
be how we treat one another.

It feels good to be back. Seventeen eventual years have passed since I have gazed across the calm waters of the Great Northern Sea to the island of my birth. The painted white house's show clearly at its eastern end and I will visit soon when spring returns, but now I have to get settled into my new accommodation and I have so much unpacking to do as I only moved in today.

I hate my precious possessions to be shut away in boxes and bags. But first, I thought that I would steal five minutes to go onto the beach and look out across the still water and gather my thoughts. This late in the season there are few visitors to this seaside resort and most that walk along the ancient promenade appear to be locals, either walking the dog or just taking a casual stroll. Some of the people entertain their children on the small area of sandy beach that still exists amongst the pebbles and I can hear the children laugh and scream in excitement. Thoughts of unpacking and getting my life organized start to fill my head and with a sigh I turn away. Crossing the wide road that runs alongside the promenade I hurry up the steep steps counting each one as I ascend. Reaching the top and number fifty-two, I stand still to catch my breath and look up at the front windows of my lodgings. They look dirty and will need cleaning as will the balcony, but not today.

A dog barks as I run across the road and I see a small white haired terrier wagging its tail as it barks defiance at me from the window of the ground apartment. I hope the little dog does not yap at every passerby as I had just moved away from a barking dog and have been looking forward to a bit of peace and quiet for years.

I had viewed the accommodation three times over a period of several weeks before I decided to take it and on each visit all I had heard was peace and quiet. The exterior walls of the building are over twelve inches thick and the internal walls are as solidly built. The building is a large block of three houses, comprising large basements and five floors. It was built several centuries ago when this seaside town was created for the sole purpose of the holidaying rich and became very popular.

The building has been sturdily built to last for hundreds, if not thousands of years. The main front door is seven feet high and three feet six inches wide and made of a solid heavy wood that is appropriately painted gloss black on the outside. Opening the large front door I step into the castled porch way and shutting the door behind me continue into the hall. All is quiet and I climb the two flights of stairs up to my lodgings. My door is on the first landing which is brightly lit by an adjacent large sash window that is eight feet high and four feet wide. The window overlooks the narrow street below and also the beach and lifting my gaze I look once again at the sea and the ancient pier which is barely holding its own. Almost destroyed in a big storm over seventy years ago the pier now only stretches into the sea about half a mile. The end of the old pier still remains and can easily be seen about a mile and a half away as everything in between has been washed away.

Movement below me catches my eye as a male dog walker and scruffy little mongrel hurry towards the beach. With a reluctant sigh I turn away from the window and reaching into my pocket for the keys I unlock my front door and let myself in.

Stepping through the small hall I open the lounge door and look at the boxes and bags that need unpacking. I already feel tired from the move and the hectic weeks that have gone before – ahh, the joy of moving.

The rest of the building is as sturdily built with solid heavy doors, large rooms and high ceilings that portray an amazing atmosphere. Memories of the past appear to linger in the air and I imagine many of the people from centuries ago dressed in their finery looking out of the front windows at the sea below, just like I am doing now. The thoughts of the past, which appear more joyful, fill me with enthusiasm and I start to unpack my belongings.

Recovering from the move several days later I explore the town and seafront. Much has changed in the town in the years I have been away with mostly new shops taking the place of the old. The Banks are still in the same places, as is the greengrocers. Charity shops replace the newsagents, the jewelers and the craft shops. Where the butchers' shop used to be a modern café now serves tea and coffee and pie and chips. The main street itself is different. Where cracked tarmac and wobbly pavements used to be there is now red ornamental bricks and small ornamental gardens which all look clean and new.

Taking familiar narrow side streets (that still have the tarmac and wobbly pavements) to the seafront, memories of times gone by make me smile and it is good to see that not all has changed. The same hotels line the promenade, set back from the main road they boast cut lawns and exotic plants and look as prosperous as when I was here last. The promenade has had a total facelift and is built of new concrete, along with ordered gardens that portray a futuristic appearance in being clean and new.

Closed circuit cameras are everywhere; in the clock tower, the seafront bars and cafés and even on the walls of buildings. I do not stay long and keep walking as even though I am doing no wrong I hate to be watched, and by all appearances by so many. The walk along the promenade to my new home feels good as it feels like I am on holiday and I realize that this can now be a permanent feeling. Living so close to the beach is also a blessing as it will only take me a few minutes to reach the sea and I imagine myself walking across the mudflats when the tide is out.

Closing my front door on this strange new world of security cameras and watching eyes is a relief. I had not noticed that there were so many security cameras when I had visited the town before on my visits to my new apartment. But, admittedly, time had been short on each occasion as I remember. Coming from the countryside where there are no security cameras to watch your every move made me only look for wildlife and the seasonal changing of the flora and not to look for every spy eye that is invading my privacy. I hope that the cameras are not going to be too much of a problem to me and spoil my enjoyment of what this delightful town has to offer.

I realize that life and the town has changed, some of the places are the same but it is now a different town that has replaced the one of my memories.

Chapter Two

The ringing of my mobile telephone interrupts my thoughts and I look in its direction where it sits on the coffee table. Walking across the room I instinctively reach out for the phone, accept the call and put it to my ear; "Hello" I say in a gruff voice as I have never felt comfortable using a mobile telephone. "Patrick!" says a happy familiar voice.

I had been tempted not to answer the ringing of the telephone but on hearing Debbie's voice I am so glad that I did. My mind races back to the first time we had seen each other and I guess it to be about twenty-eight years ago now. We were both working at a shop that sold outdoor clothing, especially rubber and plastic rainwear. In my innocence I had not seen anything unusual in the clothes that we sold, but had noticed the high amount of rubber and plastic clothing we were selling even in the dry summer months.

This had appeared odd to me, especially when the sun was shining, but Debbie had always encouraged me by saying I had a nice easy going manner and that I was to serve the younger customers; especially those who appeared very nervous and shy. I was always glad to help and there were many who appeared to lack confidence and would ask whether the materials softness would last and was it easily washable. Being a salesman and not realizing that rubber fetishes existed I would of course reply that the material was of the highest quality and would last for many years. Rarely did I fail in making a sale and as each sale was on a bonus system I made good money.

Debbie, being my manager, was delighted with me each time I made a sale and this did puzzle me. Her enthusiasm did not appear false as each time I made a sale (and a high bonus that would cost her money) she would go out of her way to praise me and encourage me to sell more. I could only assume that being a business partner in the company had a lot more going for it than being a good salesman. I had thought that maybe her salary was so high that she did not need the extra money; not realizing and being naïve at the time that each sale I made was putting more money into her pocket - as well as her silent business partner.

We had become firm friends after only a few short weeks and I had thought that here, finally, was a job that I could enjoy. The variety of customers who came into the shop made each day different and often funny and Debbie had never taken advantage of my innocence in anyway and I made good money and was definitely happy.

But life changes, many times beyond our control and when the shop closed and started to sell only online I found myself joining the many unemployed.

"Debbie? Is that really you?" I exclaim and ask stupidly.

"Of course it is. How are you?" she replies in an impatient voice.

"I'm fine thanks and that is strange, you phoning, I was thinking about you the other day as it has been so long and I was wondering what had happened to you."

"I am keeping busy as always. Hey, it sure is good to hear your voice again."

"And yours." I reply hastily; "how long has it been? Must be about five years since we last saw each other and you sound very happy, I hope life is being kind to you?"

We had been very close when we worked at the shop. Debbie had been married at the time and had always appeared happy and content. I knew I had deep feelings for her and had regarded her as a part of my family; and still do.

The past twenty- eight years had not been a lot of fun for me. Debbie had gone to university learning physics and formed new friendships and we drifted apart and the sparkle went out of my life. We still did meet occasionally but life itself became mundane and boring. I found that most other people I came into contact with were either after my money or were those who could not live life on their own and anyone would do to spare them the loneliness they suffered.

"Yes I am happy." Debbie replied and I could imagine her smile; "Now that I have managed to contact you again. Would you like to go fossil hunting with me at the weekend?" she asks as my heart fills with unbelievable joy.

"Yes of course I would, and anyway I want to see what you look like after all this time." I answer with a laugh; "That is if I am not too tired, I have only just moved in and I am back in the old town where I used to live."

"Glad to hear it. When did you move in?"

"Only a few days ago and I still have loads of unpacking to do."

"That is strange," Debbie replies; "That must be why you have been on my mind lately."

"Moving is such hard work as you may remember? Enough about me as it is wonderful to hear your voice again."

Debbie's career had grown along with her new knowledge of physics and of matters which few of us can understand. She had also grown in confidence and found an independence that her husband had abhorred. Debbie's marriage hit difficult times and eventually failed. It had been about ten years since her divorce and the strength of her character had grown as she travelled the world going from country to country teaching at schools and universities. Debbie had appeared to be enjoying herself though she had become more serious and then suddenly she packed it all in for reasons only known to her and took up further training and became a nurse at her local hospital. The career change did her a lot of good in retaining her cheerful outlook and also giving her a worthwhile purpose in life in helping others.

Debbie replies in a serious voice as if she has just made a business appointment; "I have not changed that much, well I don't think so. It would be good to see you too Patrick and to see if your hair has turned gray and if you have any added wrinkles. I am still at the same place and a good time to come round would be this coming Friday about eleven o'clock and then we will leave straight away, if that is ok with you?"

"Sounds good, yes I will see you then." I eagerly reply.

"I will be ready." She laughs and stays silent for a few seconds; "Tell me honestly Patrick, have you missed me?"

"With every bullet so far." I reply with as serious a voice as I can muster.

Debbie laughs; "I will see you then and I'll make you a special soup."

"Would you be offended if I brought my own, just in case?" I had experienced Debbie's homemade soup many years before and could still remember the stomach pains.

"Don't worry I won't poison you, well not until Saturday." she replies in a soft voice.

"I thought you said the weekend; but you did say Friday?" I ask with a nervous laugh.

"I thought that you might like to make a long weekend of it and spend a couple of nights here and then drive back late on Sunday." Debbie answers in a softer voice.

This is unusual as there had never been any sex or romance between us, only the occasional hug. An invite to sleep over was a first and I wonder if she has an ulterior motive; "As long as you promise to behave." I answer uneasily.

"I promise to be good. Don't worry," she laughs in reply.

"I am not so sure about that answer." I say sternly; "See you Friday then, bye." I reply in a gentler voice as I disconnect the call.

Hearing from Debbie has lifted my heart and life once again appears a happy place. Old feelings resurface and I remember how much fun and laughs we had when we were together. That our spirits joined would be more of a way of putting it and the feelings that we shared could by many, be interpreted as a kind of love. But to me it was always a deep friendship of that I am sure. We were similar in our thoughts and how we saw life, and this in itself creates a bond.

Whether Debbie felt the same way about me as I did about her was never spoken. This somehow had made our friendship stronger and purer and we had always known that at least we could depend on each other in times of crisis. That she had something in mind appeared obvious and as today was Wednesday I had only two more days to wait before my multitudes of questions would be answered and already I was impatient to see her again.

The next two days dragged, even though I had so much unpacking and it seemed more like two weeks had passed before Friday finally arrives. I showered and shaved and prepared my walking boots, a few sandwiches and a bottle of spring water ready all packed neatly into a large lightweight rucksack. Leaving early to allow for traffic and any delays, I take the next sixty miles at a steady rate and arrive outside Debbie's house twenty minutes early. I park and quickly lock my car and walk along her front path that is lined with lavender bushes, creating the most pleasant aroma and knock loudly on the front door.

No answer!

I knock again and there is still no answer so I take my mobile phone out of my pocket and dial her house number. I can clearly hear her telephone ringing and after a few rings I disconnect the call. Going back to my car I unlock it, get inside and decide to wait. The side road she lives in is busy with people walking to and fro the town which is at the end of the road about five hundred yards away. Sitting in my car I feel self conscious as *everyone* who walks past looks and stares in at me as if I was a burglar or alien monster from outer space. After fifteen minutes impatient waiting I decide to join the throngs of people heading for the town. The town centre will be familiar to me and I can remember the river that flows through the town to the sea.

Quickly getting out of my car I lock the door and make my way to the town at a brisk walk. Eager to see the river again I ignore the shops I pass and soon reach the riverbank. The slow flowing water is crystal clear with a healthy growth of weed on the river bed and also floating on top of the water. White flowers bloom everywhere on the floating weed as a pair of mallards swim slowly past. The river is severely restricted by concrete walls and there are few places to sit and rest and enjoy the river. Walking slowly along the brick and concrete riverbank I begin to see rubbish that has been thrown into the river; plastic bottles, crisp packets, magazines, chip cartons and cardboard cups along with a multitude of other rubbish.

The river no longer looks at all attractive anymore so I walk on hoping to find a secluded place to sit and rest. The river continues its slow pace between the concrete and brick walls and a rusty chain link fencing begins to border the path. The view changes from the backs of houses to the backs of dirty warehouses and larger buildings and in disgust I turn around and retrace my steps.

What a dismal place the river has become.

Turning into a side street that leads to the town I cannot help but notice that the buildings either side of me are dirty and poorly kept. I quicken my pace until I reach the busy main street that has banned all motor vehicles and is decorated with the same red bricks that are used across much of this country's public areas. Most of the shop fronts are brightly painted with happy smiling shoppers looking to buy their wares, with many entering the shops. My sad mood lifts when I see the smiling faces and join them as they walk along the wide pedestrian street. Many of the shops look new and prosperous and I look forward to doing some serious shopping on my next visit.

Reaching Debbie's house thirty minutes later I see that her old car is parked close to mine. Knocking on the door with a bit more optimism I soon hear footsteps coming along the hall.

The door opens to a smiling Debbie; "Patrick!" she exclaims as if I am a total surprise; "Come in," she smiles as she opens the door wide.

As I step past her Debbie reaches out and gives me a big hug and I am so surprised that I am slow in responding but do manage a quick hug back. Looking at her after all these years brings back even stronger how I really feel about her. The friendship is still strong and pure and I know that we will be friends until the end of eternity, wherever we may be.

She looks to have put on about a stone in weight but this accentuates her beauty. Her long blonde hair caresses her angelic face and the extra weight suits her tall frame. Debbie is still a few inches shorter than my lanky six feet two and I find that my face has adopted a permanent smile.

Debbie's smile appears as wide as she says; "It is so good to see you again and my, you do look well. You look even more handsome than the last time I saw you. Go on into the lounge where the fire is; we will have time for a quick cup of coffee before we leave."

"That sounds good, thank you," I answer as I make my way along the long corridor. On entering the lounge I am shocked to see that it is so sparsely furnished. A dining table of waxed pine and two hardback chairs, possibly of oak, stand against one wall. One low cushioned stool and one upright armchair with a thick cushion and red picnic rug crowd the small fireplace. The upright armchair makes it the most comfortable chair in the room and I hold back waiting to be invited to sit down.

"Sit where you like," Debbie says from the doorway and makes her way to the kitchen.

Being a selfish man with a bad back I sit myself onto the armchair and look around at the curious room. Antique pine double doors are set into the wall facing me that lead into the front room. I had visited Debbie many times before, from when we worked at the clothing shop together up until about five years ago and realize I had never been shown the front room; and had never asked. I feel that to see it would have been an intrusion and also feel that maybe it was a room set aside for a family member who had died.

Behind me white plastic double glazed doors lead into the yard and back garden. The yard is fairly clear but the garden is piled high with rubbish and building rubble. Debbie had always talked about converting her large house into several self contained apartments and it looks like her dream is becoming a reality. I look forward to seeing the work that has been done when we get back from our fossil hunting. Several of Debbie's fossil finds are displayed on the mantelpiece and I stand up to look at them. Ammonites in various sizes are arranged in a neat straight line alongside fossilized seashells and a small broken flint arrowhead. Directly in the middle of the mantle is a very old sweet tin, maybe a hundred years old, which had once held lozenges. Now it contains a neatly cut piece of cotton wool with a blackened finger bone set in the centre. The black finger looks gruesome and I quickly look away as Debbie enters the room carrying two mugs of steaming coffee.

"You have been looking at my finger bone. Do you like it?" she asks with a broad smile.

"Yes; where on earth did you get that?" I ask with a weak grin.

"I found that about two months ago and where we are going to in a little while. It is a human forefinger and I took it to the police to see what they thought about it. I took that broken arrowhead with me as I found that about two feet away from the finger at the same time. The police were amazed and confirmed it was a human finger and one of their experts said that it was possibly Neolithic. The arrowhead clinched it really as it is of an early Neolithic design which later became improved on."

I feel a small pang of jealousy as I reply; "I am impressed as I would love to find something like that, even though it does look a bit gruesome."

"That black coloring has been caused by the soil that it had lain in for all those thousands of years and it is actually turning into a fossil."

"Wow" is all I can think of saying until I look further along the mantle; "I see your ammonite collection is increasing, and they are all in excellent condition."

"I went down to the beach area where we are going to a couple of days after we had a big storm. The waves must have been huge as the beach was lower by at least twelve feet compared to what it is in the summer. Anyway enough of talking fossils tell me how you have been. You are looking well and how goes the unpacking?"

"You don't look so bad yourself," I quickly reply; "I may look good and as handsome as the last time we saw each other but it is all on the surface. The truth is life has been a bit of a nightmare; what with a collapsed lung, irritable bowel syndrome and a really bad back and I even had a mild heart attack about six months ago. Apart from that I am fine thanks, still happy and living each day as it comes, and the unpacking is nearly all done. The move has been tiring but it will be all worth it. I changed my diet quite a while back as the irritable bowel was killing me as it hurt so much and it caused me so much stress that I think that was what gave me the heart attack. I am even on filtered or spring water these days and am very careful what I eat and avoid those ready meals and have been a lot better."

Debbie's face loses a bit of its color; "Oh Patrick, are you fit enough to go for this walk? I do not want you collapsing down there as we will be miles from anywhere."

"Of course I am; if I thought I was not fit enough I would not be here. Anyway now I am eating better all my innards appear in good order. I think the heart attack was really down to me not eating as I was too scared to eat and that caused extra stress, if you know what I mean?" I ask with a confident laugh.

"Sadly yes, I have seen a lot of that in the hospital."

"Let's drink these coffees and go get some fresh air," I say eager to change the subject as I pick up the mug of hot coffee, which tastes good.

Chapter Three

An hour and a half later under a blue sky with a few cumulus clouds drifting by, we are walking across a shingle beach towards mudflats that stretch for a short distance before they meet the sea. The mud is firm underfoot and I walk towards a small gulley that I can see that stretches for several hundred yards before merging into the flattened mud.

"Patrick, do not go that way, we are looking for fossils, not cockles."

"It looks good to me, might be the remnants of a Neolithic stream, like the one where you found that finger bone." I reply in an indignant voice, pretending to be hurt.

Debbie laughs; "That mud is only a few thousand years old, we have about a half mile to walk yet before we get to the older layers."

Having a firm interest in conservation, along with an extensive knowledge of geology, Debbie is the ideal fossil hunting partner. Her passion for the history of the land and sea that stretches back millions of years has always amazed me. Knowing how old a rock is or how long a stretch of black mud has lain there obviously helps when looking for fossils.

"Please remember I am an old man and cannot go as fast as you. A gentle stroll would be nice."

"You are not old," she scoffs; "But we cannot go too slow as we have arrived a bit late and the tide will turn in about half an hour."

"Time and tide wait for no man, especially me," I quote; "If I start to slow down you can go on ahead as I can cope on my own."

"I know you can," laughs Debbie; "Patrick, you have not changed a bit."

"What do you mean by that?" I ask, though I know the answer as I have never been able to grow up and be serious too much when we are together.

The walking is easy as the mud remains firm and flat and we soon arrive at a large depression in the mud. Covering an area about the size of a large room the level of the mud is about eight or nine inches below the level of the mudflats.

"Why has this formed and why doesn't it fill up with silt and stuff?" I ask.

"There is silt at the bottom covering a very hard Greensand Rock. The rock probably extends over this whole area and is about one hundred million years old," replies Debbie with a broad smile and continues; "Why this small area is exposed is down to a broken down yacht that anchored here for about a week at the beginning of the summer. The movement of the anchor chain scoured away the top surface as the tides are very strong here, even in the summer. The owner of the yacht thought he was going to get swept out into the channel the last night he was anchored here as we had an unusual storm. He went to the harbor the next day and was more than happy to pay the mooring fees," Debbie smiles at the memory; "Anyway there are some conservationists think that most of this damage was caused that one stormy night and have now managed to get all anchoring of boats along this coast banned."

I look down at the shallow depression and ask hopefully; "Do you think we will find any dinosaur bones here?"

"No one has ever found any along this beach that I know of," Debbie disappointedly replies and seeing the disappointment on my face continues hurriedly; "But we should find plenty of ammonites, mollusks and fossilized reptile and fish bones; maybe even a whole fish skeleton." Sweeping her arm over the area including the exposed mud and low cliffs that border the shingle beach she continues with real excitement in her voice; "This whole area used to be an ancient sea in the cretaceous time, about one hundred and forty million years ago. The hard rock you can see is compressed sand and is called Greensand Rock. The clay that makes up the cliffs is the sediment and there are a lot of ammonites in there but they are very fragile. The sea was called The Gault Sea and the clay is named after it and it is described as Gault Clay."

"Lucky I brought you along," I laugh; "Is that all you know?" I ask trying to keep the envy out of my voice.

"I do not know much more" Debbie admits; "Other than where we are standing now when The Gault Sea was here we would have been about where The Mediterranean Sea is now."

"Wow" I say with excitement in my voice.

Debbie looks hard at me and detecting no sarcasm waves me forward towards the depression in the mud; "Come on, we have not got a lot of time as the tide has turned. My guess is we have about an hour before this is all under water."

I hurry forward and join her in the small depression; "What are we looking for here?"

"Mainly ammonites which have been washed out of the cliff onto the rock and then get covered in silt. As you can see we are lucky as the silt is only about two inches thick, so we should find plenty."

I keep it to myself that we have suddenly gone down from finding reptile and fish bones or mollusks and fossilized reptiles down to just ammonites. The silt is thick and compact and I scan the surface with my eyes looking for anything out of the ordinary. The regular pattern of a small ammonite catches my eye and I bend down to pick it up. The fossilized ammonite shell is only the centre of a much larger shell that has broken up under the beating of the waves but I do not mind and cannot help but exclaim in a loud triumphant voice; "Hooray, I got one."

"Show me," demands Debbie.

"Find your own," I reply holding the ammonite tightly in my hand.

"I will," she replies with a laugh as she bends down and suddenly shouts in a louder voice; "So have I, you can look at mine, I don't mind," she says holding her hand out towards me.

I can see that the one she holds is twice the size of the one I have; "Don't want to," I pout as I reach into my pocket for a plastic bag Debbie had supplied earlier. Opening the bag quickly I put my ammonite inside; "We will have a look at each other's at the end as we have not got the time now," I say, suddenly an expert on tides and time.

Debbie had watched me put my small ammonite in the bag and laughs; "Ok Patrick, maybe you will find a larger one."

"Maybe is a definite. By the way Debbie, I have been thinking about dinosaurs and a lot of archaeologists are forming the opinion that dinosaurs had feathers and that birds are the descendants of dinosaurs."

"Yes, so they say," Debbie agrees; "So, what have you been thinking then Patrick?"

"Well, after all these hundreds of millions of years of evolution all they have achieved is to become a bird that has adapted to its environment and can fly. Well …. is that it?"

Debbie laughs, straightening up from her crouched position she looks me in the eye with a puzzled expression on her face. Her eyes suddenly glint in the afternoon sunshine as she suddenly laughs again; "You know there is more to it than that," she states in a disapproving voice, as if it was a stupid question, though her laughter continues.

"Well, we humans are different from evolution, but from the point of the bird, say a seagull, its evolutionary path has led it to be half starved all the time. If you have ever tried to eat a bag of chips or an ice cream on the seafront you get mobbed by the seagulls as they are so hungry, even starving. That applies to a lot of wild creatures really; like fish and wolves and maggots. They appear to be always starving hungry!" I reply, joining in the laughter.

Bending down Debbie picks up something from the mud and looks at it closely. I can see that whatever it is it is about the size of a tennis ball; "What have you found Debbie – a dinosaur eyeball?"

Debbie raises her gaze and looking me in the eyes smiles triumphantly; "A good ammonite." Turning her gaze to the sea she says;" We have not got much time, I'll show you later, maybe you will find even better," she challenges.

I immediately stoop down and search the mud and silt and bending forward I can see the outline of an ammonite, smaller than the one Debbie has just found but worth picking up.

Sitting on the beach later we look at each other's finds, which are all ammonites. The electric blue color of I assume, the mother of pearl that lines the inside of the ammonite, has me bewitched. Imagining The Gault Sea as it was all those millions of years ago, filled with ammonites and ancient fish, and especially the clean air makes me wish to have existed back then. Life would have been much harder then admittedly, but it holds a certain magic that comes with leading a simpler life.

"You look lost in thought Patrick; dreaming of The Gault Sea?"

"Yes, how did you guess?"

Debbie laughs; "Easy really; especially when I do it myself."

"Are you going to take me to where you found the Neolithic finger bone and arrowhead now?" I ask impatiently.

"It is getting a bit late for that now as there is already a chill in the air as you have probably noticed. It won't be long before it will be getting dark," she replies looking up at the sky as she zips her jacket up to her neck.

I find it hard not to show my disappointment but agree it is getting colder and acknowledge that this time of year the days are a lot shorter than in the summer time. We walk slowly back to the beach and eat our sandwiches as the sea quickly covers the mud and is soon lapping against the pebbles of the beach.

Looking at the cliffs we find little to interest us and with the cold wind starting to blow stronger we agree to go back to a warmer place, being Debbie's home.

With the wood burner giving off almost immediate heat Debbie's living room soon warms up. The pepperoni pizza we got from the Take Away is sitting comfortably in my stomach and the tired feeling you get from visiting a sunny, windy beach fills my head and body. Closing my eyes I drift off to sleep.

Dreaming of The Gault Sea the noise of a crackling log makes me jump and brings me back to the present day. Debbie looks as tired, though she appears to have a lot more energy than me as she opens the wood burner door and puts on another log.

"Do you want to sit here?" I ask as I am sitting in the comfortable armchair again.

"No, I am happy here thanks, on the stool. We will go tomorrow where I found the finger bone, if the weather is fine," she replies as she reaches for her laptop. Switching it on she waits for it to warm up, then checks on tomorrow's weather; "Bit like today really with the wind not as strong," Debbie says with a smile; "We'll leave a bit earlier tomorrow at about ten in the morning. That is if you are up for that?"

"Sounds good to me," I reply in a tired but happy voice as I drift off to sleep again.

"Patrick, wake up." I hear Debbie say and open my eyes.

Debbie is standing in front of me with a patient smile on her face.

I stretch and rub my eyes; "What time is it?"

"It is nearly eleven. Do you want me to show you where you are going to sleep?"

I open my eyes wider; "Eleven? Oh no, I am so sorry, I have slept the entire evening, how boring for you."

Debbie's smile broadens; "To be honest Pat, I have been asleep too. Now, do you want me to show you where you are going to sleep, or are you staying there?"

I get to my feet and notice that the fire has died down; "Yes, please. I am really sorry it must have been all that fresh air and we did walk a fair way."

"Stop apologizing, I expect that it is the move to a new apartment that has taken it out of you. Follow me and I will show you your room."

I obediently follow Debbie out of the door and up the stairs. Taking me to the back of the house she leads the way to the spare bedroom; "You will be comfortable in here," she says as she opens the door.

The spare bedroom is comfortably furnished with a modern wardrobe and matching chest of drawers. There is a small white finished portable television on a small stand. The remote control is on a bedside cabinet that also has a kettle, cup and milk jug and sugar placed neatly on it.

"This is great, thank you," I say in real appreciation: "I hope that I can sleep as I have spent the entire evening sleeping."

"Don't have the television on too loud," Debbie orders; "See you in the morning."

"Yes, good night," I reply as Debbie walks out of the room and quietly shuts the door.

I feel embarrassed for falling asleep and get undressed and get into bed. Having forgotten to turn the main light off I turn on the bedside lamp and get out of bed and turn off the light. Not so sure that I will sleep the entire night I get back into bed and turn the bedside lamp off. My head fills again with happy thoughts of the Gault Sea and I am soon asleep.

Chapter Four

I awake in darkness and can see by the luminous hands of the clock it is either twenty minutes past midnight or it is four in the morning. I lay in the bed cursing my earlier weakness for falling asleep in the evening. Looking at the clock more closely I can see that it is four in the morning and resign myself to be laying awake until daylight.

I lie there quietly and realize that I can hear noises coming from downstairs. That must have been what awoke me as the noises are quite loud. There is a lot of banging about and (I presume) it is Debbie who must be tidying or cleaning. She is not being very considerate and I decide to go and see what she is doing.

I get out of bed and quietly get dressed and go downstairs without turning on any lights as I intend to surprise her and maybe make her 'jump'. Standing outside the lounge door the noises continue and I notice that only a feeble light is shining through the gap in the bottom of the door. Opening it as quietly as I can I peer in and see that it is someone shining a torch and they are throwing Debbie's ornaments into a cardboard box that it is on the floor.

It is not Debbie – it is a burglar!

"What the bloody hell do you think you are doing?" I roar in my loudest, deepest voice.

The burglar, a scruffy individual aged in his mid twenties looks at me in alarm. Shining the torch into my eyes I see the light obscure quickly as he throws Debbie's Neolithic finger bone in its tin at me.

I try to duck out of the way but the tin hits me in my right cheek and I step quickly into the room with fists upraised and then run towards him; "You fucking bastard," I yell as I take a wild swing at his head.

The burglar steps back into the small pile of logs stacked near the fire to try and avoid my blow and my fist gets him in his left eye. Swinging with my left I hit him in the jaw before he can regain his balance and take another swing with my right as he ducks down and my fist hits him painfully on the top of his head.

"Arghh," he yells and moves quickly to his left aiming a punch at my face and his fist hits me in the side of the face as he kicks out with his right foot, getting me in the shins. Moving quickly forward he takes another swing at me and punches me on the forehead and stars explode inside my head and the room goes dark as he drops his torch.

Ducking to one side I kick out at him and kick him somewhere on one of his legs and lash out blindly with my fists. Several punches connect with his face as my vision clears as he suddenly runs at me and shoves me to one side. I take several steps backwards and collide into the armchair as the burglar makes a run for the lounge door. Swinging it open wide I hear him run into the kitchen as I try to regain my balance and run after him. The back door crashes into the internal wall as he throws it open and I reach the kitchen and see him run into the back garden.

Following him quickly I run into the back garden as I see him jump up onto the garden wall and disappear into the street. I run to the back gate and pull it open to see his shadowy figure running away into the darkness.

"Patrick," Debbie yells from somewhere inside the house; "What the fuck is going on?" she shouts, her voice appearing even louder as she appears in the kitchen doorway.

"Burglar," I gasp, trying to regain my breath; "run off down the road."

"Are you alright – did you have a fight with him? I could not believe the racket you were making." Debbie continues to shout.

I manage a sarcastic laugh as I walk towards her; "And I thought it was you."

"Me – what are you talking about?" she asks in a quieter voice, though she still sounds loud in the quiet of the night.

"He was making a lot of noise, woke me up. I thought it was you making a lot of racket."

"What would I be doing making a lot of noise at four o'clock in the morning? Really Patrick, you are the limit sometimes!" Debbie snaps - then asks looking concerned; "Are you alright?"

"I got a few bruises, but I think I am ok." I reply, suddenly feeling very tired.

"Come in and let me look at you," Debbie says as she steps back into the kitchen and turns on the light.

I follow her into the kitchen and walk over to the sink. Turning on the cold water tap I pick up a mug that Debbie had served me coffee with in the evening and throw the dregs into the sink. Not bothering to clean the mug I fill it half full with water from the tap and take a large swig. My mouth feels sore and I can taste blood from where it is obviously bleeding.

"Let me look at you," Debbie orders and I turn to face her.

"Oh Patrick," she exclaims as she takes a hand towel from the rack and puts it under the cold water tap which still has water pouring out. Soaking part of the towel in water she wrings it out and starts to wipe the blood from my face. It hurts and I jerk back; "Leave it out will you," I growl; "I have had enough pain for one night."

Debbie laughs sympathetically; "I have to clean it, you have a nice cut on your face and a few bruises."

"Well, be gentle about it," I plead.

"Sorry, would you like a drink first?" she asks.

"Yeah, a coffee would be nice, please." I reply in a gentler voice.

By way of an answer Debbie walks over to the kettle and seeing that there is still water inside she switches it on. Reaching into the cupboard above the kettle she takes down a clean mug and puts coffee and sugar in. The kettle is about to boil and she quickly turns it off and pours hot water into the mug; "It is not too hot," she says as she stirs it and taking out the spoon she hands the mug to me; "There you are, hero." she says with a broad smile.

I take the mug from her outstretched hand; "Wounded hero," I answer as I lean back against the sink and take a tentative sip of the coffee; which is a bit too hot to drink. My head and face hurt along with my leg and I hope that no permanent damage is done.

"Do you want to go into the lounge and sit down?" Debbie asks sympathetically.

"In a minute, best you clean me up first as I don't want to bleed on your carpet." I reply, suddenly feeling sorry for myself.

"I am not bothered about that, go into the lounge. I will get some antiseptic for that cut."

I walk into the lounge, straighten the armchair where I had been pushed into it and gratefully sit down. Taking another sip of coffee I put the mug down near the fireplace and look around the room. The burglar had not been too neat in his searching for valuables as most of the room is a mess. The cardboard box of his spoils sits in the middle of the room and is nearly full of Debbie's prize possessions, including her laptop. I am glad he did not manage to steal anything, unless he had put some things in his pockets.

Debbie walks into the lounge carrying a bowl of water, towel and bottle of antiseptic; "Let me clean you up Patrick. What were you doing wandering round my house at four in the morning?" she asks in an accusing voice.

"I wasn't," I angrily reply; "I was asleep and the noise he was making woke me up. I have told you that already."

She makes no reply as she puts the bowl of water and bottle of antiseptic on the floor. The accusing look in her eyes gets my back up and I do not say anything. To avoid her eyes I look away and pick up the mug of coffee.

"Put that down," Debbie orders; "let me clean that blood off your face."

Feeling too tired to argue I obediently put the mug down and turn my face towards her, keeping my eyes from her face I direct my gaze to the cardboard box; "I don't think he got anything," I say in as calm a voice as I can muster.

"I will have a look, after I have cleaned you up," Debbie replies as she kneels down on the floor in front of me and gently wipes my face with the still wet towel. Using the warm water in the bowl she wipes away the blood and then dries my face using the dry part of the towel; "That cut will have to have a plaster on it," she says as she gets to her feet; "Do not move, I will go and get one." Still looking at me with an accusing stare she walks out of the lounge and I hear her go back into the kitchen.

Returning a few minutes later with a first aid box Debbie once again kneels down in front of me. Opening the first aid box she rummages through the contents; "It has been a long time since I used this," she says, referring to the first aid box; "I hope the plasters are ok."

I make no reply as she takes out a large, hygienically wrapped plaster and a bag of cotton wool; "This looks to be the only size of plaster I have," she says with a laugh.

The plaster is big and will probably cover half of my face and I have to object; "That is a bit big Debbie, can you cut it in half or something?"

"Maybe," she replies and then sighs as if it is all too much trouble; "I will have to go and find some scissors," she tells me in an irritated voice.

"If you wouldn't mind, please," I say in almost a whisper.

The look of concern returns to her eyes as she asks; "Are you sure you are alright?"

"Yes, I am ok. Do you want me to go and get the scissors?"

The look of concern changes to one of puzzlement; "No, I will get them, you stay there," she says as she turns away and walks out of the lounge.

I can understand her being upset with having a burglar in the house but feel angry with her for apparently taking it out on me. If it wasn't for me she would have lost a lot of her stuff. Debbie breaks my train of thought as she returns carrying a large pair of kitchen scissors; "These will have to do, I cannot find anything smaller," she tells me as she picks up the large plaster and tears open the paper seal. Looking at the cut on my face she cuts the plaster in half which makes the cotton padding show on one side; "Will that be alright for you?" she asks in an apparently bored voice.

"Yes, thank you, that will be fine," I answer, matching her tone.

The look of puzzlement returns to her face as she puts the plaster down on the first aid box and takes out some cotton wool. Opening the bottle of antiseptic she soaks the cotton wool and bends forward and roughly wipes the cut on my face.

I make no comment and sit patiently as she applies the plaster. Pushing it firmly on my face she gives a wry smile; "There, that should do it," she says triumphantly. Putting the lid back on the bottle of antiseptic Debbie asks; "Have you anymore cuts?"

"No, well I don't think so. Thank you."

Nodding her head Debbie picks up the first aid box, scissors and towel and starts to walk towards the door. Turning to look back at me she asks; "Can you bring the bowl of water out please?"

"Of course," I reply as I pick up the bowl and get to my feet and follow her slowly out into the kitchen.

"I think everything is still here," Debbie says as she empties the cardboard box; "No, wait a minute. Where is my finger bone and tin?"

"I think it is over there," I reply, pointing to the far wall.

Debbie turns and looks in the direction that I am pointing. Seeing the tin and spilt cotton wool she asks angrily; "How did it get over there?"

"The burglar threw it at me, that was how my face got cut," I reply.

"What – that tin cut your face?" Debbie asks sarcastically.

"Not the tin, the finger I guess," I answer in a bored voice.

"Well, where is the finger?" she snaps.

"Must be over there somewhere," I reply as I look away and pick up the remains of the coffee. Only a little remains in the bottom of the mug and which I give my full attention as I feel my anger rising, once again.

Debbie walks over and picks up the tin and cotton wool. Looking around she sees the finger bone about six feet away; "How did it get all the way over there?" she asks in agitation as she walks over and picks it up.

"Bounced off my face, I expect. Is it alright?" I ask, feigning concern.

She looks closely at the finger and places it gently on the cotton wool and puts it back in the tin; "Yes, it looks ok," she replies as she walks over and puts it back onto the mantelpiece.

"Is there anything missing?" I ask in the same concerned voice.

Debbie looks around the room; "No, well not that I can see," An angry look suddenly appears in her eyes; "The next time you hear a burglar in my house, you let me know."

Trying to keep the sarcasm out of my voice I stare into her eyes; "As I told you before, I thought it was you down here. How do you think he managed to get in?"

"I don't know, maybe he forced the back door open," she replies breaking my gaze as she looks in the direction of the back door.

"You left it unlocked," I accuse.

Staring back at me with the angry glint still in her eyes she says with clenched teeth; "I locked it."

Still staring into her eyes I can see that she is lying; "Well if there is a next time, I will bang on your door," I answer, failing to keep the sarcasm out of my voice.

Debbie's cheeks suddenly flush red and I feel an unexpected fear in my stomach as I realize I may have gone too far – and I also realize that this is one dangerous lady.

"I am going to make a coffee. Do you want another one?" she asks as she starts to walk out of the lounge.

"Yes, please," I reply to her departing back.

Debbie makes a lot of noise as she prepares the coffee, banging the mugs down onto the worktop and slamming the cupboard doors. Suddenly I feel trapped and glad that we are not in any kind of a relationship – and even happier that we are not married.

Several minutes later Debbie comes back into the lounge carrying two steaming mugs of coffee. Handing me one she asks in a voice that is now under control; "Do you still want to go and see if we can find anymore Neolithic fingers or other evidence?"

I cannot keep the surprise out of my voice; "Yes, but only if you want to. Don't you want to call the police? I expect you will be worried about getting burgled all the time we will be out there."

"No I do not want to call the police, it is a bit late for that now and I guess that I will have to get used to that feeling," she replies as she sits down on her stool.

"I notice that you do have door bolts on the back door and you have two locks on your front door, that should keep anyone out," I answer, hoping to reassure her.

"I will have to find the other key," she replies as her brow wrinkles in thought. Suddenly she gets to her feet and hurries out of the lounge and up the stairs. I hear her bedroom door slam and a few seconds later hear it open and slam again as Debbie comes back down the stairs. Stamping her way to the front door I hear her open it and noisily try the mortise lock, operating it a few times. Slamming the door shut she locks it again and comes triumphantly back into the lounge; "I just need to put it on my key ring," she says as she takes her keys down from a small shelf and puts a large key onto the ring; "Now let's see them try to get in," she laughs triumphantly and sits back down and picks up her coffee.

After coffee Debbie asks me to help her make sandwiches for our day out and we prepare an assortment of ham, lettuce and strawberry jam sandwiches and pack them into our rucksacks. Bottled spring water is the only liquid we take and Debbie suggests we stop at a café somewhere on the way back. I am in total agreement and soon impatient to leave.

Debbie still appears to be in a dark mood and I speak only when spoken to and hope her mood lightens soon or it will make it a difficult day. It is not long before I impatiently wait for Debbie to get dressed into suitable clothing and unable to wait indoors for her I tell her I will meet her outside and will wait by her car.

I decide to say nothing about locking and securing the back door.

Chapter Five

The drive to the Neolithic site is spent in silence as I let Debbie concentrate on her driving. The weather is not as good as yesterday with an overcast sky and occasional drizzle, yet the weather report had been for fine weather and I can only hope that the skies will clear. The window wipers are monotonous in there regularity at times and I hope the rain does not spoil our day.

The Neolithic site is about five miles further along the coast and several miles inland than where we went yesterday, Debbie tells me, when we are sitting waiting in traffic. They are the first words she has spoken since leaving her house, which is maybe a sign that her dark mood is finally lifting.

The rain stops, almost on cue as she turns off the coastal road into a narrow country lane and drives inland to a hilly area. Due to the steep hills, farming of any fruit or vegetable crops is almost impossible and we exit the car to the sound of sheep bahhing all around us.

After locking the car Debbie leads the way over a stile and across a field and down one of the hills to a steep valley. Turning to face me she smiles in obvious anticipation; "This had a stream running through it back in Neolithic times and was obviously a good place for hunting and fishing," she tells me, her bad mood now just a memory.

I smile back and try to imagine what this area would have been like all those thousands of years ago. There are only a few low bushes here now in what must have been a wooded area before man cut all the trees down. With no significant root system to hold onto the rainwater the water from the surrounding hills soon drains away making the valley more suitable for grass and ideal for the grazing sheep.

"Where you found the finger bone and arrowhead, do you think that was a Neolithic camp site," I ask, trying to imagine the hunters sitting round a campfire.

"That is certainly possible," she confirms as she looks along the valley; "This way," she says as she starts to walk further inland along the bottom of the valley.

I eagerly follow her fast pace and after several hundred yards Debbie stops and looks around and turns back to look at me; "It was around here, Patrick," she says, excitement filling her voice.

"Where exactly?" I ask.

Debbie smiles knowingly but does not give anything away and waves her arm around to cover the area; "Around here I found them. Look for any disturbance, especially near rabbit burrows and at these flattened areas where there might have been a small hut or fire. But don't go digging," she warns.

"Why no digging?" I ask, not understanding why not.

"The farmer will throw us off for causing damage if he sees us, but really we should find clues on the surface; and then maybe we can do a little digging."

I try to think like a Neanderthal hunter and try to imagine deer grazing amongst the now, non-existent trees and fish swimming in the now, non-existent stream.

Looking intently at the ground Debbie starts to wander alongside the valley bottom. Not wanting to crowd her I decide to walk in the opposite direction, but keep just off the valley bottom as Debbie is doing. Sheep and rabbit droppings litter the short grass and I look for the rabbit burrows, hoping that they may have dug up some arrowheads whilst digging their homes.

About fifty yards further along I come across evidence of rabbit activity. Small depressions have been dug in the ground where the rabbits have dug down for edible roots, but I see nothing resembling anything Neolithic. Looking up one of the slopes I can see several rabbit holes with piles of freshly dug earth at some of the entrances. Hoping my luck will change I walk up and search the freshly dug earth. Not seeing anything on the surface I get down on my knees and using my hands dig through the loose soil but have no luck, except for a few odd pieces of flint and several flint flakes.

The bigger pieces of flint just look like stones to me as I can see they have not been 'worked' in any way. Feeling optimistic I continue my searching at the other entrance burrows, but once again find nothing of interest. I spend about an hour looking up and down the valley, as does Debbie, and disappointingly we do not find any human remains or flint weapons.

About midday we sit together on the grass and eat our sandwiches and Debbie talks of the ways of the ancient hunter gatherers. Moving with the seasons they would follow the game and also visit the coast in their search for food. The way Debbie explains it makes it appear to be an idyllic way to live compared to our modern fast way of life that we lead now.

The old friendship between us returns making the burglary incident and her angry words and manner appear as a distant dream. Smiling with excitement Debbie reaches into the pocket of her rucksack and takes out something very small; "Look what I found," she says opening her hand so that I can see what she is holding.

It is a small flake of flint about three eighths of an inch long and I look at it in confusion as it appears to me to be nothing exciting.

"Where did you find that?" I ask, hoping that its location might enlighten me to its significance.

"It was near to where I found the finger bone; it is a flake, probably from where they sharpened one of their tools."

I look at her not believing a word as it could have been formed by a rabbits claws or sheep's hoof where it stood on a larger piece of flint; "I have to admit you have a better imagination than I have," I admit; "I found quite a few of them further along and wouldn't have thought them to be manmade."

"Where?" Debbie almost shouts at me.

"Further along," I repeat and pointing along the valley to where I had found them.

Quickly putting the remains of her dinner back in her rucksack Debbie gets to her feet; "Show me," she demands.

Still eating a sandwich I stand up and leaving my rucksack where it is I start to walk along the valley with Debbie following close behind. We soon reach the area where I had seen the flakes and spend several minutes trying to locate them. Debbie searches impatiently with me until I finally see them; "There they are," I say pointing at the half a dozen or so flakes.

Debbie pushes past me in her eagerness and bends down beside them and looks around the area where they are; "There is another," she says and picks up one that is so small I can hardly see it; "And another;" she laughs and returns her attention back to the half dozen or so other flakes.

"Why are you getting so excited?" I ask, totally baffled by her behavior.

Debbie replies in a very sarcastic, condescending tone of voice; "These small pieces of flint are from where an axe or a flint knife has been sharpened Patrick."

"Leave it out, will you. You do not honestly believe that – and you are telling me that they have remained here for thousands of years until the rabbits dug them up? I do admire your imagination," I laugh.

Debbie looks up at me with fury in her eyes and her face turns a deep red in anger; "Don't you laugh at me *mister*. I can see clearly what they are."

"All they are is where the farmer has run over a bit of flint with his tractor," I exclaim as her sudden anger and treating me as if I am stupid is getting my back up; "Manmade, yes, but not by some savage from thousands of years ago, that is ridiculous."

"You can bloody well walk back," Debbie shouts as she starts to pick up the tiny pieces of flint.

Stunned by her outburst I stare at her as she picks up the flint and searches through the grass with her fingers. It is a long walk to the main coastal road from here and many, many miles back to my car that is parked outside her house. Taking some deep breaths I calm my anger and ask in a soft, friendly voice; "Are you serious Debbie – you are going to make me walk back?"

"Yes, I bloody well am, if you think you can talk to me like that," she replies, as she continues searching through the grass.

This is certainly not the Debbie I know and remember and I can only assume that she is still upset over the attempted burglary and has become a bit unstable. To walk back to her house would probably take the rest of the day unless I 'thumbed' it and got a lift. The town where she lives is not on a direct route from here and I would have to rely on several good natured people to give me a ride back. Despite my efforts to calm down I still feel angry with her and realize I need her to see some kind of sense.

Further argument with her will only antagonize her further and I can see that the only way out of this predicament is to lie; "I am sorry Debbie, I certainly did not mean to insult you. I am sure you know much more about these things than I do."

Debbie looks up from her searching and I can see in her eyes that she has calmed down – a bit; "You can be very insulting when you want to be Patrick. I should make you walk home to teach you a lesson."

"I can only apologize for my foolishness; I am really sorry. Are those really chippings from where a Neanderthal hunter has sharpened his tools?"

"Yes, they more than likely are," Debbie confirms as she gets to her feet and puts the chippings into a pocket of her rucksack; "I want to go home now. I will give you a lift back providing you do not insult me anymore."

A feeling of relief sweeps through me and I know I must calm her further; "Of course I won't; and I did not mean to insult you in the first place," I reply in a subservient manner and also try an apologetic smile.

Debbie stares into my eyes and returns the smile, though it is more of a tightening of her lips. Putting her rucksack over her shoulder she starts to walk slowly in the direction of her car and looking down at the grass at her feet as she walks.

I turn away from her and walk quickly back to my rucksack. Picking it up I sling it over my shoulder and walking fast to catch her up I know that I must try not antagonize her further, or she will strand me in the middle of nowhere. As I approach her I slow my pace and keep about twelve feet behind her. Debbie is still searching the grass and does not acknowledge my presence. When she reaches the end of the valley she turns and starts to make her way up the hill, glancing briefly back in my direction she once again makes no sign or acknowledgement of me.

We continue back towards her car, scattering several sheep as we go. Climbing the stile Debbie looks back in my direction and a brief smile crosses her face; "Do you want to stop at a café on the way back?" she asks in a friendly voice that does not imply we had only recently had harsh words.

"Only if you want to, I guess you are a bit anxious about your house?"

Debbie shrugs her shoulders; "I cannot see that anything would happen during the day."

I smile in genuine relief; "Coffee it is then – and a scone."

We stop at a small teahouse a few miles along the coast; it is expensive, catering to the more prosperous passerby or holidaymaker. We both sit outside and watch the passing traffic as Debbie talks of the history of the area we are in. She must have done a lot of research as she can recount the influential people who transformed this land many years ago.

The coffee, served in a coffeepot containing about four cups of coffee, and the scones are however excellent. Debbie appears to have forgotten our earlier disagreement, much to my relief, and talks of the countryside around us and what it was like many thousands of years ago. A large marshy area used to be where we are sitting now that covered most of the coastline for fifty miles in each direction. It was drained several hundred years ago to provide pasture and farmland and many small villages sprang up. These were short lived as the landowners saw more profit in sheep than in people and the people were forcibly evicted, to go to who knows where. Debbie knew of several of these abandoned villages and suggested that some time in the future we would go and explore these.

Due to her outburst at the Neolithic site and her attitude towards me at her home I have become very unsure of her but smile in agreement at this suggestion. I could not see this happening, but knew that if it did, I would use my own car.

We sat at the teahouse for about an hour until we finally head back to Debbie's house. The going is slow due to an increase in traffic but Debbie does not seem to mind and chats away to me as if she does not have a care in the world.

When we arrive at her house Debbie parks her car quite close to mine. Turning the engine off she turns and looks me in the eyes; "Are you hungry Patrick? I hope you are, as I took a beef joint out of the freezer before we left and which should have defrosted by now. How does roast beef and roast potatoes with fresh carrots and runner beans sound to you?"

Really I want to go home as her changing character I find is becoming most disturbing. Knowing that refusal would offend and upset her I take the coward's way out; "That sounds great Debbie, I hope you will let me help you prepare it?"

"There is not a lot to do, except to clean the carrots and beans and put everything on to cook."

"What about the spuds – won't they need peeling?"

Debbie laughs; "No, they are frozen ones, all that is needed is to take them out of the packet and put them in the oven with the joint. You can make fresh coffee whilst I put everything on to cook."

I smile in agreement and get out of the car and stand by the front gate as Debbie locks and secures her car. I see a flicker of apprehension cross her face as she sorts out the front door keys and I wisely keep quiet as she walks along the front path to her door.

Unlocking the door she opens it wide and walks quickly along the hall and enters the lounge. There are no cries of anguish so I follow her in, shut the front door behind me and walk into the lounge.

Everything is as we left it and I put my rucksack onto the floor by the door. Debbie is sorting through hers and reaches into the pocket for the flakes of flint; "Now look at this Patrick, I told you I was right," she says as she places the flint next to the arrowhead. Turning to face me she triumphantly says; "Come over here and you tell me that some of those flakes did not come off this arrowhead?"

I walk over trying to keep my face impassive as I look at her small collection.

"You see," Debbie says; "the flint is the same color as the arrowhead and these little indentations at the edges show they have been worked."

I look more closely and think that she is certainly crazy and also color blind, but of course do not say anything to contradict her. Instead I smile in agreement; "Yes, you are right. That is amazing and I can only assume that those little bits of flint were in the same area as the arrowhead?"

A big triumphant smile covers Debbie's face; "Within twenty feet or less," she confirms; "and now to get the dinner on, I am starving."

The roast dinner is excellent and Debbie had refused to let me help in anyway and would not even let me load the dishwasher. The friction between us apparently has passed and we spend a pleasant evening together. Debbie has convinced herself that the flakes of flint have come off the arrowhead and persists in proving to me that that was where they came from. Several of the flakes she 'matches up' to the arrowhead but to me the flint is of a totally different type. I wisely keep quiet and pretend to agree with her in which Debbie appears to accept.

When the evening comes to a close I thank her for an interesting day and make my excuses and go upstairs to shower and go to bed.

The following morning, it being a Sunday, I lie in bed for a few extra hours and show my face about nine-thirty. Debbie, by all appearances has been up for hours as she is already dressed ready to go out and is sitting on her stool using her laptop when I enter the lounge;

"Good morning Patrick, I hope you slept well. Where would you like to go to today?" she asks with a beaming smile on her face.

The arguments and bad feelings we had yesterday appear forgotten by her and I wonder if staying with this obviously unstable friend is such a good idea. To refuse her hospitality and friendship may provoke her into another rage and is something I do not want to experience;"Good morning Debbie. Are there any woods nearby? I reply, returning her smile.

"That is a good idea Patrick; we can collect some mushrooms while we are out. There is a great stretch of woodland at the edge of town, but we will need some rubber boots as it will be quite muddy and wet out there."

"Nice one and easily sorted," I smile in reply; "My boots are in my car, I'll have a quick breakfast and then we'll get away."

"Sit down, please let me get you some breakfast – what would you like?"

"Only coffee and toast, and no need for you to get it, you are not my slave." I answer, but get the feeling that I am saying the wrong thing; once again.

Debbie's face changes and her eyes take on that glint of anger; "I am no one's slave and it would be my pleasure to get you breakfast. Sit." She orders and not giving me the opportunity to reply she puts her laptop on the floor and hurries out to the kitchen.

I sit in the armchair cursing the bad start between us and not understanding her mood swings. Vowing to think first before I open my mouth I sit in the armchair and await my breakfast.

Debbie returns several minutes later carrying a tray with toast and coffee. The short time that it took her to prepare my breakfast implies that she had got most of it ready before I got up.

"Thank you Debbie," I smile as I reach out for the tray; "this is a good start to the day."

"Sit back," she orders as she puts the tray in my lap; "I will go and find my boots while you are eating. "Do you want to stay out for a long time, or come back here for dinner?"

"Depends on how big the woods are; and how many mushrooms are about," I reply around a mouthful of toast.

"I will pack us something to take with us and then we can take our time," she smiles appearing happy and excited at the prospect, of I assume, picking mushrooms as that is one of her favorite hobbies.

I stand outside next to my car while I wait for Debbie to lock the doors of her house. Seeing me waiting as she walks down the path and I see the now familiar angry glint in her eyes.

"Please let me drive you today Debbie," I say hurriedly; "it is the least I can do; and you can take it easy."

Staring into my eyes I get the feeling she is going to argue the point – and she does; "But you do not know where the woods are."

"You can give me directions on the way; it is my turn to look after you today as you did a lot of driving yesterday." I reply in my friendliest voice.

Suddenly her face changes as she smiles and the angry glint fades; "Thank you Patrick, that is thoughtful of you." She opens the back door of my car and puts her rucksack and a wicker basket onto the backseat before getting in the front seat whilst still holding on to her boots.

I have already taken my boots from the trunk of the car and put them on the floor in front of the backseat, where I can reach them.

The drive to the woods only takes about twenty minutes with Debbie giving directions all the way and I finally pull up in a muddy car park; "I see what you mean about the mud, totally different to the grass of yesterday."

"The fields are on the far side of the woods and have long grass this time of year which will help wipe the mud off when we get there."

"How big are these woods Debbie?"

"Only about ten acres and they are a bit domesticated with well-marked paths and even a few benches scattered about."

"Does that mean we will have to keep to the paths, or can we run free?" I ask with an impish grin.

Debbie returns my mischievous smile; "We can run free, as you put it. There are quite a few edible mushrooms in the woods which will mean we have to wander off the paths."

"You will have to show me what is edible and what isn't as I have never picked mushrooms in the woods before. I am too frightened of poisoning myself."

"I won't let you do that," Debbie laughs; "Come on, what are we waiting for?"

Debbie quickly changes into her boots and leaves her trainers on the floor in the car. Getting out of the car she opens the back door and reaches in for her rucksack and basket. Closing the back door with a gentle slam she slings her rucksack over her shoulder and carrying the wicker basket walks slowly across the muddy car park to a path that leads into the woods.

I quickly put my boots on and lock and secure the car and hurry after her as she disappears out of sight around a corner.

Catching her up I slow down to match her pace; "At least it is not raining today," I comment, looking up at the blue sky that has a few large white cumulus clouds drifting by.

"The weather report for today is good," Debbie answers not bothering to look up at the sky; "We turn off onto a path soon which can be a bit slippery, so watch yourself."

"Thanks for the warning. I assume that you know these woods well and where the best mushrooms are; and why the basket and not a carrier bag?"

"Yes, I have been here lots of times. To collect mushrooms properly it is best to have an open basket, one like this made of wicker, so that the air can circulate around them. If you use a plastic carrier bag the mushrooms not only get squashed they sweat; and you find that when you get back home a lot are ruined as they can turn into a slimy mess. It is still early in the season so we should get plenty of freshly growing ones. The path is just up here."

Debbie leads the way onto a narrow path and I am forced to walk behind her or get brushed by the trees. Debbie appears happy carrying the wicker basket as well as having her rucksack over her shoulder and I decide that the best option is not to volunteer; if she wants me to carry anything, I feel sure she will let me know.

Soon there is wet clay underfoot and I slip several times but do not fall. Debbie laughs at my stumbling efforts and appears as sure footed as a mountain goat. Leading the way past the clay we come to an area of silver birch trees that are adorned with bracket fungi. The birch trees that have the most bracket fungi growing out of their trunks are dead and the fungi look like little shelves awaiting some pixie or elf to put something on them.

Debbie laughs and points at the many red spotted fly agaric toadstools that are growing everywhere on the ground.

"They are poisonous aren't they Debbie?" I ask in wonder as the quiet of the woods and the amount of red toadstools make it appear a special, magical place.

"Most of the books describe them as poisonous but I have never heard of anyone dying from eating them."

"Why do they describe them as poisonous then?"

"They contain a psychoactive ingredient called muscarine among other things, and which is an alkaloid that can make you hallucinate. One way of taking them is to partly boil them in water which leaches out some of the poison before you fry or bake them. The effect they can give is that you can feel drunk and like the effect alcohol has on a lot of people they can make you lose control. You can shut your finger in a door and break it and not even be aware that you have done it, which makes them a bit dangerous hence why they are described as poisonous."

"Sounds like it," I agree; "Have you ever taken them?"

"Yes, a couple of times, some that were partly boiled and put in whiskey and stored for a few months."

"What happened?"

"Not a lot really, I got drunk on the whiskey, which is about all I can remember. I went out with a hippy type just after my divorce and he used to eat them raw. His way of doing it was to take a bite and chew it slowly before swallowing and rely on the body's natural defense against eating a poison. When he had eaten enough his throat used to close up so that he could not swallow anymore."

"Sounds a bit drastic," I say, not having any desire to do such a crazy thing.

"He used to assure me that by doing it that way the body would not allow you to take too much. He regarded himself as a complete expert; but he did die of liver failure a little while ago."

"Best we give them a miss then," I reply with a grimace.

"Yes," Debbie agrees; "anyway there are much better ones to take if you want to do that sort of thing and without risking your life."

Looking at the red and white spotted fly agarics spread out across the woodland makes me think that the color red is a warning color; "It surprises me after what you have just said that most children's fairytale books that have mushrooms in them, show the red mushroom with white spots. It is almost as if they are saying to the children that they are ok."

"Yes, it is definitely a mad world we live in, mind you, there is a lot of folklore about the fly agaric and some cultures regard it as having a religious significance. The witches of olden times would add fly agaric and other hallucinogenic mushrooms to their pots along with eye of newt and ear of bat," Debbie laughs in a nervous sort of way.

"Yes, I have heard of that before; the eye of newt and ear of bat bit. I have seen a few cartoons with that in them; something else for the kids."

Debbie appears uncomfortable; "Shall we move on then?"

"Yes, by all means; but what about the bracket fungi that is growing out of the trees; is that any good to eat?"

"They are a bit tough and woody; they used to use them in the olden days for sharpening cutthroat razors."

"I have not got one of those anymore, I used to have one when I was a Teddy Boy. I use an electric razor these days."

"You were a Teddy Boy? I didn't think you were *that* old Patrick."

"I'm not if you are thinking back to the fifties, there was a Teddy Boy revival in the seventies, but I expect you are a bit young to remember that?"

"Patrick, you can be so nice at times," she laughs and follows the path which leads us into a large depression in the topography of the land. The path suddenly becomes very wet and the sticky clay sticks to my boots trebling their weight, making it difficult to walk. Sedges and reeds grow in the waterlogged soil and even though it is October mosquitoes rise up from the stagnant water and swarm around our heads. Several fly at me, attracted by my movements and the carbon dioxide in my breath, and I wave my arms around in agitation, hoping to drive them away. Several persist however and fly at my face and head avoiding my swinging arms, suddenly I can hear a loud buzzing in my right ear which just as suddenly stops. I go mad and slap my ear several times, convinced that the mosquito has landed on me and is sucking my blood. The thought that the mosquito has flown past my ear, which is why I cannot hear it anymore, takes time to penetrate my panic and I finally stop waving my arms about.

Debbie finds my antics highly amusing and makes no effort to control her laughter; "It looked like you were trying to take off," she says between laughs.

"I hate 'em, hate them," I say in anguish; "they carry diseases you know."

"I doubt that you are going to catch malaria or contract West Nile fever in this country Patrick," Debbie sarcastically replies.

"I am not so sure about that, all you have to do is think where the mosquito had its last meal; and what it landed on," I answer, making myself shudder at the thought.

"It is only the females that suck blood you know," Debbie knowledgably replies, appearing to find the subject fascinating, rather than abhorrent.

"What do the males eat then, or do they just go hungry until they die, like Mayflies do? That sounds about right to me, as females in most species appear to be much better off than the males; and they tend to live longer as well."

Debbie starts to laugh again; "Really Patrick, the way you think at times."

"Well, I am after all nothing special you know; I am after all just a man," I jokingly reply.

Quelling her laughter Debbie tries to look serious; "The male mosquito eats flower nectar mainly, I do not know what else they eat, I know it is not blood."

"That is good to hear; can we get out of here please?"

By way of an answer Debbie turns away and follows the path which leads uphill and away from the boggy area. Large oak trees, hundreds of years old dominate, and it is with relief that we pass amongst them. Being so large with outstretched branches, nothing much can grow underneath them and the ground is covered with old leaves and a few acorns. Suddenly a noise above me makes me look up and I see a gray squirrel running for cover. Its claws make a definite scratching sound as it runs along a branch and up the trunk of the tree.

Debbie is also looking at the squirrel and smiles; "I love squirrels," she says and squeals in delight as the squirrel runs around the other side of the tree trunk and disappears from sight.

"Yes, they are really cute," I agree. Looking at the base of the tree I see more bracket fungi that are in various shades of brown, even black in places. Walking closer I can see that a brownish liquid covers a lot of it, making it look like someone has had a pee over it; "Look at this Debbie, looks like we interrupted that squirrel when he was having a pee."

Debbie steps closer; "That is not pee, Patrick. That type of fungi exudes that brown liquid as I think retaining a lot of moisture will make it rot quicker."

"What about those black ones; are they a different type?"

"No, it is the same fungi but those ones are older fruiting bodies that are going rotten."

"What about that brown liquid, is that any good for anything?" I ask, hoping that I have found a new elixir or medicine.

"I don't know; I would not like to drink it as oak trees are full of tannins that would probably not do you any good. I know where we might find some edible bracket fungi, come on," she encourages and quickens her pace.

Debbie leads the way through the oak trees and the trees become more scattered as different varieties start to show. I recognize more silver birch; with a few fly agaric toadstools growing amongst them. We keep on walking and the trees become more mixed with conifers and beech growing out of a multitude of bushes and long grass. We keep on walking towards some large trees with outspread branches – and which I recognize as horse chestnut trees. Many of the leaves have fallen and 'conkers' cover the ground as not much vegetation grows below them.

Pointing to a whitish bracket fungi growing from the trunk of one of the chestnut trees Debbie indicates that I follow her; "That one is edible Patrick," she tells me as we get closer; "but the trick is, is only to collect the fresh growth. This one is called an oyster mushroom and as you can see it is similar to the bracket fungi but this one grows in clumps."

The fungus does have the coloring that is similar to oysters and even adopts a shell shaped structure. The clump Debbie is pointing to is composed of ones at different stages in their growth and I can see what she means by only picking the fresh ones. Some look old and are even turning brown with age with yellowing gills and would probably give you the belly ache if you ate them.

Picking some of the fresh ones Debbie puts them in her basket and I notice that there is no real stem to their structure and that the gills are a pale white.

"These are good," she confirms; "and we are lucky to find these as they are becoming rare in these woods as people keep picking and eating them."

"Like us," I smile; "those ones do look good," I agree; "I guess that picking wild mushrooms is similar to picking mushrooms in the greengrocer's; you avoid the older ones and only pick up the fresh ones – if you are allowed the choice."

"Yes, that's right, I know of a few people who have got sick eating edible mushrooms because they picked the older ones that were already decaying. The decayed part has toxins in it that make you sick, just like any other food that is rotten and will also make you sick."

Leading the way through the horse chestnut trees Debbie looks at a few of the tree trunks but we see no more oyster mushrooms. Following a faint trail the woodland appears to get brighter and I realize that we are approaching fields of grass and with sheep in them. The woodland has a barbed wire fence where it meets the fields and prevents the sheep that are grazing from entering the woods.

Climbing over a stile we leave the trees behind and almost straight away Debbie is picking large field mushrooms and putting them in her basket. Turning to face me she tells me the ones to pick; "These are the wild variety of the edible mushrooms that you can buy in the supermarket and these are called horse mushrooms." Picking one out of the basket she turns it upside down showing me the gills underneath; "As you can see Patrick, the gills are a light brown meaning that this is edible. Do not pick any that have white gills as they are known as the Death Cap; and as the name states they will kill you."

Turning the mushroom back over Debbie explains further; "Unfortunately from the right way up the Death Cap looks almost identical to the wild horse mushrooms and the only way to be sure is to check the color of the gills, preferably before you pick them. Just because it is poisonous to us does not mean that you have to destroy them. Anyway you would only be destroying the mushroom which is what is called the fruiting body. The main plant or roots, called mycelia, is spread out under the ground and one plant can stretch for hundreds of yards.

If you are unsure what I mean, look at the mycelia as you would, say an apple tree, and the mushrooms are the apples. Picking apples from a tree does not kill the tree and it is the same way with the mushroom, or toadstool mycelia."

I try to picture the root system of mycelia spread out underneath us like the roots of a tree and have to ask; "So those oyster mushrooms, even though they were growing out of the trunk of the tree, have a similar root system to these field mushrooms as well as the Death Caps."

Smiling encouragement Debbie agrees; "Yes, they are just the same. Some mushrooms or toadstools, even though their root systems infect the tree, can live in harmony with the host plant. If you remember back to the silver birch trees, the bracket fungi growing out of the trunks was growing out of mainly dead ones. That is because the mycelia of the bracket fungi kill the birch trees and then feed on the rotting wood."

"So I assume that the red spotted fly agarics are doing the same thing?"

"Yes, but I am not sure what the fly agarics are feeding on, they are usually found growing amongst the silver birch so I would not be surprised if their mycelia are feeding on the root system – but don't quote me on that."

"I wouldn't dare," I laugh.

"Oh and one thing more," Debbie continues; "we will probably find horse mushrooms the size of side plates, even dinner plate size, which may look good but being several days or even a week or more old are usually full of maggots. So do not pick those."

I nod my head in acknowledgement and start to scour the grass for edible mushrooms. There are a lot scattered amongst the grass and, only picking the small ones, many of which are mere 'buttons' the basket soon starts to fill up.

Debbie has a good eye for them and in my eagerness I soon get ahead of her and find a small group that look very fresh. Squatting down I look at the underneath before picking and see white gills; which means they are the Death Caps, so move on several yards further and concentrate on picking a few small buttons of horse mushrooms.

Having several in my hand I turn around to see where Debbie is so that I can put them in her basket. Debbie is crouched over the group of Death Caps; and is picking them!

Chapter Six

Debbie is not only picking the smallest but has picked several that have caps about two to three inches in diameter.

I walk back towards her and put the button Horse mushrooms in her basket. Feigning innocence I comment; "Hey Debbie, we are doing well, at this rate we will have the basket full in no time and be eating mushrooms for the rest of the week. I see that you have picked some larger ones, aren't you worried about maggots?" I ask as I pick up one of the Death Caps and turn it over so that the white gills show;

"Hey, you have picked some Death Caps," I exclaim.

Debbie looks up at me and then at the Death Cap in my hand; "Oh, n'no I meant to p'pick them, she stutters, not meeting my gaze; "I have a bit of a mouse problem at home; will save me buying some mouse killer."

"The mice will not eat them, will they?"

"No, not as they are. I will dry them out a bit and them cut them into small pieces, cover them in honey and lightly bake them," she replies, still not looking me in the eye; and I notice that her face is slightly flushed red.

"Sounds like you have done that before. The Death Caps will kill them then?"

"Oh yes, I will not have any mice for months," she replies, finally looking up at me and looking me in the eye.

"As long as you don't get them mixed up in the soup, or however you are going to serve the edible mushrooms."

"No," she scoffs; "I am not that stupid. Dying from Death Caps is meant to be a painful way to die."

I notice that even if I have insulted her and did not call her stupid and that there is no angry glint in her eye.

"What about the mice; won't they die a painful death?" I ask innocently though my mind is racing and I feel fear twist my stomach. Had Debbie any intention of feeding *me* the Death Caps after yesterday's arguments?

Regaining her composure the red flush of her face fades as she continues to look me in the eye; "No more than if I had bought poison for them. Some of the poison you can buy dries up their blood; and that sounds painful," she says in a more positive voice.

Suddenly I do not want to pick any more mushrooms and put the Death Cap back into her basket; "How many more do you want to collect?"

Looking at the basket Debbie nods her head; "We have probably got enough there, we can fry some as well as put some in with a stew. Anyway we do not want to collect too many as the horse mushroom can be a bowel and bladder irritant if you eat too many."

"We'll stop now shall we? I do not want any problems like that."

"Ok," Debbie smiles; "I am sure that you have heard of magic mushrooms? There should be some of them growing on the other side of the field."

"Yes, of course I have heard of them, but never tried them. I assume that you know what they look like and have tried them before?"

"Of course," she replies, the familiar angry glint returning to her eyes; "have taken them dozens of times. I am surprised that you haven't taken them before Patrick. They were very popular back in the seventies."

"The seventies? You are forgetting that I was a Teddy Boy back then, magic mushrooms and rock around the clock did not exactly go together."

"Oh yes, and Teddy Boys were meant to be quite violent; is that why you used to carry a cutthroat razor?"

"I never said that I carried one did I?" I protest and then decide that honesty is the best policy, with the hope that admitting violence will make her more cautious of me. And hopefully would make her think twice if she was going to poison me; "Well I did, sometimes. But not all Teddy Boy's were violent you know. To be honest we were just happy bopping and dancing to rock 'n' roll most of the time. The violence only used to happen when other people used to pick a fight with us."

This seems to be taking an insane direction and Debbie continues looking at me and I can read uncertainty in her body language. Suddenly she straightens her back and her confidence returns; "Magic mushrooms won't make you violent, in fact they will have the opposite effect. Would you like to do some with me tonight? That is providing we can find some."

"What is the kind of effect will they have on me then? They won't turn me into a hippy will they and make me call you man or should I say chick,"

Trying not to laugh but failing Debbie bursts into happy laughter; "No, Man."

I laugh with her and ask again; "What will they do to me?"

"They should make you laugh like you have never laughed before, and also they will make you hallucinate."

"The laughing sounds good but I don't fancy seeing any gnomes or fairies or anything like that."

Debbie laughs again; "No, Patrick you shouldn't, but they do affect people in different ways. When I say hallucinate I mean that everything will look different to you."

"What a chair will look like a table?"

"No; wait and see, trust me."

"OOhh – I was doing alright until you said that," and laugh; "Of course I trust you Debbie; and I always have," I reassure, but are thinking; am I that desperate to keep a friend?

Smiling happily Debbie turns away and starts walking quickly across the field.

I hurry to catch up; "What is the hurry Debbie?"

"It has been years since I have done mushrooms," she says and looks me in the eyes; "doing mushrooms should be fun. The main thing with doing a drug like that is to do it with the right people and doing them with you should be a lot of fun as I trust you as well."

"Thank you, that has got to be the best thing you have said to me in years," and I smile but the warning bells in my head are ringing; "What happens if you do mushrooms with the wrong people?"

"I will tell you tomorrow, come on, we are wasting time," Debbie says as she quickens her pace.

Reaching the other side of the field which is separated from the next field by more barbed wire Debbie suddenly stops and crouches down, indicating I do the same.

"Even though they are called mushrooms, they do actually look like toadstools and they are also very small. Crouching down like this we should be able to see them a lot easier; ahh, there are some," she stands up and walks about twenty paces when she crouches down again to pick some very small pale white toadstools. How she had managed to see them from twenty paces away baffles me as they are no bigger than matchsticks.

Using her right thumb nail and forefinger she neatly cuts the stem and puts them in her left hand as she picks. After picking ten or more she opens her left hand wide for me to see them.

"There they are Patrick. As you can see they are more like toadstools than what we call mushrooms," Picking one up by its stem she shows me the gills underneath; "They are similar to horse mushrooms in that they have slightly brown gills." Turning the mushroom the right way up the shape is not at all similar to edible mushrooms as it has a protruding tip; "As you can see on the top is a nipple, in fact the whole mushroom looks like a ladies breast," she tells me as she twists the mushroom in her fingers so that I can see all around; "To be rather blunt about it, the fresh ones look like a young girls breast and as they get older they resemble the female breast as she gets older; to droopy when they are really old," Debbie suddenly laughs hysterically and her face flushes red in embarrassment.

I take the tiny mushroom from her fingers and look at it more closely and with a slight stretch of the imagination agree that it does look like a young girls breast (eighteen and upward!!).

"Come on, there should be loads around here," she encourages; "you look for them as well."

Now that I know what I am looking for I can see several growing in the grass and take several steps towards them and bend down.

"Do not pull them Patrick, use your thumbnail like I did and give a clean cut."

"Why not pull them?"

"One, you will pull the root up which will have dirt on it, which is what we don't want, and second, if you cut the stem that way and come back in a couple of days another will be growing in its place. If you pull the root, or mycelia to use its proper name, and come back in a couple of days there will be nothing."

I reach out for one nearest me and do as I am told and cut the stem and continue with the others, putting them in my left hand; "How many will we need?" I ask, suddenly engrossed in picking.

"About seventy each should do it, we will make tea out of them as they can make you feel a bit sick if you eat them," Debbie replies, appearing as engrossed as I am in picking the tiny mushrooms.

Soon I have a whole handful and after crouching down for so long have to stand up; with leg and back muscles aching. Looking around I cannot see Debbie at first and suddenly panic fills me until I see her several hundred yards away crouched down. Every now and then Debbie looks anxiously around, especially focusing on the distant woodland. Walking over to her I hold out my hand of mushrooms; "I don't know how many I have picked, but I have a whole handful here."

She stands up, not appearing to have acquired the aching muscles like I have and looks anxiously around before turning towards me and looks at the mushrooms in my hand;

"You must have about fifty there Patrick, here put them under these," she says as she moves some of the horse mushrooms to one side. Picking up the Death Caps she throws them down; "We won't have those after all."

"I am glad you did that," I say with a smile and put the magic mushrooms into her basket; "Won't they get squashed in there?" I ask.

"Not much," Debbie replies; "but we do not want anyone seeing them."

"I noticed you looking around, why do you want to keep them a secret?"

"It is illegal to have magic mushrooms. The law is a bit vague in places whereas you cannot get done for picking them, but to prepare them, that is to dry and process them is against the law. You can go to jail if the judge does not like you."

"Yes, I thought they were against the law, but we have not got that many. How many do you have to have to qualify a jail term then?" I ask.

Debbie looks nervously around before replying; "I haven't a clue; but I have never wanted to put it to the test."

"Going to jail would spoil our day," I agree; "how many more shall we pick?"

"These are really small," she answers as she puts her mushrooms with mine in the basket and puts several horse mushrooms on top; "If we get a couple of handfuls each that should do us as we want to have enough."

"Ok, I will go back to that area where I was as there are loads there," I say as I turn away.

"Keep your eyes open as well please Patrick," Debbie says in a worried voice.

Looking around the only movement I can see is the sheep grazing and a faint breeze blowing the tops of the trees; "Looks like we have got the place to ourselves, but I will keep my eyes open," I say as I walk back to where I had seen lots of the magic mushrooms.

Picking the tiny mushrooms is obsessive and I am amazed how I can see so many, some from maybe thirty yards away. They are easy to see now that I have got my eyes focused on the pale white that appears to stick up like a beacon amongst the green of the grass. Even though my legs and back aches I soon pick a large handful and make my way back to Debbie, who is now several hundred yards away. Hiding them under the horse mushrooms in her basket I can see that Debbie also has a large handful.

"You have got enough there, haven't you Debbie?"

Debbie looks at the mushrooms in her hand; "Yes, I think so, but I love picking them as much as I do taking them."

"That bodes well for tonight then as I have had a lovely time picking them as well."

Debbie stands and walks over to her basket, moving the larger mushrooms out of the way, she puts her mushrooms in the basket and covers them with several of the horse mushrooms and looks at me; "We have been lucky today Patrick, and also they are not too wet which will make them easier to sort out when we get back. Go back to the car shall we?" she asks.

"Yes, good idea. Back the same way?"

"Probably be best as being a side path we should not meet any dog walkers or whoever may want to look in my basket."

"Lead on," I say waving my arm in the direction of the woods.

Walking back across the field is slow going as the magic mushrooms appear to have sprouted behind us and neither of us can walk past them without picking some.

By the time we reach the woods we must have put several hundred more into the basket and I have to ask; "What are you going to do with all the extra ones Debbie?"

She looks into the basket and laughs with excitement; "I will dry them out and then put them in honey and they will last for years – unless we eat 'em of course"

I find her laugh and mood contagious; "I hope they are good enough tonight for me to want to do them again, as we have worked for it."

"They will be," she reassures me with beaming smile.

Chapter Seven

"We never did eat the sandwiches you packed," I say to Debbie as she puts her rucksack and basket of mushrooms on the worktop.

"Never mind, we will have them later if we get hungry," she replies with a wide excited smile.

"I am hungry now, what did you make?"

"Only tuna and some salad, I'll put them in the fridge and cook up some of these mushrooms with sausages and bacon."

"I'll go along with that," I smile; "I am starving, would you like some help?"

"No, I can manage; you can sort out the magic ones we picked."

"What is it that you want me to do?" I ask, walking over to look in the basket of mushrooms.

"Wait there, I will get you a couple of tea towels," Debbie tells me as she hurries out of the kitchen and I hear her go upstairs.

I take the opportunity to look quickly through the basket as I was not convinced she had thrown all the Death Cap mushrooms away in the field. Moving some of the horse mushrooms to one side I can see some remaining Death Caps lower down, Hearing Debbie coming back down the stairs I put the horse mushrooms back where they were and walk over to the kettle. Unplugging it I put it under the cold tap and turn the water on as Debbie comes back into the kitchen.

"That is a good idea Patrick; I could do with a cup of coffee."

I fill the kettle up and put the plug back in and turn the kettle on as she spreads out clean tea towels onto the worktop; "What is it you want me to do with them?" I ask, baffled as to what she has in mind.

Reaching into the basket Debbie takes out the horse mushrooms that are covering the magic ones and puts them on the worktop. Taking out handfuls of magic mushrooms she places them onto one of the tea towels; what I want you to do is to lay them one at a time on this other towel side by side in little rows, but make sure they are not touching one another."

"Sounds easy enough, then what?"

"That will take you long enough and I will show you what happens next when you have done that. Once you fill up one towel, put the remainder onto the second towel."

The kettle boils as she finishes speaking and I walk over and make coffee for us both and try not to make it obvious that I am watching her as she starts to empty the rest of the basket. Deliberately turning my back when she has about reached the Death Caps, I see, in the reflection of the chrome kettle, that she puts them in the cupboard above the worktop and ensures that she closes the cupboard door quietly.

I make no comment as I put her mug of coffee next to her and look at the mushrooms she has spread out on the worktop; "I did not realize that we had picked so many, they look good enough to eat as they are."

"They can be eaten raw but I much prefer them cooked lightly in butter," Debbie says as she turns towards me with a beaming smile; "Show me the ones you want."

I step a little closer and pick out four nice sized button mushrooms; "I will not have too many as I remember you saying they may be an irritant and I want no problems, even little ones, to spoil the evening."

"Good thinking Patrick, I will put the rest, along with the oyster mushrooms in the fridge and we can have some with our breakfast," she replies as she puts five more button mushrooms next to mine on the worktop.

Getting several bowls from the cupboard underneath the worktop Debbie puts the remainder in the bowls and puts them in the fridge as I start to separate the magic mushrooms and put them gently onto the tea towel.

Curious as to what their effect maybe upon me I ask; "What is it that makes these ones magic then Debbie?"

"They contain a chemical called Psilocybin, which when you eat it is converted into Psilocin which is what causes the hallucinations, among other feelings."

"Why does the mushroom make the chemical then?"

"To stop you from eating them," she laughs; "If you noticed, the sheep leave them well alone. Unfortunately for the Psilocybin mushrooms we humans like them and they are getting slowly wiped out as so many people are picking them and picking them wrong by constantly damaging the mycelia. There are not that many places these days where they do grow."

"This one looks different," I say, holding one up for Debbie to see.

Debbie walks over and takes it from me; "Now you can see why they need to be sorted out Patrick, where did you pick that one from?"

"I think that was one of a few I found in the woods on the way back."

"In the woods? You must never pick them in woods because so many woodland species look very similar. How many did you pick?"

"Not many, half a dozen maybe."

"Well make sure you find them Patrick as they could easily be poisonous."

"Looking at that one now it does look so different in here compared to the others, but they are only little, surely they won't do that much damage?"

Debbie laughs, but in a cold sort of way; "You would be surprised, I did a lot of reading and research about mushrooms because I wanted to be sure I knew what I was putting into my body. A lot of poisonous toadstools can cause permanent liver damage and there are some that affect the joints in your body, like the elbows and knees. They are really scary because they can make your arms and legs fall off."

"Wow," I exclaim; "that would spoil your day if you are walking down the road and your arm falls off."

"I do not think that it would happen that way, but really Patrick, it is better to be safe than sorry. Don't look so worried, this one," she says holding up the little toadstool; "looks like ones I have seen in the books that they describe as inedible – which usually means they taste really horrible. Even the magic mushrooms could be described as having 'an acquired taste' a bit like caviar, which have a very strong fishy taste that a lot of people don't like."

"And I am one of them; I have tried caviar and did not like it at all."

Looking at the magic mushrooms on the tea towels Debbie pushes the point she has made; "Make sure that you sort them out properly Patrick – if in doubt – leave it out, or throw it out in your case!"

"You have frightened the life out of me now, thinking back I am sure that I only picked six in the woods and looking at that one I know I can find them."

Debbie says no more as she picks up one of the button horse mushrooms and starts to peel the skin off.

"I am surprised to see you do that Debbie, I have never bothered when I buy mushrooms from the supermarket."

"Well I could wash them, but that will make them a bit soggy. I just think about what might have peed on them, makes me peel the skin off every time," she laughs.

I return to my sorting and soon find the other five dodgy ones and after showing them to Debbie, throw them in the bin.

The smell of cooking bacon and sausages fills the kitchen as I spread out the last of the mushrooms on the two tea towels. After washing my hands I switch the kettle on and make more coffee as Debbie dishes up the food. The button horse mushrooms have cooked to a golden color and their aroma, along with the bacon and sausages and fried bread, make my stomach grumble.

We eat in the lounge with the plates balanced on our laps and I have to admit, though it is a simple meal, it is one of the best tasting meals I have ever had. The mushrooms taste good being so fresh and I congratulate Debbie on her cooking as I sit back and let the food digest.

Thinking about the magic mushrooms I feel excited about doing them even though I am not sure how they are going to affect me. I had heard of them before but have never met anyone who has taken them and filled with curiosity try to get more information about them from Debbie who's only comment is; "Wait and see."

We sit and talk of other things as she does not have a television in the lounge, the only one in the house is the small portable television in the room I am using. Debbie is of the opinion that too much time is wasted sitting in front of a TV all day when there are so many other things to do. I do not argue with her, even though I disagree, as most of my knowledge is derived from watching TV and it can also make good company.

We check on the magic mushrooms several times as the tea towels absorb the moisture, turning some that had become wet a light brown color, to a pale creamy white as they dried. The purpose of putting them on the tea towels is now apparent as it is a way of double checking that we have picked the right ones. Also by drying them out, it will make them more suitable for absorbing the hot water when we make a tea out of them. After a couple of hours Debbie changes the tea towels for clean, dry ones which helps dry the mushrooms out even more.

Not all adopt the creamy white coloring as some stay a light brown, showing that they are not the psilocybin ones that we want and they get thrown in the bin. Several maggots have also crawled out of the mushrooms and these get washed down the sink. Some of the mushrooms have blackened areas and though small, are an indication that part of the mushroom is rotten, so they get thrown out as well.

As evening approaches and the mushrooms have been drying for about four hours with many having shriveled and now resemble common toadstools, Debbie finally counts out about two hundred and puts them in a warm ceramic teapot. Boiling fresh water, she pours it into the pot and tells me that we need to let it brew for at least five minutes.

While we are waiting for the mushrooms to brew Debbie prepares the fire in the lounge, ensuring that there is enough wood stacked for the evening. Moving the armchair, stool and coffee table back from the fireplace Debbie clears the floor of old magazines and her shoes and anything else that we may trip over. Sorting out several cassette tapes she laughs with excitement as she presses 'play' and Watcher of the Skies by Genesis fills the room.

"Tea?" she asks, with beaming smile and walks out to the kitchen.

I follow closely as she warms two mugs and puts two heaped spoonfuls of sugar into one of them; "I will put sugar with yours in case you do not like the taste and anyway the sugar will help make it a happy time."

"Why aren't you having sugar?" I ask.

"I quite like the taste as they are," she answers as she puts a small tea strainer over my mug with the sugar and pours the mushroom tea into it. The tea is very dark and the strainer prevents a lot of black powder, which I assume are the spores, from going into the mug. Filling the mug about three quarters full she transfers the strainer to her mug and pours out the rest of the tea.

Removing the strainer, she takes the lid off the teapot and turning the strainer upside down, bangs it on the edge so that the spores and other small parts of the mushrooms go back into the pot. Looking at me with excitement in her eyes she stirs mine vigorously with a spoon and hands it to me; "Drink," she orders; "the food of the gods."

I take the mug from her and take a small sip, even with the sugar the tea tastes absolutely disgusting, like stagnant water, and I am not so sure that I will be able to drink it all.

Taking a large swig herself Debbie laughs; "Come on, we will go and make ourselves comfortable in the lounge."

The room is warm when we enter with the fire burning well and Debbie indicates I sit in the armchair. We sit quietly and I do my best to drink all of the tea but as I get down to the dregs the taste becomes more intense and I can see that the tea strainer has not worked that well, as a lot of the black spores line the bottom of the mug.

Leaving about half an inch of tea in the bottom of the mug I put it down onto the coffee table. Debbie has already drunk all of hers and looking into my mug says; "You have left some Patrick, don't you want that?"

"I see what you mean about an acquired taste as that is really disgusting. I will have to leave that last bit."

Debbie picks my mug up and laughs; "Cannot see it go to waste," she says as she drinks it down; "we can always do another brew if you want some more."

Peter Gabriel is singing about people having to be four feet tall as I sit back and wait to see what happens. Debbie is singing along under her breath and the music moves on to the next track as Peter sings of scattered pages of a book by the sea.

"I love Genesis, I hope you like them Patrick? Sorry I do not have any rock 'n' roll."

"That is fine; I have to admit I do like Genesis. I have got all their albums from when Peter Gabriel was with them and this album has to be one of the best, this, and Selling England by the Pound have to be my favorites."

"I have got that one as well," she confirms as she looks up at the pile of cassettes she has ready for the evening; "But when these came out you were a Teddy Boy then weren't you?"

"Yes, it was about then, but I used to listen to these and many others that weren't rock 'n' roll when I was at home. I think that was why I stopped being a Ted as I got a bit bored with the rock 'n' roll and used to spend most of my time listening to these and Pink Floyd, Hawkwind, Stray, Budgie, Caravan, The Pink Fairies….; and the list goes on," I smile.

"The Pink Fairies? I am surprised at you Patrick. I have got one of their albums somewhere, what is it called?" she says as her brow wrinkles in thought; "Oh yes, I remember; What a bunch of Sweeties."

"Yeah I got that one and also Never, Neverland, what a great band they are," I reply with real enthusiasm.

"Yes I agree, a bit controversial at the time as I remember. You surprise me that you liked Hawkwind; I have got quite a few of theirs on tape."

"One of the original hippy bands, but the album In Search of Space is awesome; I played that until the needle wore it out. It was lucky I also had them on tape and then CD's came along."

Looking up at her pile of tapes and old cassette player Debbie's face drops; "My CD player is broken, that is why the tapes."

"I still have a lot of mine on tape; not got much rock 'n' roll left," I reply as I feel my face go numb and my stomach seems to turn over.

Debbie is looking at me strangely and then bursts out laughing; "You said that at the wrong speed Patrick."

"Wrong speed, what are you talking about?"

"It sounded like you were talking slow, are you feeling anything yet?"

"My face feels a bit numb and I feel a bit sick," I reply as I try to focus onto her face, which now looks a bit blurred.

Standing up Debbie wobbles a bit as she picks up both of the mugs; "I will make us a drink; that will help settle your stomach."

"I don't think I am going to be sick, just feel a bit queasy."

"I will make us a drink anyway, won't be long," she tells me as she walks slowly out of the lounge.

The fire cracks and I look over at the flames, which appear to be moving fast as Peter Gabriel sings; 'Six, Six, Six is no longer alone,' and the music has increased in tempo and I wonder what happened to the rest of the album. Looking away from the fire I look at the coffee table which appears to be in a vivid three dimensions. The place mats on it look very sharp and clear and I have to look away. I next look at the carpet which also appears in a vivid three dimensions as the music slows – but sounds amazing. It is almost like I can feel every note reverberating in the air and I have to sit back and close my eyes.

And have to snap them open again as the colors inside my head whirl and dance and to see the calm room, that is not moving, is a relief. Wow, this is not what I expected, I had been drunk many times before, sometimes so badly that I could not walk, but this is nothing like it.

The music stops as Debbie comes back into the lounge carrying two mugs, walking over to me she hands me one; "Get that inside you, will help settle your stomach, I have put some milk with it and extra sugar."

I reach out for the mug and take it from her hand; "Thanks," I say as I take a swig. The coffee is only warm, but very sweet, and I drink some more.

"The music's stopped," Debbie says, looking at her pile of cassettes; "I know what you will like," and she turns quickly putting her mug onto the coffee table; "Don't need that," she says and reaching out Debbie takes a cassette from the pile, opens the player and replaces the tape and pushes 'play'.

Peter Gabriel sings 'Can you tell me where my country lies?'

"Nice one Debbie," I say as I recognize the first song of Selling England by the Pound.

"This is a good album," Debbie replies; "I like Peter Gabriel's lyrics, very fairy tale."

"Yes, it was a shame they split up," I answer, referring to when he left after them after only making seven albums.

"Blessing in disguise for the band really, as they went from strength to strength after he left; Are you listening to me Patrick?" Debbie asks in a loud voice as I realize I had closed my eyes.

Snapping them open I look up at her; "Of course, just drifted for a few seconds. Thanks for the coffee, it has helped already."

"Glad to hear it, I turned the heating on when I was out there, as it felt a bit cold in the hall. Are you warm enough?"

"Yes fine thanks; that log fire is really good, I watched it for a while but the flames were going too fast and I had to look away," I tell her with a laugh; "I have got a gas fire at my new place." I say, as if it is very important.

"A gas fire is less work, but I do like a real fire. How are the mushrooms Patrick?"

I watch her as she sits down on her stool and picks up her coffee as I try to find the words;

"Amazing. Thank you. I was listening to the music when you were out making coffee and just could not believe it. It felt like I was part of it, every note seemed to come out into the room and I could almost see it floating on the air. Then I closed my eyes and wow! I did not realize just how much was going on in my head – I had to open my eyes again – really frightened me," I start to laugh and then have to put my coffee mug down onto the coffee table as the laughter suddenly continues and I find I cannot stop.

Debbie laughs along with me and reaches out for her mug of coffee; and misses – by several inches which makes me laugh even more.

Blushing with embarrassment or blushing because she is laughing so much makes me continue laughing more and more and I have to bend double as my stomach starts to hurt. It feels like several minutes before we can stop laughing and I manage to straighten up but by then my jaw is really hurting and putting my hand to my jaw mumble; "Orhh, my jaw hurts," which makes me laugh again. Finally I manage to stop and pick up my coffee; "Thanks for the coffee Debbie, or have I already said that?" and I cannot help but laugh again.

Debbie is also laughing and between the laughter only manages to say; "You did," before she bursts out laughing again.

It is several minutes before we both calm down and trying to breathe properly we both manage to drink our coffees.

Everything is in that vivid three dimensions as Debbie had said and she stands out in relief from her surroundings as the music grabs my full attention once again. It is an instrumental part from 'Firth of Fifth' and I find myself getting drawn in and close my eyes – and have to open them again as I feel myself falling in towards it.

Debbie is watching me; "Are you alright Patrick?"

"Yes thanks, thought I was falling down a big hole."

"They do change your perception on things," Debbie laughs; "Would you like some more?"

The effect had worn off slightly from that first intensity and I agree to 'half a mug full'.

"Would you like one of these?" Debbie asks holding her hand out towards me. In the palm of her hand are two white tablets about the size of headache tablets. They look roughly made as they are quite thick and have badly deformed edges.

"What are they? You did not get them from the chemist did you?"

Debbie laughs; "No, they are ecstasy tablets, I get them from a friend who lives the other side of town."

"What will they do to me?" I ask nervously.

"They will intensify the mushrooms and take you somewhere really nice," she replies with a laugh.

I consider what she is offering me and am aware that many people have died from taking them. Their rough appearance makes them look like they have been made in some backstreet and I feel that the effect of the magic mushrooms is intense enough; "No thanks, I am having a great time as it is and I don't want to overdo it on my first time. I'll just have half a cup more of mushroom tea, please."

Debbie looks disappointed and then shrugs her shoulders; "More for me then," she says and puts the two tablets into her mouth and swallows them down; "I'll get you some more tea," she says and gets unsteadily to her feet. Picking up the mugs she staggers out of the room and goes into the kitchen.

After drinking the extra mushroom tea I find that the initial intensity does not return but things do look weird. Debbie changes the music many times, some I am familiar with like Pink Floyd and Caravan, but some I have not heard before. After several hours Debbie decides she is hungry and asks if I want something to eat? Food is the last thing on my mind but I do have a ranging thirst and just have more sweetened coffee.

Debbie staggers back from the kitchen carrying a bowl of cereal which is shredded wheat and to; "I love this stuff," puts a large spoonful into her mouth. Suddenly her face changes and she spits it out back into her bowl; "Urgh, urgh," is all she can keep saying and she claws at her mouth to pull out what she hasn't spat out. Looking at me with tears in her eyes she says in a shaky voice; "Urgh, that was horrible, it suddenly felt like I had a mouthful of worms and they were moving about inside my mouth."

This I find exceptionally funny and burst out laughing as the look on her face is most comical.

"It's not funny," she says, appearing offended.

Regaining my breath I managed to blurt out; "It is, the look on your face," and then I laugh and laugh and have difficulty stopping as her comical face will not go out of my mind.

Seeing the funny side Debbie joins in the laughter, which continues until my stomach and jaw start to hurt again.

My perception of her changes at one point as she sits happily listening to the music. Debbie suddenly appears to me to be very young an innocent. She does not appear to be lonely, but does appear to be lost and also in having little confidence. That she is alone in a very difficult world is the overall feeling that I get and this image lasts in my mind for quite a while.

The evening has to be one of the weirdest times that I have ever had; perception of not only Debbie changes but perception of myself also changes. I also feel lost in a very big world as the new feelings that I am having are at times, very difficult to understand.

There are moments when it feels like I have a fluorescent light bulb alight inside my head which makes closing my eyes impossible. My hair feels greasy and each strand of hair feels like it is a thick piece of straw. There is one time when Debbie has to shout at me to calm down as it appears I was breathing very fast and am 'going off like a steam kettle' to put it into Debbie's words.

As the evening draws to a close and the effects of the mushrooms are wearing off, I feel relieved that it is over as it feels good to be back in the real world. Surprisingly, unlike alcohol, I can remember most of what has happened and recognize that a lot of the feelings are drug induced; but in the same breath they are feelings that I have always had, they feel so real and a part of me.

The effects of the ecstasy tablets on Debbie are comical to watch as her face has become very pale and by all appearances she is finding it difficult to focus her eyes. Her eyelids flutter and then close and remain closed for several minutes when she snaps them open wide and stares at me as if she does not know who I am. I guess that she is seeing the same sort of brightness and colors inside her head that I experience when I close my eyes. That she is on a different 'level' to me is obvious and she appears to have difficulty coping with the drugs inside of her. For her, one who has obviously taken many drugs in her past and to appear to have difficulty controlling them makes me glad that I refused the extra tablet.

Getting to sleep is very difficult, if I can keep my eyes closed for any length of time I would start to drift off to sleep to be suddenly awoken by a 'twang' like the feeling of an elastic band twanging inside my head – which is most unpleasant, even painful. The fear of this re-occurring keeps my eyes open and I do not think that I got any sleep that night.

Chapter Eight

The dawn shows as a gray light through the windows and it is only then that I realize that I had not closed the curtains. Getting up to close them I decide not to go back to bed and dress quickly and go downstairs. The fire still burns as a red glow of embers so I put some kindling wood and a few small logs in the grate as it feels quite chilly.

Making myself a coffee I check the cupboard above the worktop for the Death Cap mushrooms; which are still there where Debbie had put them. As I pick up my coffee I notice that the magic mushrooms are no longer on the worktop and double check the fridge to see if she had put them inside. There is no sign of them so I go back into the lounge to see that the kindling wood has caught fire. Pulling the armchair and coffee table closer to the fire I sit down and stare into the flames.

I still feel a bit 'out of it' from the effects of the mushrooms from the night before and am glad that I do not have to go to work as I do not even feel capable of driving, let alone working. The memories of the night before are strong and I am glad of the experience; but not so sure that I would do them again.

My impression of Debbie being a lost little girl still remains and I realize that now I see her differently but not in a bad way, as the mushrooms and ecstasy had affected her in such a way that she had dropped her guard. I could only guess that I had done the same and hoped that I had not left a bad impression.

Remembering Debbie trying to eat the shredded wheat makes me smile and of the other silly things we had done or talked about. I feel that a stronger bond has formed between us and hope she feels the same way. Standing up to put some music on I suddenly feel dizzy and stagger several steps forward and have to reach out to the mantelpiece to stop myself from falling. Whether this was due to standing up too quickly or the effects of the mushrooms that were what made me lose my balance I am not sure. Still holding onto the mantelpiece with one hand I eject the cassette tape from the player, seeing that it is Ummaguma by Pink Floyd so turn it over and put it back into the player. Pressing 'play' I turn the volume down and sit back down into the armchair.

The music sounds good and I close my eyes and listen to the fire crackling and drift off to sleep.

Waking with a jump only a few minutes later as my leg feels wet and I look down to see that I have tipped the remainder of the coffee over me. Standing up quickly my head spins, but not as badly as before, and putting the mug down I go outside to get my spare jeans that are in my car.

The road is deserted as it is still early and I go quickly to my car and open the trunk and get my jeans out. As I shut and lock it I notice a man walking along the path towards me. I hurry back inside Debbie's house as I do not want him to see me with my wet leg, in case he thinks that I have peed myself.

As I close the door I can hear Debbie in the kitchen knocking crockery together and I assume that she is putting the washing up into the sink.

I walk along the hall and enter the kitchen; "Good morning Debbie," I cheerfully say; "I hope that I did not wake you when I got up?"

Debbie, still wearing her white nightie and blue low cut dressing gown turns from putting the washing up in the sink and looks at me and then down to look at my wet leg; "Good morning Patrick, no you did not wake me. I hope that you slept well?"

"No, not a wink until I got up," pointing down at my wet leg I laugh; "I tipped the remains of the coffee over me, I did not wet myself, honest."

"Glad to hear it, I have to admit I thought you had," she laughs.

"Thanks, I stopped wetting myself weeks ago."

"Glad to hear that too. Do you have your passport with you?"

"Yes, I have, it is in the car along with my credit cards and money as I have not changed the locks on my new apartment yet. I reckon that they are safer in the car than in the apartment; why do you ask?"

"Do you fancy going across the channel to the Continent for the day?"

"Across the channel – what for?" I ask.

"I have wanted to go across for quite a while but did not fancy it on my own. We can get some shopping over there and I want to go up to the Netherlands to see someone," Debbie replies rather mysteriously.

I wonder why she wants to go to the Netherlands as I am aware of the drug laws over there; "Who is it you want to see – we are not going to do any drug trafficking are we?"

Debbie laughs and her face colors slightly; "No, I just want to see an old friend who I have known for many years."

I get the feeling that Debbie is lying to me and decide that if that is what she is going across for I will not get involved. The excitement of going across the channel and to spend a few hours in another country fills me and I cannot help the smile as I reply; "Providing that you will do the driving as they drive on the wrong side of the road over there."

Debbie's face fills with delight and she smiles broadly; "Of course I will drive, it will be a good day out and will get us away from England for a few hours." Putting her cup down onto the worktop she folds her dressing gown around her tightly; "Go and get your passport and I will get changed and we may make the 9.30 ferry."

She hurries past me and runs up the stairs as I wonder what I am letting myself in for. If Debbie is getting involved in something illegal I had better go prepared and decide to take my money and credit cards with me in case I find myself alone. I go out to my car and get my bag that contains my passport and cards and put my wallet in my pocket.

I do not have to wait very long before Debbie hurries back down the stairs. She is dressed in faded jeans and trainers with a pale blue jumper and dark blue jacket; "Are you ready then?" she asks impatiently.

"Yes, all ready," I reply and I had already checked that the back door is locked.

"Come on then," Debbie says as she hurries to the front door.

"Have you got your passport and plenty of money?" I ask, noticing that she carries no bag.

Debbie presses her hand against her right breast where her inside pocket is; "Of course I have, thank you for agreeing to come with me, we will have a good day. Come on then," she says with excitement as she opens the front door and holds it open for me.

I walk past her and head for her car as she slams the door shut and locks the door. Hurrying along the path she opens her car door and unlocks the passengers' side and I get in as she starts the car with a roar.

Debbie drives quickly to Dover, many times exceeding the speed limit as she chats to me with excitement telling me that it has been many months since she has seen her friend. Her friend's name is Sally who is also a nurse. They met at the hospital when Sally was living in England and she moved to the Netherlands several years ago. She works as a nurse at a local hospital and moved there because the money and lifestyle is a lot better than in England. I ask Debbie why she had not moved there and Debbie says that she prefers England and the English way of life.

We soon arrive at Dover and Debbie drives to a booking firm for cross channel tickets and with a 'stay there' she gets out of her car and hurries inside. Five minutes later she comes out holding a small booklet and smiling broadly.

Getting back into her car she throws the booklet at me and starts the engine. Driving quickly out into the traffic Debbie tells me that we just have time to make the ferry. I open the booklet and see that it is a ticket for one car and for up to five passengers. The ticket costs over two hundred pounds, which to me is an absolute fortune for a day out and I ask if she wants me to pay half for the ticket.

With a laugh Debbie replies; "No, that is fine. Keep your money for when we get across and you can spend yours in the Hypermarket."

"What do you need in the Hypermarket?" I ask.

"Well it will be a wine and liquor store as well where we will stop. We can get some tobacco there as well and I will give you your money back when we get home."

"Tobacco – does that mean you intend to sell it when we get back?"

Debbie takes her eyes off the road and looks me in the eyes; "Of course, I need to get my money back for the cost of the ferry and for the petrol I will use. That is if it's alright with you?" And her eyes take on a familiar mad glint.

The cost of the ferry is a bit high, but to make two hundred pounds plus means we will have to get a lot of tobacco and wine! I ask as I wonder just how much we will have to get for her to break even.

Debbie returns her attention back to the road as we approach the ferry terminal; "No not too much. The tobacco is incredibly cheap in Belgium and we are allowed to bring back a kilo each which will be forty pouches. I will be able to get the ferry fare back on the tobacco alone and if we get some spirits and wine I should be able to make a profit on the day."

"Got it all worked out then?" I ask with a laugh.

"Yes, done this many times in the past. With Christmas approaching all we have to say is it is for Christmas and the New Year if we get stopped by customs."

"You think we will get stopped then?" I ask worriedly.

"We shouldn't do as it has been a long time since I went over. When was the last time you crossed the channel?"

I think back and realize that it was at least two years ago that I had visited France. I did not enjoy it much as I found driving on the right-hand side of the road very confusing and frustrating at times.

Debbie listens to my reply with a big smile as we pull up to the security post leading into the ferry terminal; "We have got nothing to worry about then," she says as she winds her window down; "Give me the ticket and your passport," she asks as she reaches into her pocket and pulls out her passport.

I hand her the ticket and my passport and putting her passport on top she reaches out and hands them to the lady security officer with a smile and a 'Good morning'.

The lady takes the passports and ticket and enters them into the computer. Bending down she takes a long hard look at me and I smile back sweetly. I can see that the security officer is not impressed with my smile as she makes no acknowledgement as she returns her attention back to the computer. Typing on the keyboard she waits a few seconds and then hands the passports and ticket back to Debbie along with a yellow ticket for displaying in the windscreen; "Have a nice day," she says with a smile.

Why Debbie should get a smile and not me I do not ask as Debbie takes the passports and ticket and puts them in my lap as she hangs the yellow ticket with H1 written in black felt tip pen from the rearview mirror; "Thank you, you have a nice day as well," she says as she puts the car in gear and we drive into the docks.

The line of cars and caravans in H1 are already moving as Debbie drives to the back of the queue. I can see numerous cars and caravans already driving onto the huge ferry and ten minutes later Debbie is parking the car inside the ferry. A ferry operator chains the car to the deck as we get out and after locking the doors we follow the crowd and head upstairs.

"A cup of coffee will be a good idea," Debbie says as we reach a lower deck and she makes her way forward into a large lounge.

We are at the very front of the ship and we look out of the windows at the harbor entrance and what looks like a calm English Channel. The weather looks good for October with large white cumulus clouds drifting over a pale blue sky.

Debbie looks towards the counter and seeing that they are not serving walks to the front windows and sits down at a table. I sit next to her as she lets out a 'Yayy, we made it.'

"That was easy enough," I say and look towards the counter where a steward readies a coffee machine; "When will they start serving?" I ask.

"Probably when we get moving," Debbie replies as she looks at her watch; "which should be in about fifteen minutes, that is if we sail on time."

I wait impatiently as my stomach feels empty and watch the steward as he cleans the counter with a red cloth and I look out to sea.

"Don't you want to go up on deck?" Debbie asks as the ships' engines start up. The vibration running through the ship is incredible as cups and saucers start to rattle behind the counter.

"No, coffee is more important, I will go up on deck when I have some coffee inside of me," I answer as the vibration reaches a pitch and the ships' engines die down to a more regular beat.

We sit quietly as more passengers enter the lounge. There are a lot of families with small children and the children run around the lounge in excitement with the parents shouting at them to calm down and to sit beside them. In one corner of the lounge there is a small play area for the children with a part of it filled with brightly colored rubber balls. Many of the children ignore their parents and with screams of delight they jump in amongst the rubber balls and some throw them about. Luckily the children's play area is surrounded by black netting that reaches up to the ceiling and no balls escape the confines of the play area. Several mothers express their dislike and walk over to their children and watch them so that no one gets hurt.

"Oh to be a parent," laughs Debbie as the noise level increases as a lot of the children scream with delight.

"Going up on deck sounds more attractive with all that noise going on," I say in frustration.

"Hey, we are moving already," Debbie exclaims.

I look out of the window and see the dock moving past us. There is no sensation of movement except what I can see with my eyes and we are soon past the dock entrance and head out into the English Channel.

Chapter Nine

The voyage across the channel is smooth and uneventful apart from seeing two other ferries outside the port as they make their way into Dover. The coffee, when served, is very hot and it is at least twenty minutes before I make it out on deck. By then the White Cliffs of Dover are a faint white line in the distance and I do not linger long on deck as there is quite a chilly breeze blowing.

When I return to the lounge I see a large group of people sitting at the table where Debbie and I had sat and I look around for her. Not seeing any sign of her I get myself another cup of coffee and sit down at a vacant table near the counter. The noise in the lounge has increased enormously with most tables occupied but at least the children have calmed down a little and there is only a small amount of excited screaming.

Debbie joins me as I am finishing my coffee and seeing that my cup is nearly empty asks if I would like another.

I reach into my pocket for some money telling her that I also want something to eat and she holds her hand up and says that she will pay. She soon returns carrying a tray with coffee and croissants and several individually wrapped squares of butter.

Just over two hours later the huge ship is gently easing into the port at Calais and we make our way down to the car. The car has already been relieved of its chains and we get in and wait for the ship to dock. We do not have to wait long as the large front door drops down and Debbie is soon driving out into the port. Security at the entrance to the port ignores us as we drive out and ten minutes later we are heading north on the motorway.

"We will stop at the tobacconists and wine shop in Belgium on the way out, in case we have any problems getting back," she tells me as we speed along the motorway - on the right hand side of the road.

"Problems – What kind of problems?" I ask.

"The traffic may well slow us down on the way back and it being a Sunday the tobacconists and the Hypermarkets shut early."

"How long will it take to get to your friends' place?"

"It will take us a couple of hours, if the roads are not too busy," she replies with a tight smile.

Debbie soon takes a turning off of the motorway and we drive into a small town. Reaching a busy junction and with the traffic lights showing green Debbie takes a right turn.

"I am glad you know where you are going, I am lost already," I confess with a nervous laugh.

Debbie smiles in reply; "Yes, I have done this a few times, the tobacco shop and Hypermarket are about a mile further on."

"Shouldn't I have changed my English pounds for Euros on the boat?" I ask.

"No, there is no need as they will happily take your English money," Debbie replies with a laugh.

"But at what rate of exchange?"

"They will not be much dearer than if you had Euros. Anyway you do not have to worry about that as I will reimburse you," she answers, still with a broad smile on her face.

Debbie soon pulls into a large car park with a large metal-clad building that proudly displays its name and the windows are covered with pictures of their goods – at 'value prices'. I am surprised to see that most of the advertisements are in English, though prices are displayed in Euros.

Debbie parks as close to the building as she can get and as we get out tells me that we will need a large trolley. I follow her to the front of the building and she points at the trolleys lined up out front underneath a curved corrugated roof with large windows at its sides.

"Won't I need some Euros for the trolley?" I ask.

"You shouldn't do, they are not as tight as our supermarkets."

I take Debbie at her word and walk over to the trolleys, seeing that they need no money to release them I pull out a trolley and follow her into the huge building.

Inside has the appearance of a very large supermarket rather than the tobacco and wine store I was expecting. As we enter an aisle tinned food is on offer along with breakfast cereal.

"Follow me Patrick," Debbie orders as she hurries along the aisle.

A half hour later and after spending over £180 pounds, I push the heavy trolley, that is loaded with a kilo more of tobacco than we are allowed to take back, boxes of wine, whisky of Scottish origin, also brandy and vodka made in France. Several crates of bottled French beer also fill the trolley and we also have several baguettes, French cheese, Belgian pizzas and a multitude of other foodstuffs.

Debbie laughs with delight as we load as much as we can into the trunk of her car and the remainder goes onto the backseat and on the floor which she covers with several bright red tartan picnic blankets; "That should keep us going for a few days." she laughs; "and it will give the English customs something to look at."

"I hope they don't confiscate anything; especially those extra twenty pouches of tobacco," I say with genuine worry in my voice.

"If they do look through and we haven't got more than we should have customs may become suspicious. Come on, we have a long way to go," Debbie tells me as she gets in behind the wheel.

I run back to the front of the store with the trolley and as I turn around I see that Debbie has parked just a few feet from me.

"Get in Patrick," she shouts and I hurry round to the other side of the car and get in quickly as she drives away.

Debbie soon drives onto the motorway and putting her foot down speeds along – but keeps to the speed limit. Half an hour later she pulls into a garage for petrol and fills the tank up with petrol that is a lot cheaper than in England!

I watch her as she pays for the petrol and notice as she leaves the shop that she uses the public telephone. There are at least ten public telephones lining the outside of the shop and many of them are being used. This is so different from English garages where there is only two or three public telephones available and bringing home that they do things very differently on the Continent – even with the expansion of the mobile telephone network.

Debbie soon finishes her call and with a big smile covering her face gets back into the car and starts it with a roar; "That is good, Sally is at home as she usually is on a Sunday. Be about another half an hour and we will be there," she tells me as she drives away from the garage and rejoins the busy motorway.

Twenty minutes later we leave the motorway and drive along a wide road lined with tall poplar trees. Beyond the trees the land is very flat and after a few miles we approach a large town that is composed mainly of large bungalows and everywhere looks clean and new.

Debbie looks across at me with the smile still covering her face; "Certainly different from England here, you can see why Sally likes it."

"Yes, it is a surprise; and you are not tempted to live here?"

She laughs; "No, even though it is nice here I cannot speak Dutch. I have a real problem trying to speak another language. I know that a lot of them do speak English but if you cannot speak their language you will never be fully accepted."

"I take it your friend can speak Dutch?"

"Yes, she speaks it like a native. Five more minutes we will be there," Debbie says and I cannot help but notice the excitement in her voice.

We drive into the main street of the town that is lined with shops; most are closed, it being a Sunday and several cctv cameras watch the traffic. Debbie turns off the main street and a few minutes later we pull up outside a large, modern bungalow. The garden is immaculate with ornamental shrubs, carefully manicured lawn and neat flowerbeds much of which has been dug over and is ready for next year's planting.

"Out we get," Debbie tells me as she switches the engine off and applies the handbrake; "I have not told Sally that you are with me. She can be a bit funny about strangers especially men, but just ignore her as we will not be here long."

Wondering about Debbie's friend and her strange comments I get out of the car and wait as she locks the doors and I follow her along the path.

The door is opened by an elderly lady who must be in her sixties. She is about five and a half feet tall and must only weigh about ninety pounds. Her black hair, which has obviously been dyed, is drawn tightly back from her face and formed into a round 'bun' on the top of her head. I take one look at her and feel an instant deep dislike and the feeling appears mutual as on seeing me she scowls ferociously; "Who is your man friend Debbie?" she demands in an angry voice.

"Hi Sally, this is a good friend of mine, Patrick, who has kindly agreed to accompany me."

"If you had told me on the telephone that you had a man with you I would not have let you come. Where is Jacky then?"

"I have not seen Jacky for a few months. I am sorry if you are offended but as you know I do not like to travel on my own, especially to here," Debbie replies indignantly.

Looking me over again Sally reluctantly opens her front door wider; "You had better come in then," she says as if it is a great honor for us.

I follow Debbie into the large bungalow which is spotlessly clean and Sally shuts the door behind us; "Go into the lounge, would you like a cup of coffee?" she grudgingly asks.

"Yes, that would be good Sally. I am really sorry that I have upset you," Debbie repeats.

"I understand, I forget that you do not like being on your own. I hope that your friend is alright?" Sally asks as she looks me up and down suspiciously.

"Of course he is. I have known Patrick for nearly thirty years and we have always been close friends," Debbie replies with an innocent smile.

"Please sit down and I will go and make you both a coffee. How do you like it?" Sally asks looking me in the eyes.

"Thank you Sally, black please with two sugars," I answer doing my best to form a friendly smile that I find difficult to do. It is her bungalow after all but I feel her rudeness is uncalled for.

"Polite isn't he?" Sally says as she turns away and walks out of the door.

"Sit down Patrick," Debbie tells me; "I will go and give her a hand."

I look around the room and see two comfortable armchairs and a large couch covered in dark brown leather. The furniture is made in the Dutch style and has thick sturdy legs and framework and is possibly made of oak, and looks like it will last for a thousand years. One of the armchairs has a Dutch magazine on the arm and I presume that was where Sally was sitting before we arrived. Deciding that the couch is the safest place to sit I sit at one end that has a small dark wood table next to it with several coasters on it depicting windmills. Looking around the room I see several scenic pictures of possibly Amsterdam on the wall and a vase of artificial flowers on a small dark wood table next to the huge window that overlooks the immaculate garden.

Raised voices come from, I assume, the kitchen as Sally vents her anger again at Debbie for bringing me. Sally expresses her concern 'and has no wish to spend time in prison at her age'.

I had guessed that Debbie had come all this way to buy drugs and hoped that she knew what she was doing; especially on our return through the English customs.

Debbie reassures Sally that I am no threat and their voices reduce in volume and I can no longer hear what they are saying. I am left waiting for more than ten minutes while they talk quietly until Debbie returns carrying a large mug that is decorated with colorful flowers.

"Here is your coffee Patrick," she says as she hands me the mug; "I am just going to talk to Sally for a little while longer, are you alright here?" she asks appearing apologetic.

"Thank you," I reply as I take the mug from her hand; "Do not worry about me, I am ok."

Debbie smiles; "Nice one, we will be with you in a few minutes," she tells me and walks back out into the kitchen.

The coffee is really bitter and tastes disgusting, but I know that I have no choice but to drink it all or Debbie's friend will criticize.

I sip at the coffee which is really hot and do my best to force it down quickly as I know that when it cools down it will taste even more disgusting. Debbie and Sally continue their whispered discussion for about fifteen minutes before they come back into the lounge. Debbie is smiling broadly and I guess that she has got what she came for.

Sally sits down on the armchair that has the magazine on the arm and looks at me with a haughty expression; "I understand that you and Debbie worked together selling rubber clothing to those who have a rubber fetish?" she asks, with a condescending smile on her lips.

I smile broadly; "Yes, that was a long time ago and I admit I was a bit naïve at the time. Thought that I was selling waterproof clothing," I answer and laugh in embarrassment.

"What is it that you are doing now?" Sally demands, looking deeply into my eyes.

"I work on a contract basis fitting air conditioning units mainly in public buildings and factories. The work pays well and gives me a lot of freedom; I am between contracts at the moment as I needed to take some time off as I have recently moved to a new apartment." I reply in the friendliest voice; "You are a nurse I understand, the same as Debbie?" I ask trying to be friendly.

"Well not quite the same as Debbie," Sally replies as she breaks the gaze then focuses her eyes back onto mine; "How did you like the mushrooms last night?"

I laugh nervously; "Oh, Debbie told you about that. Well, it was my first time and I certainly did not expect that to happen."

Sally smiles at me in a superior sort of way and I guess that she has taken them many times and considers herself an expert; "Why, what happened?"

"The most amazing feelings and everything looked so different and it was certainly not like getting drunk," I reply as I break the gaze and look down at the floor, Sally's questioning makes me feel uncomfortable, I know that she is only 'sounding me out' but I feel her questioning is an invasion of my privacy.

"How come you didn't take an 'E' when it was offered?" she asks, sounding offended.

"An 'E'? – Oh, you mean an ecstasy tablet. Those magic mushrooms had knocked me sideways and I guess I was a little frightened to."

Sally snorts in a derisory way; "You would probably have enjoyed it. I know those ones and I know they are good. Maybe next time you are offered you will consider taking one or two?"

I stare into her eyes as I reply; "One maybe the first time, definitely not two."

Debbie interrupts our conversation; "Have you finished your coffee Patrick? We have to get going or we will miss the ferry."

"Yes, all finished," I answer as I look back at our host; "Thank you for the coffee, it has been a pleasure meeting you Sally; and I love your home, you are very lucky to live here."

Sally takes the compliment well and her only reply is; 'Have a safe journey back.'

I stand up and pick up the empty coffee mug; "I will show my domestication and put this in your kitchen. May I use your toilet please before we leave? As it is a long journey back."

Sally quickly gets to her feet and holds out her hand towards me; "Give me that," she orders; "The toilet is near the front door, it is the door on the left, please do not pee on the carpet."

I hand her the mug; "Thank you," I say without snarling; "I never pee on the carpet," and make my way to the toilet.

The toilet is also immaculately clean and smells faintly of roses and I use it carefully and make sure I do not pee on the floor that has a fitted blue carpet. I wash my hands in the small basin and on stepping out the door see that the front door is already open and Sally and Debbie are already outside and talking in low tones a few yards along the path.

"Thanks for that Sally, maybe I will see you again," I say as I walk past them towards the car.

"Maybe," Sally replies; "Bye Debbie, take care on the way back."

"Bye Sally; and thank you. See you again soon," Debbie says as she turns away and walks slightly bow-legged along the path.

"Come on then Patrick, we might make the early ferry," she says as she opens the car door and gets in. Leaning across she unlocks the passengers' door and as I open it I take another look at Sally; "Bye," I say as I get in and do not hear if Sally makes any reply.

"That wasn't so bad was it?" Debbie asks me as she starts the engine.

"Not so sure about the twenty questions; and that coffee tasted disgusting."

Debbie laughs; "I agree with you about the coffee, she does like it strong. Sally is ok; she is just a bit nervous about strangers, men especially."

"Yes, I gathered that. I see she lives on her own, is she a lesbian?"

Debbie laughs even louder; "Just because she lives alone that does not automatically mean that she is a lesbian. Anyway what do you think?" she asks as she drives away.

I wisely do not reply as Debbie continues along the road. We drive through some lovely flat countryside of tree-lined ploughed fields, some surrounded by dykes until we take a turning that leads us back onto the motorway.

The motorway is packed with cars and but for the good grace of a nice man driving a pale cream Volvo who lets us out, we would have had difficulty joining the queue of traffic.

"Shit," Debbie exclaims; "It could well be like this all the way back to Calais."

We are hardly moving as we shunt and stop amongst the three lines of traffic which are bumper to bumper; "Where did all these cars come from?" I ask in dismay as on our way to Sally's the motorways were fairly clear of traffic in both directions and we had only been at Sally's for about forty minutes, but then the drive in the countryside; "It will take us hours to get back."

"The usual late afternoon traffic jam," Debbie replies and sounds really annoyed; "We will stop for a break further on and hopefully the traffic should thin out by then."

I make no answer and leave her to concentrate on her driving as the cars in front keep stopping for no reason that I can see.

The next hour is a nightmare of being surrounded by other cars, at one point we do get up to about twenty miles an hour but this only lasts for about half a mile before we are brought to a complete standstill for about ten minutes.

A service stop consisting of a large garage and restaurant appears to the side of the motorway and it is with relief when Debbie drives off the motorway. After filling up with petrol she drives around to the back of the restaurant and parks her car at the far edge of the car park near some bushes and trees and with a deep sigh turns the engine off.

After sitting with her eyes closed for a few minutes Debbie turns and looks at me; "I really need to use the toilet Patrick and I need the long walk as my legs are cramped. Will you stay with the car until I get back and then you can go? I will get us a coffee each while I am there."

"Of course," I answer; "but please do not be too long as I need to go as well."

Debbie opens her door; "I won't be long," she promises as she slams the door and I watch her bow-legged walk across the car park as she makes her way to the restaurant.

Five minutes pass slowly when suddenly a large white police van pulls up sharply next to the car. I look anxiously as a young police officer wearing the uniform of the Netherlands police gets out of the passengers' side and walks quickly over to me. Rapping the window with a bunch of keys he 'asks' me to wind my window down. I do as he asks and stare at him.

"Where have you been sir?" he demands.

I look in the back of the car at the tartan blankets before looking back at him; "Have been doing some Christmas shopping," I reply and try to keep the anger out of my voice.

He looks in the back of the car and then stares at me; "Would you mind stepping out of the car please sir?"

Knowing I have little choice I open the door and step out and stand in front of him.

"Where have you been shopping sir?" he asks.

I point in the direction of Belgium; "A few miles down the road," I answer and fail to keep some of the anger out of my voice. I hate being stopped and feel that he is just being dominating.

"You say along the road, how is it that you are here sir?"

"Me and my friend are just having a day out and we were going to go to Amsterdam but with the traffic and all we have left it a bit too late. We got about twenty miles from here when we decided it would be best to turn back in case we miss the ferry."

"Where did you turn off sir?" he demands.

I point back up the road where we had come from and shrug my shoulders; "I haven't a clue what the name of the place was as we got a bit lost before we found the motorway again."

He stares at me and appearing not to believe a word I say and I stare back at him defiantly.

"Wait there," he orders as he walks back to the police van which I see is full of police in the back. He opens the passenger door and leans in and takes out a small black box. As he walks back to me he inserts a small opaque tube into the top and holds it out towards me;

"Would you mind breathing into this sir?" he asks politely.

I look at it knowing that it is a breathalyzer; "I am not the driver mate," I aggressively reply; "Why do you want me to breathe into that?"

My reply appears to anger him and I suspect that it is not just a breathalyzer for detecting alcohol. Aware that Debbie is carrying some kind of drugs on her I look at him angrily in the eyes and then shrug my shoulders again and lean forward to breathe into his device.

"Blow gently into it please, sir, until I tell you to stop," he orders.

I do as instructed and hope that it will not detect the drug that was in the magic mushrooms. I had had little to eat, only a couple of croissants on the boat and several cups of coffee and I still feel a bit rough from the effects of last night.

As I breathe into the breathalyzer I see Debbie come around the corner of the restaurant and on seeing the police van and me being breathalyzed she walks alongside the restaurant towards a large white camper van.

The policeman instructs me to stop when I have just about emptied my lungs and he stares at the machine as it analyzes my breath and the driver shouts something to him in Dutch.

After about a few long seconds he looks back at me; "That is fine sir, thank you," and he turns around and walks back to the police van and gets in. Slamming the door shut he says something to the driver who then starts the engine and they drive away!

I stare dumbfounded as the police van drives towards the exit and then get back into Debbie's car. Slamming the door shut I think over what has just happened and wonder why he asked no questions about who the driver was and where were they?

Hearing footsteps approaching I look sharply in their direction and see that it is Debbie carrying two cups of coffee. She looks white and pale; "What was that all about Patrick?" she nervously asks.

"Can you believe that?" I exclaim angrily; "As you saw they breathalyzed me even though I told them I was not the driver and they asked me where I had been."

"What did you tell them?"

"That we had been Christmas shopping and tried to get to Amsterdam but the traffic was too busy so we turned back," I reply with a broad smile.

"What did they say about me?"

I look at Debbie, who looks scared stiff; "Well that was the puzzle, they didn't ask me anything about you."

"Did he think you were on your own?"

"I told him I wasn't but I guess that he must have thought I was. That breathalyzer must have showed negative though I was a bit nervous about that chemical in the mushrooms I took last night."

"Psilocybin," Debbie automatically replies; "Do you think he knew where we had been?"

"Well he didn't search the car or me. I guess it was just a random check which they probably make on the tourists with Amsterdam being just up the road."

"Marijuana is legal in the Netherlands and you don't have to go to Amsterdam to get it," Debbie answers with a weak grin.

I open the car door; "It's weird is all I have to say. I really need to use the toilet and pee after that. Where are they?"

Debbie looks back in the direction of the restaurant; "They are just inside the main doors."

I shut the passengers' door and hurry across the car park.

Debbie is sitting in her car sipping her coffee with a worried look on her face when I return. When I open the passenger door she visibly jumps and nearly spills her coffee.

"That made you jump," I laugh; "Sorry, what are you going to do now?"

She looks at me and I see her face is still a little pale; "What do you mean, what am I going to do now?"

"I know that you got something from Sally, I can tell that by the way you walk."

Debbie stares at me; "Only you know that. I am not going to get rid of them if that is what you are asking."

"I am not asking you to do that. I wouldn't worry too much, if they are not waiting down the road for us or waiting at the docks I would just forget about it."

"You think so Patrick?" Debbie nervously asks.

"Yeah, thinking about it and where we are parked I bet they thought I was rolling a joint or something. He looked satisfied about the breathalyzer result. If we stay here for another half hour or so maybe the traffic will have thinned out and we can get back home," I say as I take my coffee out of the cup holder. Peeling the lid off I take a big swig – and wished I hadn't as the coffee is piping hot and I burn my tongue and mouth.

Debbie stares out of the front windscreen; "I guess you are right, we haven't got much choice really."

"There are lots choices, but if you get arrested you are on your own. I know nothing and I don't know anything about us visiting Sally. We just turned off the motorway because of the traffic and stopped in a small town where you went off somewhere to pee. We then got a bit lost until we found the motorway again, is what I will say if the worst does happen."

Debbie looks at me and comes to a decision; "Yes, ok, I know you won't say anything and if I do get busted I will tell them you know nothing about it."

"You are not going to get 'busted' as you put it. I'll go and get us another cup of coffee and we'll drink that and then head back home."

Debbie smiles in agreement but I can see she is still very scared. She has calmed down considerably when I return with the coffee and after getting out and telephoning Sally to tell her of what had happened she now appears a lot happier.

About forty minutes later Debbie starts the car and we drive out of the car park and on to the motorway. The traffic is a lot lighter and she even manages to get our speed up to forty miles an hour.

As we cross the border into Belgium and with no sign of any police she relaxes further. Driving carefully and at times keeping a constant eye on the rearview mirror we drive through Belgium and into France. As we cross the French border darkness starts to fall and Debbie admits that she hates to drive on the Continent in the dark. I could not agree with her more as with the reduced visibility I soon lose my bearings.

Luckily Debbie has made this trip many times and we turn off the motorway when the bright lights of Calais docks show the way. Debbie visibly tenses up as we drive into the docks and I try to give her some words of reassurance;

"Keep a smile on your face Debbie," I advise; "If the Netherlands police knew about our visit to Sally I feel sure that they wouldn't have let us out of their country. I will put money on it that we will not get stopped here. The French do not like the English very much and I am sure that it would give them great pleasure to 'bust' you if they knew."

Debbie glances at me; "I am sure that you are right Patrick. But you won't mind if I worry a little will you?"

"If you want to waste your energy it's up to you," I laugh. The security kiosk of the docks looms before us and we join a queue of about fifteen cars; "Just remember to keep smiling. We have had a great day in their country and I bet they won't even look in the car."

I open the glove compartment on the dash in front of me and take out the ferry ticket. Putting my passport on top I hand them to Debbie; "Don't forget your passport," I laugh; "and keep smiling."

Debbie takes the ticket and passport from my hand and reaches into her pocket and puts her passport with them. I chat about the day and the awful traffic on the motorway to stop her from thinking too much as we approach the security kiosk.

Winding her window down Debbie smiles broadly as she hands over our ticket and passports to the young looking male security officer. To me her smile looks false but I am sure the security officer will not notice. He casually looks through the passports and ferry ticket and does not even enter the details into the computer as he hands them back.

"Thank you," Debbie says broadening her smile and the security officer does not even acknowledge her smile as he looks to the car behind us.

Putting the car in gear Debbie follows the line of traffic to the ferry, which is already waiting with cargo doors open and we drive on board. One of the crew points to where Debbie should park and as she turns the engine off another crewman chains her car to the deck.

"I hope that we have a smooth crossing," I say; "Shall we go to the lounge or do you want to go up on deck until we sail?"

"Do you know where the receipt is from the shopping?" Debbie asks me as she looks in her rearview mirror at the car pulling in behind us and does not answer my question.

"The receipt? Yes, it is in the same bag as the baguettes," I answer in surprise and wonder why she asks.

"And where is that?" Debbie asks nervously.

"I think that is in the trunk. Why do you want it?"

"You must have wondered why I spent so much of your money buying all that food," Debbie replies.

"Well, I did wonder about some of it as some was more expensive than in England. I guessed you had your reasons and anyway you did say you would give me my money back."

"I needed us to spend that much as that is how much I had changed into Euros on the ferry on the way out and had to give that to Sally."

Remembering that I had handed over £180 at the Hypermarket I cannot help but exclaim; "Bloody hell, you did buy a lot from Sally, no wonder you are a bit nervous."

"More than a bit," Debbie confirms as she opens her door; "Please get out Patrick, so that I can lock your door."

Putting the ferry ticket and my passport into my pocket, which had been on the shelf behind the gear lever, I hand Debbie's passport to her as I get out and shut the door.

Debbie quickly locks the door and gets out and locks her door as no central locking and she goes to the back of the car. Opening the trunk she rummages around inside and then shuts and locks it holding the large receipt in her hand.

"Why do you want that? I can remember how much I spent," I ask.

"Because the receipt shows that you paid in English pounds. I'll throw it overboard when we get out to sea in case customs ask where all the Euros went," she answers with a nervous smile.

"They won't ask, but yes, better to be safe than sorry. Shall we go upstairs?"

"Yes, let's go up on deck until we sail," Debbie replies as her smile widens.

The ferry journey back across the English Channel is uneventful, it being dark we do not get to see very much apart from other ships lights in the distance. As we exit the port and enter the English Channel Debbie tears up the big receipt and after throwing it overboard we go downstairs and into the restaurant. Debbie insists on buying the coffee and also buys two large portions of chips with beef burgers in a roll. I had not realized how hungry I was until Debbie puts the food in front of me; my stomach even growls at the sight of it.

As we pull into Dover Docks Debbie becomes more agitated and I try to appear confident before her. I challenge her to a bet of £20 that we will not get stopped going through customs but she will not take up the bet.

Returning to her car as the ship docks, we get in, fasten our seat belts and await the opening of the cargo doors. The car has already been unchained from the deck and I cannot keep quiet and offer her more advice – which is to keep smiling and to make sure that she concentrates on her driving and not to hit anything.

Debbie is in too much of a state to even acknowledge my wise words and with a pale face we drive off the ferry and follow the traffic to customs.

Handing the ticket and my passport I comment on her pasty appearance; "Say to them when you hand over the passports that it has been one hell of a day and you are knackered. They might interpret your pale complexion as tiredness rather than fear."

"I look as bad as that do I?" Debbie asks, the nervousness in her voice is plain to hear.

"Well you do to me and you sound a bit nervous as well, so don't say too much. Here we go," I say as we approach the kiosk.

Debbie winds her window down and without saying anything hands over the ferry ticket and passports.

"I do not want that," the customs officer says as he hands back the ferry ticket. Typing in the details from our passports he hands them back as he scrutinizes us.

"I will be glad to get home. What a long day I feel really tired," Debbie tells him and manages a weak smile.

"Drive carefully," the customs officer says and looks at the car behind us as Debbie puts the car in gear and we drive out of the port.

"You just didn't want to bet and give me £20," I laugh as Debbie gives a whoop of joy.

As we drive out of Dover Debbie pulls over at a lay by and putting the parking brake on switches the engine off. Removing her seatbelt she undoes the front of her jeans and unzipping the fly, and with an 'excuse me, it is riding up inside me' she puts her hand down the front of her jeans and after lifting her bum off the seat pulls out a large rubber condom wrapped package. I am amazed at the size of it as it must be an inch and a half in diameter and nearly nine inches long. Putting it on the shelf behind the gear lever she sits back down and does her jeans back up and fastens her seat belt;

"That is better Patrick. Sorry about that but it was going further up inside of me than it should. Can you put it in the glove compartment for me please?"

I look at the wet package which appears to contain a lot of white colored pills and which does not smell too good either and I am glad that I have no sexual inclinations towards her.

Debbie suddenly interrupts my thoughts; "Don't worry, I'll do it as best not to have your fingerprints on it," she says as she leans across me and opens the glove compartment. Picking the package up carefully she puts it in the glove compartment and shuts the door. Starting the engine Debbie smiles and puts the car in gear and we drive into the night and back to her home.

Arriving back at her house we quickly unload the car. Most of the shopping gets left in the hall and after putting a few things in the fridge Debbie makes coffee while I light the fire in the lounge.

Sitting down in front of the fire with coffee in hand is a relief as it has sure been a long and at times exciting day. Debbie has placed her package on the small coffee table and after a few minutes she goes out into the kitchen and comes back with a pair of scissors. Cutting away the rubber condom that encloses the package she throws it onto the fire. Now the rubber has been removed I can clearly see the white tablets that are inside a polythene bag that is wrapped tightly with more polythene. Removing the layer of polythene, which she also throws onto the fire, Debbie opens the bag and tips several out onto her hand. They look to be the same roughly made white tablets as she had before and I wonder if her saying that she had got them from the other side of town was in fact a lie.

"At last," she exclaims and holds her hand out towards me; "Don't they look wonderful Patrick?"

"I wouldn't know as I have not had anything to do with them. What are they made of, I presume that they are E's?"

"Yes, these are E's and these are the same batch as I had before. They are made of a synthetic form of ecstasy rather than the natural ingredient that comes from the rain forest. They also have bulking agents as the dose you need is very small and they are made up to be pill size."

"Not that it is any of my business, but are you going to keep all those or are you going to sell them?"

Debbie laughs; "I will probably keep these for myself, I might sell some to a few friends if I am persuaded to, but after all the trouble we went through today I think I would prefer to keep them."

"How many are there?" I ask trying to keep the surprise out of my voice that Debbie intends to keep them all.

"There should be two hundred and fifty," Debbie answers with a broad smile.

"How long would that amount last you?"

"At least a couple of years, if my friends want some I will probably go back and get some more, but that will be next year. If I go over too many times customs will take an interest in me."

"Yes, I had heard that they monitor who goes across the channel and how many times. These days of computers the information comes up almost as soon as they type your name in. But if you went over for shopping at the Hypermarket surely they wouldn't mind that?" I ask.

"Even if I was to do that they seem to only tolerate a few trips. If you go over too much it implies to them that you are selling the alcohol and tobacco rather than having it for your own use," Debbie replies with a frown deepening her forehead and showing her disapproval.

"You look eager to take some of them now. When are you going to do them again?"

"Yes Patrick, you can read me like a book. I would like to do some now but I feel too tired. Will you take some with me tomorrow, maybe in the afternoon?"

"I quite liked the mushrooms. I will do some more of them tomorrow as it should be good doing them in the daylight," I answer diplomatically as I had heard a lot of bad things about ecstasy and the deaths they cause.

"You will probably find that they will not do a lot to you as it is a bit soon after taking the others," Debbie advises.

"Really? That does surprise me you saying that. I thought that drugs were addictive and some people needed to take them every day."

"Would you want the effects of magic mushrooms every day?"

"Well, no, you would not get much done around the house and trying to fit air conditioning would probably be impossible; why all the fuss about them then as they are illegal?"

"They are illegal because a lot of people, especially the youngsters, take so many of them at a time. I know of people who have taken over two hundred mushrooms, even more, at a time and they wonder why they get head problems!" Debbie replies in frustration.

"Two hundred!" I exclaim in disbelief; "Wow that is a lot, I was totally 'out of it' on one hundred and that was in a 'tea'. What happens to you when you take so many at once?"

"You go right off your head, think you can fly and things like that. There have been several deaths because people thought they could fly and they jump out of windows. The rule is to take these things in moderation and to know your limit. It is no different to alcohol really; if you drink a whole bottle of whisky or a bottle of vodka you end up not knowing what you are doing and you can even die from what they call alcohol poisoning. If you are in a Public House and you get very drunk the landlord will stop serving you as he knows you will probably end up getting into trouble; and it is almost guaranteed that you are going to end up being very sick."

"Yes, you are right there. I remember when I was a Teddy Boy the drunks used to pick fights with us as they thought they were invincible – which they weren't. What about those E's that you have, what happens when you take too many of those?"

"Same thing really, if they are any good you should only need two or three. I have known of people who have taken ten at one time and to me that told me that what they were taking was not very strong, if they were, that amount would make them senseless."

"Scary stuff, have you ever taken too many Debbie?"

"I did once a long time ago. If you go back twenty, even thirty years when they first came into this country they were a lot stronger then. My first one was about thirty years ago and it was a mixture of ecstasy and amphetamine."

"Amphetamine – that is what is called speed?"

"Yes, that's right. Well this tablet cost me £15, which was a lot of money back then and kept me up for four days and three nights," Debbie laughs; "You have never seen the house so clean but it took me more than a week to get over it."

"When you say it kept you 'up' for four days and three nights meaning you did not sleep during that time?" I ask amazed at what Debbie is telling me.

Debbie laughs; "Yes awake for all that time and I had to take a week off work as I felt so ill."

"Thirty years ago – you were working at the shop then?"

"Yes, I had to tell the boss I had rotten flu and my husband gave me a really bad time over it. I didn't take anything for months afterwards."

"Did your husband take those sorts of things with you?"

"No, he was dead against anything like that. Mind you it was fine for him to get drunk and knock me around. That is the annoying thing with alcohol, it being legal it is generally accepted in this society for people to get drunk." Debbie frowns deeply and then shakes her head to clear the bad thoughts; "Enough of talk of drunken people, I am going to bed. Will you stay a few more days with me please Patrick? You did say that you didn't have to go back to work."

"Yes, I will stay for a few more days if you really want me to. Anyway I want to try some more of those mushrooms tomorrow."

"Mark my words they will not have the same effect as they did last night." Debbie smiles, the tiredness obvious to see on her face; "I am going to bed and I will see you in the morning." Debbie says as she gets to her feet and after putting the E's back in the bag which she still holds in her hand she then folds the bag carefully so that none will fall out and takes them with her as she goes upstairs to bed.

"Goodnight Debbie, sleep well," I say as she walks out the door.

"I think I will, I feel really tired. Goodnight Patrick."

Chapter Ten

The smell of frying bacon wakes me in the morning and I turn over and look at the clock. I cannot believe the time as I see that it is 9.30 a.m. three hours past my usual wake up time and I throw back the covers and get out of bed.

"Is that you getting out of bed Patrick?" Debbie calls from the bottom of the stairs.

"Yes and it's a bit late for me."

"That is alright, you are allowed to. Do you want some breakfast?"

"Yes please, I will come right down," I shout and reach for my clothes.

As I walk into the kitchen Debbie starts to fill a plate with bacon; "Good morning Patrick, I take it you slept well?"

I yawn loudly, "Excuse me, yes I did. Good morning Debbie, I hope you slept ok too?"

"Yes like a log," Debbie replies as she puts a fried egg, mushrooms and a fried slice onto the plate. Picking up the plate and a knife and fork she hands them to me; "Your coffee is behind you, go into the lounge I will be right behind you."

"Nice one thanks," I answer taking the plate and cutlery from her hand. Turning around I see two mugs of coffee and I take the one with no milk and go into the lounge.

The fire is burning brightly and by the looks of it Debbie has been up for an hour or more. Sitting down in the armchair I tuck into my breakfast as Debbie walks in carrying hers.

"Looks like you were up early this morning?" I ask.

"Yes, I woke up about 7a.m. and thinking about what we are going today filled me with excitement and I could not get back to sleep, so I got up," she replies with a beaming smile.

"Yes, I am looking forward to this afternoon," I say around a mouthful of bacon and look out of the window at the gray morning; "Do you know what the weather is going to be like today?"

"They have forecast rain later on, but it will only be about twelve degrees."

"That is a shame as I was looking forward to going down the town this afternoon."

"After you have taken your mushrooms I presume? That is not such a good idea as your aura will be different; and people will know that you are 'out of it' and which may lead to problems."

I feel disappointed at her answer; "You know best, your back garden is ok. Let us hope it does not rain too much," I answer as I continue to eat my breakfast.

We finish our breakfasts in silence and I stand up and hold out my hand for Debbie's plate; "I will go and wash these up and then go and have a shower."

I am surprised when Debbie hands me her plate and empty mug as I expected her to object to me doing the washing up; "Thank you Patrick, can I have another coffee please as you are going out there?"

"Of course, that was a lovely breakfast, a good start to the day," I smile broadly as I go out into the kitchen.

Returning with her coffee I see that she has her bag of ecstasy tablets on the table; "Here is your coffee Debbie, when are you going to take your E's then?" I ask.

Debbie takes the mug from my hand and looks back at the tablets; "I am thinking of doing a couple with this coffee."

"Early start then," I laugh; "May I look at one of them again please?" Last night when Debbie showed them to me they had looked slightly different and I want a closer look.

"Of course, are you thinking of doing some with me?" Debbie replies as she opens the bag and takes out two and hands them to me.

"No, I am looking forward to those mushrooms again," I answer as I look at the tablets closely. I was right in my suspicions, though made as roughly as the tablets Debbie showed me the other night these are definitely different. They are a lot thinner and appear to be an off white where the other night's ones were a pure white.

"They look good don't they Patrick? I can hardly wait," Debbie laughs with excitement; "Are you sure that you will not do some with me?"

"I do not want to put bad thoughts in your head but to tell you the truth I am a little scared of them. I have heard of so many bad things about ecstasy. A lot of people have died from taking just one and to be honest I would be terrified."

"Ahh, you shouldn't always believe what you read in the papers. Yes some people have died, but that is because they do not look after themselves after they have taken them. They can dehydrate you and the trick is to have a lot of fluid. A lot of people go to night clubs after taking them and those places charge £2, even £2.50 for a small bottle of water. Well with prices like that a lot go without or buy beer or spirits, which is not advisable. Anyway they buy the pills from someone off the street and who knows what they are made of? Some people have no scruples, I remember a few years ago there were a lot of yellow tablets around which were reputed to be a good speed and they turned out to be what they feed the chickens. They were some kind of hormone tablet and they had no real effect; and I didn't hear of anyone laying any eggs," Debbie laughs loudly at her joke.

Surprised at her flippant attitude I look more closely at the two tablets in my hand; "These are slightly different to the ones you had the other night, are these ok to take?"

"Sally said they were the same batch. I have bought from her for years and she has already tried them and said they are ok."

"Have you got any from your last batch?"

"No, they were the last. Don't worry Patrick; I know what I am doing. You should try them, you will probably find that you like them – a lot," Debbie giggles in excitement.

Handing them back to her I consider Debbie's words and then dismiss them as pure madness. To put your life at risk just to have a good time appears foolish to me. I do not want to worry her with my dark thoughts so smile broadly; "I am sure that you do know what you are doing, maybe I will take some with you another time," I lie, but with a smile on my face.

Debbie takes them from my hand and shrugs her shoulders; "Your loss Patrick, there is nothing to fear except fear itself. I am going to have a good time today and I do know what I am doing," she answers as she puts the tablets in her mouth and washes them down with a mouthful of coffee.

"Hey," I laugh; "Don't start the party to early without me. Give me fifteen minutes to have a shower and I'll be back."

"I've already started," Debbie laughs and takes another mouthful of coffee.

When I come back down Debbie is still sitting on her stool staring into the flames of the fire. Hearing me entering the room she looks up at me; "All clean now?" she smiles.

"Yes, thank you. That is a good shower you have there. Would you like another coffee?" I ask as I pick her mug up from the table.

"Yes please Patrick. You will find the mushrooms in a jar in the cupboard above the worktop next to the sink," she tells me with a wide smile.

I look at the clock and see that it is only 10.30 a.m.; "I was going to have a little bit more to eat and do them this afternoon as they did make me feel a bit sick the other day."

"That is a good idea, they can have that effect on you and plenty of food inside you will make you feel better. Help yourself to whatever when you are hungry, there is plenty of food out there in the cupboards and in the freezer."

"Thanks Debbie, I am not forgetting that we bought some baguettes and French cheese yesterday. Will you want anything when I get it ready?"

"Maybe, I'll let you know," Debbie laughs and her eyelids flicker and I can see that the tablets are already taking effect.

I go out into the kitchen to make more coffee as I hear music from the lounge and a loud 'Yayy' from Debbie.

Debbie spends the rest of the morning sitting on her stool mostly with her eyes closed and listening to the music. I try several times to talk to her but she seems to be 'somewhere else' and I feel that after I have taken some magic mushrooms I will be on the same level as her and we will be able to communicate more easily.

I make myself several French cheese sandwiches using a whole baguette and prepare some for Debbie. Putting it on the table in front of her with another mug of coffee I tell her that 'dinner is served'.

Debbie opens her eyes and taking the mug of coffee in her hand mumbles a 'thank you' closes her eyes again and drifts off to the place where she seems to be very happy.

About an hour after eating I take down the jar of dried mushrooms in the kitchen and look at them closely. Now that they are dry they are all shriveled up and do not look at all appetizing. Preparing the teapot I warm it up with boiling water and count out about one hundred of the magic mushrooms. It is difficult to get an accurate figure as they are all tangled up together but I estimate I have the right number. I put them in the teapot and pour boiling water over them and let them stew for about ten minutes. I admit that I am a bit nervous of taking them rather than excited, but after ten minutes I pour out the mushroom tea into a large mug and add four teaspoons of sugar. Looking into the teapot I see that the mushrooms have expanded back to their original size and apart from the gray coloring they look fine. Making another mug of coffee for Debbie I go into the lounge and put the coffee in front of her and she opens her eyes; "Thank you Patrick. When are you going to take your mushrooms?"

Holding the mug up in front of me I smile; "I have them here, cheers," I say as I take a large swig. The taste, even with the extra sugar is still absolutely disgusting.

"Well done," smiles Debbie; "I will do some more of these," she says as she opens her bag of tablets. Taking out two she laughs with excitement as she puts them in her mouth and washes them down with a mouthful of coffee; "Happy days. You should try these Patrick as they are very good. You were right about them being different as I keep drifting off to a wonderful place," she says with a broad smile.

"Yes I can see that you keep drifting away to somewhere. Happy days," I say as I take another mouthful of the mushroom tea.

I sit down on the armchair and force down as much tea as I am able to. The taste is truly disgusting and I only manage about two-thirds. Putting the mug down onto the table I notice that Debbie has closed her eyes and drifted off again so I sit back and await the effects of the tea.

Forty minutes later my legs start to ache and this is followed by the most intense backache I have ever experienced. Vision becomes blurred and I find that I cannot stop yawning. The yawns are so deep and long that my jaw locks up several times and is really painful. I find that I cannot sit still as my muscles ache something bad and I find that I am not having such a good time after all; in fact I am having a terrible time.

Debbie notices my discomfort; "I seem to remember telling you that the effect would not be the same. I see that you keep moving about in your chair and yawning, that is because you have not taken enough," she tells me with a knowing smile.

"Not enough?" I ask; "but I took about a hundred and I thought some chemicals can remain in your system for up to seventy-two hours."

"Maybe not Psilocybin, if I was you I would go and make yourself some more tea using about another fifty mushrooms."

The suggestion fills me with horror as I am having a bad enough time as it is and to take more and to intensify the feelings seems absolute madness.

"I'll give it a bit longer," I reply; "and see how it goes. How are you doing?"

She shrugs her shoulders and then smiles; "I am having a wonderful time," and her eyelids flutter and she closes her eyes again.

I laugh loudly; "I notice that you cannot keep your eyes open, you are not going to sleep on me are you?"

"Hardly," Debbie answers, not opening her eyes.

The aches and yawns continue and I feel most uncomfortable and really wish that I had not taken the mushroom tea. I certainly do not want to take anymore as already I feel out of my depth and am eager for the effects to wear off.

The afternoon passes in a blur of pain and of feeling uncomfortable and after about three hours I tell Debbie that I am going to bed for a few hours as I feel totally wiped out.

Debbie smiles; "By all means Patrick do what you feel. I will be here when you come back down as I am very tempted to do some more of these," she says and waves her hand towards the bag of tablets.

Debbie looks very pale and I notice that there is a bead of sweat on her forehead and her neck also looks wet with sweat.

"I just need to close my eyes for an hour or so then I will come back down," I tell her as I get to my feet. The room starts to spin and I suddenly feel very sick; "Be back soon," I say as I stagger out of the door.

It is difficult climbing the stairs and I am glad there is a handrail which I have to grip onto tightly to stop myself from falling back down the stairs. Reaching the room where I am staying I open the door wide, stagger forward and without removing my clothes fall down on the bed face first and I think I pass out for a while.

My aching legs seem to bring me back to consciousness and I fold up into the fetal position as a terrific yawn takes over. My jaw locks tightly and I am unable to close my mouth and the pain from the locked jaw muscles penetrate my brain and I pray for release.

Release is a long time coming as I lay on the bed and twist and turn in agony and worry that I will never feel normal again. I have to get up and I stagger quickly to the toilet and throw up. Retching painfully tears fill my eyes and I wish for an end to this horrible nightmare.

Debbie makes an appearance in my room sometime later and puts a mug of coffee on the bedside cabinet.

"Are you alright Patrick? Try and drink your coffee, I have put lots of sugar in it and a little milk. The milk should help to bind the effects of the mushrooms. Come down as soon as you can as I am getting lonely down there."

I turnover and face her; "Thank you Debbie, I do feel a little better than I did earlier. I feel sure I will come down soon. Thank you for the coffee and thank you for caring."

"My pleasure and come down soon," she says as she walks out of the room, leaving the door wide open.

I sit up as best I can and picking up the coffee I take a sip. It is very sweet so I drink some more, put the mug back down and lay back and close my eyes and fall asleep.

How long I had slept I do not know except that when I drink some more of the coffee I notice that it has gone cold. I force the rest down and have to get up to use the toilet. Looking in the mirror at myself I notice that my hair is in a total mess and my eyes are badly bloodshot.

'Why do I do these crazy things?' I ask myself and manage a weak smile. After relieving myself I manage to walk back into my room. Aware that Debbie is probably worrying about me I brush my hair and after splashing cold water onto my face carefully go back downstairs.

Entering the lounge I notice that Hawkwind is playing 'Master of the universe' Debbie is still sitting on her stool and I see that she has eaten the baguette and cheese. A full mug of coffee sits on the table in front of her and on hearing me enter she opens her eyes and smiles; "Well done Patrick. I was beginning to think that you were going to stay up there for the rest of the day."

I look at the clock on the mantelpiece and see that it is 4.45 p.m. which surprises me as I thought it was a lot later.

"Really sorry to duck out on you Debbie, I feel a whole lot better now thanks to the coffee, even though I drank most of it when it was stone cold."

"You're welcome," Debbie smiles; "I have just made myself a coffee, if you want another one the kettle has just boiled."

"Thanks," I reply as I realize that I have left my empty mug upstairs; "I'll do that before it gets cold."

I go out into the kitchen and get a clean mug from the cupboard, as I cannot manage going back upstairs, I make myself a coffee. Wondering if the milk did help me I add milk from the fridge and put plenty of sugar in.

Debbie is still sitting on her stool when I get back and I sit on the armchair gratefully and sip my coffee as 'Master of the universe' ends. Debbie smiles at me; "You do look a lot better Patrick, take it easy there."

"Thanks Debbie," I reply noticing that she is still pale and appears to be covered in sweat; "You look hot, do you want me to open one of the French doors and let some air in?"

"Yes, I am a bit hot," she admits; "Yes please open one of the doors, but not too much as I think it is raining out there."

I get up and walk slowly over to the French doors and after unlocking them, open one a few inches. It is raining hard and I feel a cool breeze wash over me and stand still for a while before I turn and go back to the armchair. Sitting down I take a mouthful of coffee and smile weakly at Debbie who has been watching my every move.

Debbie laughs and reaches into her bag of tablets and after taking one out puts it in her mouth and swallows it without the help of any coffee.

"I see that you are still having a good time," I say with a broad smile.

"Yes I am thank you Patrick. Would you like one?"

"No, no thanks," I laugh; "You are forgetting that I am only a lightweight."

"Yes I was forgetting," Debbie giggles as her eyelids flutter and she closes them for a few seconds before snapping her eyes open wide. Giving a little shudder she reaches out for her coffee and takes a large mouthful; "That's better," she says and giggles again.

The rest of the afternoon and evening passes in a bit of a blur for me. Many times I find that I have drifted off to sleep sometimes for only a few minutes. Debbie remains mostly seated on her stool with her eyes closed listening to the music. The silence when the music finishes wakes me several times but each time Debbie gets up and turns the cassette tape over or puts another one on. By the end of the evening a pile of tapes, not returned to their cases, remains next to her cassette player.

Each time I am fully conscious I make coffee for me and Debbie. I remember what she had said about needing fluid when under the influence of those tablets and I endeavor to keep the coffee flowing.

Debbie takes many more ecstasy tablets during the evening; sometimes every hour on the hour. The effect upon her does not appear weak and to my mind she is overdosing. I think it best to make no comment as she has taken these things for many years and must know what she is doing to herself. To object and make her aware that she is, to me, taking more than she should could cause more problems and wisely I keep my thoughts to myself.

I manage to eat more baguette and cheese in the evening but Debbie only consumes coffee and ecstasy. About ten-thirty Debbie makes a strange noise and falls backwards off her stool and lands with a big thump onto the floor. She is oblivious to this as she has totally passed out. I untangle the stool from her feet and lay her out on the floor in some kind of comfort. I check her pulse which appears to be strong and go and get a blanket from the airing cupboard. I cover her and make her as comfortable as possible.

I sit beside her for another hour as the fire dies down and after switching off the cassette player I shut and lock the French doors. Putting the safety guard in front of the fire I check that the back door is locked and that everything in the kitchen is switched off safely and go upstairs to bed.

Lying in bed I do worry about Debbie's condition but feel that there is little I can do. That she might need hospital treatment does cross my mind many times but to call for an ambulance and have her taken to the local hospital where she works, could be a very big mistake.

Her stomach would probably need pumping out, but with her unconscious and her 'illness' being self-inflicted I could not expect any sympathy from the hospital staff. I had heard before of people taking drugs and needing hospital treatment and of the staff having no sympathy for them and using the biggest stomach tube available; and not being too gentle about it.

Debbie is a big enough girl to take the consequences of her actions and I just hope that I wouldn't find her dead in the morning. With these troubled thoughts passing through my mind I toss and turn for several hours before sleep finally claims me.

Chapter Eleven

Hearing a noise in my room in the morning I wake up to find Debbie standing just inside the door. She looks very different to me somehow and even has the appearance of being a complete stranger. Dressed in a bright pink T-shirt and matching pink dress, she has obviously had a shower and cleaned herself up and she appears to be twenty years younger than she really is. To complete the picture she has tied her hair back into two tight pig-tails and I sit up and smile weakly; "Good morning Debbie, you fell asleep on me last night."

Not acknowledging me in any way she curtly asks; "Are you going to come shopping with me later, or do you want to go home?"

"Shopping sounds good" I answer automatically; "Where are you going?"

"I have to go to the supermarket and then we can have a wander up the town."

"What after all that you got when we were in Belgium? Anyway I should be fit in an hour or two. You look good this morning I take it you slept well?

"Like a log. Would you like some breakfast before we go?"

Putting my hand on my stomach I reply; "My stomach is still a bit queasy from yesterday, I think all I would be able to handle is toast and coffee."

A few hours later, after she has locked and secured the house, I go out the gate and start walking in the direction of the town when Debbie stops me.

"We are going in my car Patrick, I am not going to carry all that shopping, and anyway, the best supermarket is along the coast. While we are there we can watch the ferries, I know a great place from where we can watch them."

I make no complaint as it will make the shopping trip a bit more exciting. Getting into her car we buckle up and are soon on our way. The drive of about thirty miles along the Kent coast is slow going as there is a lot of traffic about and it takes almost an hour to get there.

Debbie drives through the town past several supermarkets and I ask her why she has passed them?

"We can sit on the cliffs for a few hours before we do that," she tells me with a smile as she takes a turning off the main road. We drive along it, passing through a picturesque village with oak beamed houses from the seventeenth century and then drive down a steep hill cut into the cliffs that leads to the coast.

I look at Debbie and then back at the cliffs as we approach the beach; "Debbie I thought you said we were going to sit on the cliffs to watch the boats?"

Debbie laughs, not taking her eyes off the road; "They are ships Patrick, and yes, we are going to sit on the cliffs."

"But they are over two hundred feet high here; wouldn't it be easier to park back up there?" I ask, indicating back up the road the way we came.

"Where is the fun in that? It is not much of a walk and I know a good place and we should have it to ourselves."

I make no comment as Debbie drives into a large car park and drives to the far end and parks the car close to a path that meanders up the white cliffs. I get out and she locks the doors and with a beaming smile starts walking towards the path. Seeing that I am not following she stops and turns around. The smile has now gone and an angry glint is in her eyes; "Come on Patrick, you are not frightened of a little walk are you?"

I smile back at her and look up at the cliffs; "Of course not, but that is not a little walk."

"I will walk slowly for you," she replies in a condescending voice; "it will be worth it and there is a café at the top where we can get a cup of coffee."

I can see that any arguing would only antagonize her further and wish that I had gone home after all. Putting on a brave face I follow her up the path.

The weather is fine with a faint breeze blowing off the sea and the walk up to the top of the cliffs is arduous and I have to stop several times to rest and catch my breath – much to Debbie's annoyance. After stopping the fourth time she loses her temper and almost shouting says; "Will you come on Patrick? I thought that you were a lot fitter than this, I can do it all right, why can't you?"

I have to take several breaths before answering her and I try to keep my voice calm; "You are forgetting that I do not do hiking as a hobby and I bet you have walked up this path a lot of times, where this is my first time and it is really steep to me."

Snorting with disgust Debbie stares at me with angry eyes and I stare back as calmly as possible, though I feel furious with her. She has certainly changed her character since yesterday, though I am surprised that she is able to walk so easily up these cliffs considering that she passed out unconscious last night. Suddenly the angry glint fades and Debbie suddenly smiles;

"I guess I am being unfair to you. It was probably a long night for you last night and yes, I have walked up and down this path many times."

"Thank you Debbie; and you are also forgetting that I am after all, just a man."

"Yes I was forgetting that Patrick. Let me know when you are ready."

Having caught my breath I smile and say in a firm voice; "I am ready now."

She nods her head towards me and turning away starts to walk up the path at a slower pace. I keep a few steps behind her and it is not long before we reach the top of the cliffs.

The walk to the top is definitely worth it as the view is truly awesome. Looking out across the sea I can see France in the distance. The air is clear and looking across the water I can even make out several high rise buildings and the port of Calais. It looks like there are several ferries in the port and I can see that one that is steaming towards us and is about half way across the channel.

Looking along our coast I can see the port of Dover with four ferries berthed which are being loaded or are unloading. A stream of lorries are leaving and arriving at the port and suddenly I have the holiday atmosphere inside of me and wish that I could be crossing the sea again; but this time to go on a long holiday. The vastness of the continent seems to beckon me and I am fully aware that once across, I could drive for days, even weeks and not have to drive the same road again.

Memories of several holidays, where I did just that, come flooding back and I can see myself driving the open road without a care in the world.

Happy days; and no reason why not that there should be more. The trip across the channel with Debbie the other day is now but a faint memory and it would have been good to do more than a day trip.

Debbie moves beside me and reaches out and holds my arm; "What are you thinking Patrick? The look on your face makes me think you want to get on a ferry again."

I look at her and cannot help a beaming smile; "Yes, how right you are. Wouldn't it be wonderful to go across and then explore Europe for the next couple of months?"

"I guessed that is what you were thinking – I would love to, but not this time of year. Maybe we can go next year in the spring?"

I get the feeling that it will never happen and feel my smile fade a little but reply; "I will have to save up for it, but three weeks would probably be a max."

"Yes, the pressures of life. Isn't it annoying that we cannot just get up and go; bills have to be paid and we have to earn the money to pay them."

"Now you are getting depressing;" I say and I widen my smile; "but we can dream can't we; and maybe one day we will be able to go for a long holiday."

"Yes, definitely, shall we find the café? It is only a few hundred yards further on."

There are several tables set up outside the little café which looks like a small bungalow that was built at the turn of the last century; and we have it all to ourselves. The unavoidable closed circuit television camera watches our every move, but this time I do not mind. We sit quietly and drink our coffees while we look out over the calm sea and watch the ferries for about an hour before Debbie starts to get restless. My legs still ache from the climb and I would be happy just sitting here for a lot longer but do not get the opportunity as she gets to her feet;

"Come on Patrick, I have shopping to get," she says as she starts to walk back the way we came.

I make no comment as I reluctantly stand up and have to walk quickly to catch her up. Debbie is definitely taking the dominant position in our friendship and I can see that it is leading to her eventually treating me with contempt.

The walk down the cliffs is almost a run and by the time I reach her car Debbie is already sitting behind the wheel with the engine running. I get in beside her and shut the door, and not giving me time to fasten my seatbelt, she drives out of the car park with wheels spinning. The drive to the supermarket is filled with irritation as Debbie swears at slow drivers and her fingers tap the steering wheel in frustration every time we have to stop at a road junction or at traffic lights.

Parking the car as close to the supermarket entrance as she can Debbie exits the car as if it is on fire and waits impatiently as I get out more slowly. Leaning back in to lock the passengers' side Debbie slams her door and locks it with a frown covering her face; she does look to be in a bad mood and I assume that it is the 'come down' after yesterday's high. Walking over to the trolleys she pulls one out from the rack. Pushing it towards me she almost shouts; "You can push it around Patrick," and not giving me a chance to reply hurries through the main doors.

Keeping up with Debbie's rush around the supermarket is difficult and I upset several other customers as I cut in front of them with the trolley. After what seems only a few minutes we are queuing for the till and Debbie finally fully acknowledges me and looks me in the eyes; "When we get back I will make you some dinner and you can have a nap if you want to."

What I want to do is go home as there is that mad glint in her eyes and once again she appears to be a different person. I do feel tired after the climb up the cliffs and this mad rush around the supermarket, but feel that after a rest of a few hours I will be fit enough to take the long drive home. Debbie empties the trolleys' contents onto the conveyor belt not letting me help and waits impatiently with her back to me as she watches the customers in front of us get served.

As her shopping gets scanned she quickly puts it into the bags and puts the loaded bags back into the trolley. The final item gets scanned and the shop assistant, a young girl of about eighteen years with blue streaks in her hair, reads out the total. Debbie tuts in annoyance at the price and then searches through her purse for her credit card (being in such a hurry I would have thought that she would have that all ready). The young girl looks at me with trained patience and I can see by her eyes that she has the same thoughts as me. I smile and nod my head in tired acceptance as Debbie finally finds her card and puts it into the machine. Typing in her security number she looks around the store as the machine accepts her details and she pulls out her card. Not looking at the assistant she reaches out for her receipt and snatching it out of the girl's hand walks quickly towards the exit.

I follow as quickly as I can with the loaded trolley but Debbie rushes ahead of me as I have to slow down to let other shoppers pass in front of me.

Waiting for me at her car she already has the trunk open and lifts the bags out of the trolley and almost throws them in the trunk. Emptying the trolley Debbie slams the lid down and gets into her car leaving me to return the trolley.

The drive back to her home is once again filled with impatience and irritation. I sit quietly beside her in the passenger seat and hope that she does not hit anything in her agitated state. While we are waiting in a long queue at traffic lights I can stay quiet no longer; "You seem in an awful hurry Debbie, what is the rush?"

Debbie has a strange look in her eyes as she moves her head to meet my gaze; "I have a surprise for you this afternoon," she says.

"A surprise; what kind of a surprise?" I ask nervously.

She smiles a cold smile that sends shivers up my spine; "It would not be a surprise if I told you would it? Wait and see," she says in a stern voice as she returns her attention back to driving as the lights change.

Returning to her home a hurried emptying of the trunk follows and just as quickly Debbie puts everything away and not letting me help, orders me into the lounge while she prepares dinner.

Cleaning out the grate I get the fire ready with old newspaper and kindling and sit quietly vowing to go home as soon as the opportunity arises.

The lounge door soon opens and Debbie walks in carrying a tray with a 'fry up' dinner of bacon, sausages, baked beans, mushrooms, fried slice of bread and a steaming mug of coffee. Putting it in my lap she smiles; "Eat up, I hope you like the coffee as it is a new kind I bought at the Hypermarket the other day."

I settle the tray in my lap and take a sip of the coffee that has a slightly unusual taste; "That tastes different. What is it?"

"An Italian blend, I hope it is alright?"

"Could do with a bit more sugar, apart from that it tastes fine," I lie as it tastes horrible. I start to lift the tray from my lap with the intention of going into the kitchen for more sugar.

"Stay there; I will bring the sugar when I come back with my dinner."

"I do appreciate you waiting on me like this Debbie, but as I said before you are not my slave. I hope that you will let me do something like the washing up? And I am still wondering what this surprise is that you have for me?"

Debbie laughs; "You will have to wait and see, there will be plenty of time for doing the washing up later on Patrick; eat up," she tells me as she walks out of the lounge.

I look at the cooked mushrooms with suspicion, turning them over so that I can see the color of the gills, which look black and are the right color for fried edible mushrooms; I hope. Doubt remains in my mind as I turn them back over and taste the coffee again. Never having an Italian blend before I assume the unusual taste is normal and put the mug back down onto the tray and await more sugar.

Debbie soon returns with her dinner, which is the same as the one served to me and with a cup of sugar and teaspoon. As she sits down she tastes her coffee; "Yes, it is a bit sharp," she says pulling a face as she spoons in extra sugar. Stirring her mug of coffee she puts the wet spoon into the cup of sugar and hands it to me.

As I take the sugar from her hand she makes a great show of tasting her coffee again; "That is better with the extra sugar, it won't do my teeth any good though," she laughs.

I put in two teaspoonfuls of sugar, stir and take a sip. The strange taste has been covered up by the sugar making it drinkable and I take another sip.

"Better?"she asks with raised eyebrows.

"Yes. That tastes good thank you," I answer as I put the mug back down and stab a mushroom with my fork and put it in my mouth.

"The mushrooms are still good, I am going to make a stew with them later on," Debbie says as she also puts a mushroom into her mouth.

The rest of the meal is eaten in silence as we are both hungry after our busy morning. Debbie eats her meal a lot faster than me and as I finish the last mouthful she stands up in front of me putting her hand out to take my tray; "Take your coffee Patrick; and yes, you can do the washing up in a little while."

Obediently taking the mug from the tray I hold it to one side as Debbie picks up the tray from my lap; "Would you like some more coffee?"

I take a big swig as the fry up has made me thirsty; "Yes please."

"Stay there I will bring the pot in and I will bring the sugar back."

Debbie does not join me in drinking more coffee and several times I see that she is watching me with a curious stare as I drink and I also notice that the mad glint has returned to her eyes. I get the feeling that something is not quite right but put it down to her being unsure whether I like this new brand of coffee, which must be a cheap brand as it still retains the horrible taste.

Chapter Twelve

I slowly open my eyes to a darkened room that is totally black. My back and legs feel battered and bruised and hurt terribly and I try to move to a more comfortable position. My legs feel exceptionally heavy and as I move them something that is attached to my ankles rattles and moves with them. I feel as if I am still asleep as I feel groggy and realize that I am lying on my left side on cold concrete.

Quickly coming to my senses I sit up and also realize that there is something around my neck. Putting my hand up I can feel a cold metal ring circling it. The ring is about an inch wide and about an eighth of an inch thick and is secured at the back by a small padlock that is fixed to a heavy chain. Reaching down to my ankles I can feel that they are also encircled by metal rings and that they are also securely fixed together by heavier padlocks.

Getting to my feet I can feel the heavy chain lying on my spine and reach behind and follow the chain back down to the floor. The chain feels as if it is secured to a metal hoop in the floor also by a large padlock and I take several short steps away from it. The metal ring around my neck pushes painfully onto my Adams apple restricting my breathing and I have to take a step backwards.

I am in total darkness and start to panic as I become fully awake and realize what has happened to me.

I have been chained up like some dangerous wild animal!

The darkness is absolute and I can see nothing at all as I explore my bonds with shaking hands. My back and the backs of my legs are extremely painful and it is with some small consolation that I am still fully clothed. I can only surmise that I have been dragged into this prison which has caused the pain in my back and legs. I suddenly feel weak as my legs start to tremble and turn to jelly and I have to sit down onto the cold concrete floor.

I try to think as to how I have got into this position but my brain refuses to work properly. The last thing that I can remember was eating the fry up and drinking the strange coffee.

Panic suddenly hits my mind as I think back to the Death Cap mushrooms and think of the possibility that I have been poisoned. Apart from the pain in my back and legs my body feels all right except a little groggy. My brain works frustratingly slowly as I try to think and come to the conclusion that maybe I have been drugged rather than poisoned.

It must have been something in the coffee my mind tells me as the next thoughts surface into almost a shout – Where am I and Why?

That Debbie is responsible for putting me in this position I am convinced, but why she has done this to me I have no idea. We have, or should I now say had, been friends for more than twenty years. Yes, we held different opinions on life but not serious enough to warrant this treatment.

But it appears Debbie feels differently.

I pull at the metal hoop that secures me to the floor in a futile attempt to get free. The hoop is set deep into the concrete and feels about a half inch thick and is as solid as rock. Picking at the rings around my ankles is just as pointless and drives home that I am trapped. A wave of self pity washes over me and I pull again at the hoop set into the floor. This only gives me the confirmation that only a sledgehammer or crowbar will set me free and causes the tears to flow down my cheeks.

I sit and cry in frustration for several minutes as a deep anger within me starts to stir. Focusing on the anger gives me strength and I let it build up within me until I shout and scream at the top of my voice. I might as well be shouting for help on the moon as no sound greets my shouts and I do not even have an echo to comfort me.

The cold of the concrete is seeping into my bones and I get to my feet. Putting a few fingers between the metal hoop that is around my neck and my Adams apple I take several short steps before the tightness affects my breathing again and I am forced to go back. Stepping to the right I feel emptiness and continue to shuffle round in a circle. Four steps later my left shin bangs into something cold and hard. Reaching down I put my hand out and feel a cold smooth surface. Following the shape I can feel that it is a cold porcelain toilet that has no plastic or wooden seat. Turning around I back onto the toilet and gingerly sit down and straighten my back. The metal ring around my neck pushes against my throat, but though I am in an awkward position I manage to keep my bum onto the cold ceramic. Well, at least I will be able to go to the toilet in some kind of comfort I think in a mad abstract thought as if everything is fine. Debbie, or whoever it is that has me chained up here does not want me to have to sit in my own toilet waste. Getting to my feet I step away from the toilet and closer to the metal hoop and find I am able to straighten my back. I shuffle around with the chain at my ankles restricting my steps and making the shackles around my ankles rub painfully onto my skin. I manage to shuffle eight steps in a restricted circle until I arrive back at the toilet.

I sit back down onto the cold porcelain and wonder what I am going to do next. There are not many options; I could try and smash the toilet with my shackled ankles, create a sharp piece of porcelain and cut my writs or the jugular vein in my throat. Or I could sit and wait.

I decide to sit and wait.

Maybe fifteen minutes later the cold of the porcelain toilet is penetrating through my jeans and skin and is seeping to the bone. I stand quickly and rub some kind of feeling back into my bum. Walking 'the circle' I keep the blood flowing through my legs but am unable to move quickly due to the shackles and the short chain between them and my feet remain cold.

The constant darkness makes me lose track of time and to keep my mind occupied I once again count the steps in the circle. All I can manage are eight small steps from toilet bowl edge to toilet bowl edge. The pain in my ankles as each shackle tightens and rubs against the skin with each step gets worse. The pain at the backs of my legs and in my back has me sitting down onto the toilet after about a dozen circles. To try and keep warm I keep up this ludicrous shuffling walk until the pain in my ankles becomes too much and tiredness forces me down onto the cold concrete floor.

The cold concrete soon forces me to stand again and the hopelessness of my position causes the tears to flow once again. How many hours pass as I am forced to keep constantly on the move could be as little as two and could be as many as ten, I have no real idea, except to be aware that I am becoming very tired.

The tiredness eventually forces me to sit onto the toilet as sitting presents only a small part of my body to suffer the cold and I manage a very troubled sleep. Sleep does not come easily but it is only for a short time until I am forced to my feet by the cold and shuffle the eight steps again. Hunger and thirst begin to distract me from the cold and I become obsessed with the dream of eating a large hamburger with all the trimmings and washed down with a mug of hot coffee. The dreaming of food makes my mouth water and I hope that soon Debbie, or whoever it is who is keeping me a prisoner, will bring me some food.

Pain in my bladder makes me aware that I have not passed water since I became aware that I am shackled. I guess that it is the fear that has prevented my bladder from working properly and I turn towards the toilet and unzip my fly. It is pure guesswork that I aim into the toilet and as the urine gushes out I am rewarded by the sound of it striking water. Trying the best I can I keep the urine flowing until my bladder empties and giving a it a shake put my penis back into my trousers and zip up my fly. Reaching out above the toilet I cannot find the cistern only a flat wall. Moving my hand over the wall I feel a curved metal button about an inch and a half in diameter and press it hard into the wall. The toilet flushes and when the noise subsides I can hear the cistern filling with water several feet above me. Whoever is keeping me here wants me to remain reasonably clean and I grope around the toilet for toilet paper but can find none.

Sitting back down onto the toilet my stomach grumbles in protest and I wonder when I am going to be fed. All is quiet and I sit not making any noise and straining my ears for the faintest sound. The quiet, like the dark, is absolute. I could easily be in a cave far underground but my senses tell me that I am in the basement of somebody's house.

Casting my mind back I picture myself walking around Debbie's house and try to think where the door to the basement might be. The only logical place is in the hall and I can remember a door under the main stairway. I had always assumed that it was a door that led to a cupboard, but thinking about it I am now convinced that I was wrong in that assumption.

Presuming that it is the door to this basement I should be able to hear Debbie walking about above me; and hear any visitors that she has. I am surprised that I cannot hear the traffic passing by her house and can only assume that I have awoken during the night and that only a few hours have passed and that I am in a different basement. My internal clock and the short stubble on my face tells me that that train of thought is wrong and that I have been chained up for at least ten or twelve hours. The mystery of why my world is so quiet will only be solved by a visit from my jailor; whoever and whenever that may be.

The hours pass slowly by and with a raging thirst constantly invading my thoughts I bend down to the toilet and using my nose test it for cleanliness. The toilet smells of old urine and the thought of flushing the toilet with my hand held under the flow to get a drink suddenly holds no appeal. I tell myself that no matter how desperate and thirsty I become, to drink that toilet water might well cause even bigger problems. The chance of contracting some kind of disease that may linger in the bowl could cause untold damage to my digestive system. The last thing that I want right now is to contract diarrhea or have trouble passing water. Keeping my mouth closed I hope my saliva will offset the thirst until water is brought to me.

I sleep on and off sitting uncomfortably on the toilet until my stomach starts to hurt. Realizing that my bowels want emptying I undo my jeans and along with my underpants push them down my legs and sit on the cold porcelain.

My bowels empty almost immediately and I grope around hoping to find the toilet paper that I may have missed before. All my fingers find is a cold wall and cold concrete on the floor and I know that I am going to have to wash my bum using my left hand. I had heard of people doing this when no toilet paper is available and that afterwards they only eat with their right hand but have never had to do that before.

Partly standing up I search behind me for the metal button until I eventually find it. Pushing it hard I squat back down quickly and put my left hand under the flow of water and wash my bum and privates as best I can. The water is cold and I know it will take ages before my bum and privates are dry. Waiting for the cistern to fill up again I once again push the button and rinse any excreta off my left hand.

I wait patiently for the water to evaporate off my skin and after about a half hour can wait no longer as more cold is penetrating and get to my feet and pull my jeans up. My bum and privates are still wet, along with my left hand and I consider removing my socks or underwear next time as the wetness is very uncomfortable.

I walk and shuffle my eight steps at a time when suddenly the light is turned on. After spending so many hours in the pitch black the bright light shining into my eyes actually hurts and I have to close them. The light shining through my eyelids is also too bright and I use my right hand to cover them.

I can hear a key turning in the door lock and lower my hand and force my eyes open. The door, faced with a single piece of plywood opens and standing there holding a tray with a plate of food and steaming mug is Debbie.

"Debbie," I shout; "What do you think you are doing? Get me out of this."

Debbie stares at me with that now familiar glint of madness in her eyes; "Why should I? Not so big and proud now are you *mister*."

"What are you talking about? Come on unlock me will you? The game is over." I scream.

Debbie's face turns a deep red and she screams back; "Game – what game? This is no game you bastard. It was a bit different when you used to lock me up down here when you went off to work. You made me suffer over the years with your insane jealousy and now it's your turn."

"How have I made you suffer – what is it that I have done to you?" I plead.

Debbie makes no reply as she puts the tray down in front of me just out of reach. Walking back to the door she reaches out and grabs hold of an old walking stick that was out of my sight. Stepping back into the room she pushes the tray towards me and stops when she reaches a white line chalked into the concrete. Looking up into my eyes the smile that forms on her face fills me with horror.

"I will leave the light on for fifteen minutes and what you haven't eaten by then you can eat in the dark."

"Debbie, please, stop doing this, I have never hurt you in the past. Why are you doing this to me?" I plead, suddenly becoming very frightened.

Making no reply Debbie turns her back on me and still holding onto the walking stick walks out of the door and slams it shut behind her. The sound of the key turning in the lock has to be one of the worst sounds I have ever heard.

Looking down at the tray I look at the two slices of bread and thick lump of yellow cheese. The mug is still steaming and by the color of the contents I guess it to be coffee. I bend down to reach the tray and cannot reach it with my hands as the ring of steel around my neck tightens and I have to straighten up a bit or choke to death. Reaching out with my right foot I manage to put my heel onto the tray and carefully pull it towards me. The tray slides smoothly over the concrete and I stop when I estimate I can bend down and reach it with my hands.

The coffee smells good making my mouth salivate and even though it is only bread and cheese it looks very appetizing because I am so hungry. Picking up the tray with both hands I slowly shuffle backwards until I am able to sit down onto the toilet. The coffee does smell good and I bend down and breathe deeply. It only smells of coffee and carefully balancing the tray on my knees I pick up the steaming mug and take a small sip. The coffee tastes as good as it smells and I take a larger swig.

The cheese also tastes good, it is strong mature cheddar that is creamy and I waste no time in eating it. The bread is fairly moist and the two slices soon follow the cheese. Drinking the remaining coffee quickly which has a bitter aftertaste I put the tray down at my feet and look around at my prison.

The walls are faced with rendered concrete and give no clue as to their thickness. I had noticed that the door was over an inch thick when Debbie had left it open and being plywood faced and with no sound penetrating, guess it to be a fire door. Fire doors are solid chipboard inside and though the description is 'fireproof' usually the fireproofing lasts for only an hour before the flames can penetrate. A solid door like that is also a good guard against noise and no matter how much noise I may make, little sound would penetrate.

Looking up at the ceiling with its single bright light bulb hanging down, I see that like the walls, it is also composed of concrete and explains why I can hear no sound above me. On visiting Debbie's house before I had assumed that her floors were of a wooden construction. The thick carpet that she had covering the floors effectively masked their construction and now when I think about it her floors had been very solid underfoot.

Looking about the room I can see that it is over twenty feet long and must stretch under Debbie's front room as well as her lounge. The room is also totally bare of any boxes or furniture which seems odd as most houses take advantage of any spare room for storage. The concrete walls are also devoid of any windows and I can see several small ventilation covers just below the ceiling at each end of the room.

The toilet is as I guessed. Made of white porcelain it is stained with old urine and faint marks of excreta and I am glad that I did not drink the water. The button that operates the flush is of shiny chrome and is set into the wall with no evidence of the piping or of the cistern above. There is also no toilet paper.

My chains and the shackles around my ankles are of strong steel and by their rusty appearance could easily be over a hundred years old. The hoop of steel that is set in the concrete does look about a good half inch thick and the padlocks are of good English manufacture, giving me no chance of breaking free.

Debbie certainly had a mad glint in her eyes and I vow on her return that I will not provoke her and will try to appeal to her better judgment. Threatening her would do no good at all and would probably have the opposite effect, giving her good reason to make me suffer more than I am already. The thoughts, though positive, appear to fail in my mind as I think them and it is with dread and fear that I face my dismal looking future.

That Debbie has a lot more unpleasantness planned for me is a more truthful thought.

Too soon the light is turned off making the blackness more acute and I stay seated on the toilet. It seems to me that hours pass slowly but in reality are probably only minutes rather than hours as time becomes distorted. I wonder when Debbie is going to collect the tray and also wonder when my next meal will be and drift off to sleep.

I awake to total darkness and hear the door close quietly and the key turn in the lock. Reaching out with my hand I can no longer feel the tray and stretch out my leg hoping it will bump into it. The tray has gone and I curse myself for sleeping through Debbie's collection of it. My head feels groggy like it did before and I get the feeling that I have been drugged once again. The drug must have been in the coffee even though I could not taste it until that bitter taste at the end and with this thought I drift off back to sleep.

Surrounded by a group of strange people with pointed heads I try to fight my way out. Swinging with my right fist at the pointed head closest to me who is female, and she ducks easily as my swing is so slow. It feels like I am surrounded by thick treacle that makes every movement appear as if it is in slow motion. I try to back away from the strange people but am stopped by a hard concrete wall. Suddenly a man with an elongated pointed head laughs at me; his teeth are yellow and pointed and have what looks like thick yellow cheese stuck between them. Bending towards me his face fills my vision and when he breathes, a dark yellow breath fills my eyes, nose and mouth. I scream in terror as his face fades, but the smell of his breath seems to cling to my skin and inside my lungs and I scream again.

Opening my eyes to the total blackness the pointed headed people are still vivid inside my head and I start to shake. Too frightened to breathe as my chest hurts and I realize it was all just a crazy nightmare. No wonder Debbie is feeding me strong cheese!

Now too frightened to close my eyes I stare into the dark and for the first time in many years pray to my god. I do believe in a god but rarely acknowledge His or Her presence by attending church as I have witnessed so much evil occurring in this world.

My mind drifts back to a conversation I had many years ago with a practicing Christian, who was also a good friend of mine. He was a great believer in God and went to church every Sunday to thank the Lord for his wonders and for life itself. The conversation we had was one of strong belief and I could not understand in his almost slavish dependence on one who has allowed so much cruelty and injustice to occur on what was reputedly His world.

My friend argued that all the evil that happened on this world was caused by the devil and that to defy the devil and all his ways and believe in God that was right and true, would bring happiness; and an eventual end to the devil.

Well right now I believed in what my friend had said to me. Debbie is evil and is certainly possessed by a devil and in this I whole heartedly agree. I clasp my hands together and pray like I have never prayed before. I actually fall to my knees and look up, to where Heaven is meant to be, and with tears streaming down my face pray for His intervention by banishing the devil from Debbie's soul.

I stay on my knees for as long as I can until the pain becomes too much and I struggle to my feet. The darkened room remains empty and cold and I feel totally alone. The feeling of being so alone frightens me and despair fills my mind as I feel the tears flow down my cheeks. I unclasp my hands as the anger returns and I swear defiance against Debbie and the devil, whoever he or she is.

Awareness of horrors to come seep through my body that make me tremble. A thought with such clarity suddenly appears in my mind and shouts and laughs inside my head and tells me that this is just the beginning.

I shake my head to try and clear the terrifying thoughts that are filling my head but to no avail. Sitting back down onto the cold toilet I beg for help, but the horrible feeling that help will not come makes me cry out in anguish.

'I have not led an evil life, why am I being tortured like this?' I shout aloud, but of course get no reply.

Sleep finally overtakes me as I sit on the cold toilet, but there is little relief from the nightmares. The pointed headed people return accusing me of something, but I cannot hear their words. The evil smell that had enveloped me earlier seeps into my every pore and I scream myself awake.

I feel cold, the cold of the room chills me to the bone and I suffer a strong feeling of defeat. The strong 'Me' that is always inside shouts at me to pull myself together. 'The only thing to fear is fear itself' the voice shouts and I stand up and take several slow deep breaths. Yes, I will face the fear that is haunting me and still feeling as if I am losing my mind I laugh at the darkness. I am made of stronger stuff than this I tell myself and laugh again. I stand straight backed and make myself think of more pleasant thoughts.

Remembering a special Christmas with my family helps and I conjure up their happy smiling faces. The world had appeared a friendly place then and as I remember I did not have a care in the world. The peace and contentment lasted well into the New Year and even the return to work after the holiday was filled with happy, smiling faces. I could feel the strength returning to me and know that I can face anything that Debbie or the devil has in their minds for me.

The thought of being in an arena in ancient Rome facing lions that are charging towards me suddenly fills my mind. It is almost as if I am there and I shout defiance at the Romans who fill the arena. Theirs is a sad life filled with cruelty and the death they had forced upon me would free me from the evils of that world and brings the promise of a utopia filled with sunlight.

The thought that I *am* losing my mind makes me shudder and I do my best to hang onto my sanity as I hear the key turning in the lock.

Chapter Thirteen

The door swings open and I can make out Debbie's form silhouetted against the light that is streaming down the stairs. She is holding a long thin cane that is about six feet long and she is pointing it at my head as she screams; "You are a bastard," and runs towards me.

The cane is pointed at one end and she jabs it forward piercing my right cheek and it passes through my skin and flesh until it finally stops when it comes up against one of my back teeth.

Screaming wildly Debbie pulls the cane out and hurriedly backs out through the doorway and slams the door. The turning of the key in the lock grates my nerves as my mouth fills with blood and I fall to my knees in shock.

Pulling out my handkerchief I press it against my hair covered cheek as I had not been able to shave and the blood pours out and soaks my jeans. She must have hit a vein as I can feel the blood quickly soak the handkerchief and I press harder to try and stop the flow.

I can feel the blood filling my mouth and push my tongue against the hole as a wave of pain flows up into my mind. My tongue starts to hurt and I can feel a sharp piece of the cane wedged between my teeth. Putting my right forefinger and thumb inside my mouth I try to get hold of the tiny sliver of cane. The angle is too acute and I have to reluctantly change hands and put my left forefinger and thumb into my mouth. Thoughts of a feces' covered finger make me gag and I nearly throw up. Forcing my mind to remain calm I manage to grab hold of the sliver with my thumbnail and press it firmly against my finger and pull it out through the gap in my teeth. Pulling my finger and thumb out of my mouth I throw the splinter down onto the floor and spit out the blood that has filled my mouth.

The thought of my dirty finger once again fills my mind and I spit again and again until my mouth is clear. Using my tongue again I press it against the hole and try to find a dry piece of handkerchief. Only a part of it has remained dry and I press it against the outside of my cheek as my head clears. Tears flow down my cheeks and get into the cut and it stings like crazy, but the thought that this will also help disinfect the wound helps a little; but not much.

Why had she suddenly done this to me? I can only think that she had been upstairs working herself into a rage and filling herself with more insane thoughts.

The bitch! Next time I will be ready for her when she opens the door; the bitch!

Debbie does not return that night; or whatever the time is as it could be any time during the day. I do not know if it is day or night or even what day it is. The bleeding soaks into my beard and stops after about a quarter of an hour and I spend the next painful hours sitting on the toilet. I cannot bring myself to wash my handkerchief under the flushing water of the toilet as I am so frightened of getting the cut infected. Instead I keep my face as still as I can and keep my mouth shut so as not to open the cut and make it bleed again.

The blood had poured out and I hope that it had washed any infection that may have got in and formed a thick coating of dried blood. My thoughts drift forward to my next meal and I know that I will have to be very careful when eating. The hot coffee, if any is served, will have to cool down to almost cold before I drink any or that could also start the bleeding again.

Many hours later and with the pointed headed people taunting me with their laughter the light suddenly comes on and wakes me with its brightness. Getting hurriedly to my feet I force my eyes to stay open and shade my eyes with my hand as the key turns in the lock and the door opens.

Debbie, wearing a tight fitting blue T-shirt, no bra and tight fitting jeans walks in carrying a tray of steaming food and mug of coffee.

The smile that she is also wearing drops at the sight of my blood-soaked face as a look of real concern covers her face; "Phillip," she exclaims; "What have you done to your face?"

I look at her as I feel the anger inside me grow to a foolish level but force my voice to remain calm; "I don't know, it must have happened when I was asleep. Why are you calling me Phillip? My name is Patrick. Patrick," I insist; "my name is Patrick your friend from the shop."

Putting the tray down onto the chalked line Debbie stands and the look of concern on her face appears genuine though the glint of madness shines in her eyes; "Eat the lovely dinner I have made for you Phillip," she answers and obviously not having heard me tell her my name is Patrick.

"I will get some dressings for that as we do not want it to get septic," she says, as she turns away and hurries out of the door and up the stairs.

The open door seems to mock me as I look at the stairs wishing I could go up them and escape this nightmare. Instead I reach out with my foot and slide the tray towards me. Picking the tray up I balance it on my knees and look closely at what Debbie has cooked for me. There are several large pieces of chicken; a leg and breast, along with roast potatoes, brussel sprouts, and roast parsnips and asparagus tips. The smell of the coffee drifts up my nose distracting me from my earlier thoughts that I should not drink it hot. Picking up the mug I take a tentative sip and keep the hot liquid in the left side of my mouth. The coffee tastes good and I examine the rest of the meal.

The potatoes and parsnips have been roasted to a golden brown, as has some of the chicken. I wonder if the golden coloring has been added rather than being achieved by simple roasting. As I am just about to take my first mouthful of brussel sprouts, which I consider safe to eat, Debbie returns carrying the first aid box.

"I will leave this here for you," she says as she puts the box down onto the chalked line; "I will leave the light on longer for you this time so that you can dress your wound. Enjoy the meal," she says and smiles as she turns away and walks out of the room shutting the door quietly behind her. I do not hear the key turning in the lock and assume she will come back soon after I have eaten.

The way that she said 'Enjoy the meal' fills me with suspicion and I look even closer at the meal. Bending down I breathe in deeply smelling the potatoes, parsnips, brussels and asparagus. Paying special attention to the roast chicken I turn each bit over and examine them more closely. With the thought that salmonella can be present in re-heated chicken I decide to give the meat a miss.

Picking up the chicken leg I pull off the meat and put it down the toilet and return the bone back to the plate. Tearing the large breast fillet into small pieces I also put that down the toilet and flush it away and rinse my hand in case Debbie comes back before I have finished the meal.

While I was tearing the chicken into pieces the meal had cooled down sufficiently for me to eat. Hoping that the golden glaze is not something ominous I eat the root vegetables and brussels and asparagus tips and wash it all down with the now barely warm coffee that has the familiar bitter aftertaste.

Cursing my weakness for drinking what may have been drugged coffee I obediently put the tray back onto the chalked line by pushing it along with my foot. I reach out for the first aid box and slide it towards me. Opening the box I look inside at the contents and see that there is one small roll of bandage, several small plasters and a crumpled tube of antiseptic cream. I flush the toilet and try to wash the dried blood out of my beard as best I can and wiping my hands on my blood soaked jeans I open the tube of antiseptic cream and squirt a little out onto my finger. The cream looks white and pure and I put it to my nose to check the aroma. The cream smells only of antiseptic cream so I smear it onto the cut on my face and unravel some of the bandage as it is far too long for my purpose. Unraveling several inches I hold the edge of the bandage in my right hand between forefinger and thumb and try to tear it in half.

The bandage remains firmly in one piece so I decide to keep it all and roll it up and make a thick pad the width of the bandage and about an inch and a half long. Using the plasters I stick the bandage to the hair on my face and after closing the first aid box push it back to the white chalked line.

The light is switched off about ten minutes later and I remain seated on the toilet as a wave of tiredness sweeps over me. That the coffee was heavily drugged is now obvious and I have difficulty keeping my eyes open and fall asleep within a few minutes.

Waking up some time later and feeling groggy, I stand up and shuffle around my eight steps several times to get the blood flowing. My face feels strange where I had been cut and I put my hand up to my face but my hand also feels strange and it feels like it is tightly bandaged. My other hand feels the same way and I bring my hands up to my face.

It is then with deep shock that I realize that they are bandaged and that I have no thumbs. I scream in anguish and a deep anger fills my soul. How can I get through life without any thumbs? My brain races with crazy thoughts and I wonder how Debbie has managed to cut off my thumbs without waking me. Yes, the coffee was drugged but it would need a deep anesthetic to knock me out that much.

Debbie must have got that kind of anesthetic from the hospital. We had never fully discussed what she actually did at the hospital and I always took it that she was a nurse of some kind. To be able to get a strong anesthetic she must have access to the operating rooms or full access to the hospital stores. Being in a trusted position she could probably easily steal anesthetic and she could have been stealing a little each time over the years so that it would not be missed.

Removing thumbs could be done with a sharp knife but if she was to steal anesthetic she could easily steal scalpels or surgeons tools. She would also know the procedure for removing limbs or other extremities, the bandages feel dry and there is little pain.

I scream in anguish again and again as tears roll down my cheeks. A deep cold fear suddenly fills my soul and I scream and sob for what I think could be hours.

After regaining my breath I raise my right hand up to my cheek to feel whether the bandage is still in place.

The wound and the skin around it feel slimy and the bandage and plasters have gone. Debbie must have removed the dressing when I was under the anesthetic. What the slime is I have no idea so I gently rub the wound with my finger and then put my finger to my nose and breathe in gently. The slime on my finger smells earthy and the smell reminds me of mushrooms. Has Debbie put some of the Death Cap on my wound – or is it something else?

I curse my stupidity for eating a meal that may have been drugged and especially curse myself for drinking coffee that I now know was drugged. I can only blame the situation and my thirst and hunger for not thinking rationally, in future I will have to go without. But how long will I last not eating and drinking?

Not long, only a few days, maybe a week. But it might be better than suffering more horrors that Debbie may have planned for me.

I rub the wound on my cheek again with a cleaner finger and sit and worry what may happen to the wound. Will it turn septic; or will a fungus start to grow and cause me immeasurable amounts of pain? Only time will tell and I continue to worry and imagine my face turning into one giant mushroom as sleep claims me and I fall into a deep troubled sleep.

The pointed headed people's heads change into pointed mushrooms and white Death Cap mushrooms sprout from their faces and bodies. They hold their hands up towards me and none of them have any thumbs. One giant mushroom person pushes the others aside as he comes towards me. He reaches out with mushroom shaped hands with no thumbs and laughs as I try to push myself into the hard ground.

The turning of the key in the lock wakes me from the awful nightmare and I cover my eyes so that the glare from the light does not burn into them. The room remains in darkness and I hear Debbie's soft steps as she walks towards me. Lowering my hands I open my eyes and peer into the gloom. I can make out Debbie's shadowy figure as she creeps towards me holding a large bowl in her hands in front of her.

Stopping at the chalked white line her eyes widen as she realizes that I am awake and takes a step backwards. Soft, hate filled words erupt from her mouth and I strain my ears to try and hear what she is saying and can barely make out the words as they are said so softly;

"I hate you Phillip, as I hate all men who think that they can push me around. Just because I am a woman you think that I am weak and feeble. Well, look at you, you bastard, not so tough and strong now are you? How are your thumbs?" she laughs cruelly and raising the bowl to the level of her face she suddenly throws the liquid contents at me.

The smell as it hits me in the face and chest is of soap and disinfectant. The smelly liquid, which I assume is water gets into my eyes blurring my vision and stings like crazy. I close my eyes to try and shut out the pain and hear her step forward and I try to turn away. My movements are slow as I am so distracted by the pain in my eyes which feel as if they are on fire. Pain erupts from the area where it can hurt a man the most – in the testicles, and I cannot stifle the scream that erupts from my throat and lash out with a right swing at her that misses the mark.

Waves of pain wash up from my testicles making me feel sick and I throw up as Debbie laughs again cruelly from about six feet away. I turn away and face the wall in case she kicks me again and throw up and hear some of the vomit splash into the toilet. Protecting my testicles with my hands I turn back towards her as I hear the door slam shut and the key turn in the lock.

I collapse backwards onto the toilet and sit on it awkwardly separating my buttocks. The smell of the soap, disinfectant and my vomit make me throw up again and I curse my god from here to eternity. Crazy images enter my head as the mushroom people are pushed aside by a huge red colored being with horns and hairy legs with hooves. He opens his mouth which is filled with blood red teeth and he has a mouthful of removed thumbs and he laughs as his eyes roll back into his head and all I can see is the whites of his eyes that shine like searchlights.

Aware that I am losing my mind and also aware that the crazy images are a form of escape from this reality helps banish them from my mind and my head clears. I manage to open my eyes but see only blackness as I throw up again over my legs.

What is the matter with this insane woman?

I manage to calm my hurried breathing, though each breath forces the soapy smells deeper into my body. Flushing the toilet I put both hands under the flow and splash the water over my face and wipe my neck with my wet hands. Realizing that the bandages covering my hands are now soaking wet I shout to myself that I am a 'stupid bloody idiot' as tears flow down my cheeks. Waiting patiently for the cistern to fill up again as the name Phillip shouts in my mind. This is the third time that she has called me Phillip and my mind races back over the years as I try to recall a Phillip in her life. I can remember her husband who was called Bruce and her friend Martin but I do not remember a Phillip.

I think back to her divorce and the awkward years that followed. During that time I only saw her twice as Debbie had become unstable and bitter and was difficult to talk to; as most people do that have gone through a divorce, especially if it is not of their doing. Offering her friendship I had said to her that if she ever needed me to call, but really I did not want to get involved and she never did call.

The cistern refills and I flush the toilet and cup my right hand under the flow and wash my face again, even though I feel cold as most of me is wet and I try not to shiver as I let my mind drift back.

Many years had passed since I had seen her and had met her by accident at a café outside Rhayader, a town near the Elan Valley in Wales. I had gone there on my own to get over a long love affair that had recently broken my heart. Seeing Debbie had stirred up strange emotions inside me and after talking to her as I remember, I had run away to the depths of the Welsh mountains and lived like a hermit for weeks until I could face the world and its people again.

Debbie had telephoned me several months after that and we met at Port Lyminge Animal Park and had a wonderful day out which rekindled our friendship. Our meeting in Wales was hardly discussed as Debbie had seen at the time that I was unhappy. Not wanting to open old wounds she had admitted that she had gone there for the same reasons. Since that day the subject had never been raised again and like a lot of bad things in life they are best left in the past and eventually forgotten. We had lost touch again over the years as with work pressures and Debbie living so far away, seeing each other was sometimes difficult. People change as they get older too by having different interests and the years separate old friends, even if we do not want them too.

That she sees me as Phillip is now painfully obvious. Phillip, whoever he was, had hurt her so badly in the past that memories of him were making her lose touch with reality. When a man and a woman get together a battle for dominance can sometimes ensue. This battle for dominance can be taken to extremes with one becoming unreasonable and turning into a complete bully, which they themselves cannot see. Debbie had obviously been bullied and I wondered if Phillip had treated her in similar ways to which she was now treating me.

The human mind can easily become unbalanced under such extreme pressures. Debbie's reactions to seeing me as bullying and ridiculing her over the flint flakes may have been the trigger and obviously overdosing on those ecstasy tablets had pushed her over the edge. Her moments of instability and unpleasantness I have witnessed these past few days had shown me she was not happy with our friendship and she had tried to adopt the dominant position. Maybe a deeper relationship was forming without me realizing it. The magic mushroom trip had brought us much closer together and I had seen her in a new light and maybe had come to see me differently; one that her psyche rejected. My refusal to take the ecstasy with her she could have interpreted that I did not fully trust her, even though I had admitted that they scared me.

I knew that somehow I had to get her to see me as Patrick her friend, not as Phillip her enemy. How I was going to achieve that was going to be difficult to say the least.

I close my eyes and ask for forgiveness of my god, for the abuse I had hurled at Him earlier and for Him to show me a way out of this madness.

The soaking I had received made the cold basement feel even colder and I could no longer suppress the shivers. Several cold hours pass until sleep once again claims me and I sleep for quite a while until I start to slip off the toilet.

Chapter Fourteen

Rubbing my back painfully on the front of the toilet as I slip to the floor wakes me with a start and I stiffen my legs to stop myself from falling further. My clothes and bandages are still damp but I feel better after the long sleep and could almost see a light at the end of the dark tunnel I was in. That I had hit on the cause of Debbie's behavior made me a lot happier, but the solution was still difficult to see.

My back hurts like hell and I try straightening myself up to ease the pain but it makes no difference. Shuffling the circle does not help either as my ankles hurt, so I try to find a comfortable position sitting on the toilet. A cramp starts to develop in my right leg which hurts more than my back so I stand up, but the pain continues. I have to bend down to massage my leg with my sore hands which makes my back hurt even more, so I try sitting down again.

The hours that pass with me constantly moving make me feel tired and I end up hunched and staring at the darkness below me. My clothes and bandages have almost dried and I hope that Debbie will not give me anymore wet surprises.

My patience is being stretched to the limit sitting in the dark waiting for Debbie's next visit. I become very hungry and know it will be difficult to flush my next meal down the toilet as I am so hungry. My mind feels alert and I do not want it dulled by the sleeping drug that Debbie is adding to the coffee and maybe to the food as well.

I try to compromise in my mind by telling myself that I would only eat the food and not drink the coffee. But the thought that it may be the food that is drugged and of what she might do to me next time fills me with horror and I fall asleep with thoughts of dismay filling my mind.

I awaken some time later and the determination that grows inside me feels strong at times but as the time passes, with the hunger gnawing at my belly, the determination fades to nothing. I feel totally at her mercy and can only hope that the next visit will make her see sense and that she will set me free.

The hours of constant darkness seem to go on forever, I have emptied my bowels twice in that time and estimate it has been over twelve hours since her last visit. I can feel the hair on my face and almost smell my cheesy feet through my trainers. I so want her to open the door so that I can convince her that I am Patrick and not Phillip and I rehearse my lines again and again until I am sick of them.

Waking after a sleep of many hours and with no sign of Debbie makes me call out for her. I shout and scream but she does not come, which makes me shout even louder until my throat hurts and I finally subside into silence. The hours still flow past and after emptying my bowels for the third time despair drives me into a panic. I pace as best as I can and try to ignore the pain in my ankles. I wave my arms around but the limitations of what I can do makes me fall asleep and enter into the netherworld of crazy dreams.

The pointed headed and mushroom headed people with no thumbs do not return but in their place I dream of a forested world populated by talking animals and those that should have thumbs have none. I roam the forest with several golden deer that wear cloth boots over their hooves. They complain when their boots get wet and complain when their boots are dusty and dry. A dark green fox that is with us also wears cloth boots over its paws and complains when the sun shines and also when it is cloudy and the sun does not shine.

Hiding in a large cave we all look out over the forest which is multicolored like the colors of autumn. The forest stretches for miles until it becomes lost in a multicolored horizon and the green fox then complains of back ache. One of the golden deer complains of hoof ache while another complains of ear ache until I wake up and know that I am going mad.

My head now seems to exist of several different people all arguing amongst themselves. One is saying that this is not madness and that the dreams are a form of escape. Another laughs in a crazy way and tells me that I *am* going mad. Another holds the opinion that the dreams are real and that the reality of being chained up is the dream.

The thoughts remind me of an old Chinese saying or proverb. The proverb tries to explain the illusion that is our lives and asks if I am a butterfly - dreaming that I am a human – or am I a human, dreaming that I am a butterfly?

The proverb helps bring some kind of sanity to me and I know that this is not some crazy illusion that is happening inside my head. My back and legs would not hurt so much in a dream. To clarify reality I touch the wound on my cheek and can feel the rough texture and have to prod it quite hard with my fingers to get a feeling of pain. The wound is obviously healing and I try to think back to how many hours have passed since Debbie pushed the pointed cane through my cheek. Where my thumbs have been removed feels numb and the stubble on my face has grown to almost cover the lower half and I now have a short beard. Thoughts about time are difficult as I have no idea whether it is day or night but I guess that four days and nights have passed but someone in my head disagrees pointing out that my fingernails have not grown very much.

The arguments start inside my head with everyone shouting at once and I shout out loud for them to stop. Silence reigns for a few seconds until a voice in my head says in a matter of fact way; "You are going mad mate" and frightens the hell out of me. Memories of the movie 'One Flew Over The Cuckoo Nest' with Jack Nicholson make me shudder as I do not want to go mad.

Cheech Marin an American comedian suddenly pops into my head of when he was in a strait jacket in the movie 'Nice Dreams' shuffling about on the floor screaming that his balls itched, no longer appears funny. Tommy Chong in the same movie saying 'Don't worry about it' over and over again wakes me from the images that are taking over my head. I cannot stop shaking, a shaking that starts to envelop me and takes over my whole body and I scream for it to stop, but the shaking continues.

I feel ill and weak and know that I am going into some kind of shock which I fight against and wish that Debbie would visit, if only to torture me; as it would at least get me away from the madness that is taking over my body and mind.

A voice suddenly shouts in my mind; 'STOP. It is you that is driving yourself mad. Stop thinking of pointed headed people of talking animals and of crazy movies. Prisoners in solitary confinement do not all go mad.

Stop remembering times gone past I tell myself and make your mind think of something that cannot harm you.

Of course! I used to be able to recite the times table; think of mathematics and I picture the word mathematics in my head. I used to enjoy math's and time used to fly past when I had a mathematics problem to think about. Admittedly I am in no condition to do algebra but I can do my times table.

Starting with the two's I start to recite and imagine each set of numbers in my head as I progress to three, four, five and six. Stumbling with seven times eight I start back at the beginning once again picturing the numbers in my head and am soon past the seven's and into the eight's.

My body and mind relax and the shaking stops; even the pain from my back and legs fade as I continue to recite the numbers in my mind. I become a little bored with the lower numbers and soon progress to the thirteen and fourteen time's table and the time fly's by. It becomes difficult to only picture the numbers but I do not allow other thoughts to distract me and fall asleep picturing fourteen times fourteen.

My grumbling stomach and a raging thirst wake me some time later and I fix my mind back onto the times table. I do well for what must be over an hour but thirst pushes aside the images of the numbers in my head and is replaced by flowing water. Twenty-four hours must have passed since Debbie's last visit my thirst tells me and I consider drinking some of the flushing water from the toilet.

I put this thought aside and return to putting numbers back inside my head and start at the six times table. I reach the twelve's in no time at all when the thought of drinking the water returns as my mouth is so dry. Picturing the bacteria filling my mouth helps and I return to the twelve times table.

Debbie is becoming conspicuous by her absence and a vision of her face drifts into my mind. She has mad, staring eyes but is holding a mug of steaming coffee in her hand.

Where was I? Oh yes; twelve times seven – surely it would be better to die of the bacteria than it would be than to die of thirst?

I fight the urge to drink and push thoughts of Debbie out of my mind as I try addition; one hundred and forty-four add two hundred and fifty-six and picture the sets of numbers one above the other and come up with an answer of four hundred. Trying to think of the same sum I forget the first set of numbers and wish that I could have a drink.

I try adding more sets of numbers but my thirst and dry, sticky mouth keep interfering. Suddenly making up my mind I turn towards the wall and push the button that operates the flush. Putting my right hand into the flow of water I allow some water to pass through my fingers and then cup my hand even though I can feel the bandage become soaking wet. Pouring the small amount of water into my mouth I swill it around and then spit it into the toilet. I wait until the cistern is full again and then flush the toilet again cupping my hand under the flow and pour it into my mouth. My throat seems to work under its own volition and opens and I swallow the water.

Water has never tasted so good, it may be full of bacteria but I no longer care – well at least I will not die of thirst.

I turn around and sit back down onto the toilet and feeling a lot better and starting at the two's recite the times table all the way up to the fifteens before I stop.

The drink has revitalized me and I stand up and flush the toilet and drink again. Sitting back down I close my eyes and reciting my tables fall into a deep sleep.

The grumbling in my stomach wakes me and I get to my feet and then sit down again as I need to empty my bowels.

My legs still ache from sitting in the same position and after emptying my bowels and washing, trying to avoid getting both my bandages wet; I stand up and take a step forward. I then step sideways and try and walk the circle with the eight short steps. Both my ankles hurt where they are shackled and I reach down to try and shift them to a better position. The right ankle feels moist and I put my finger up to my mouth and taste the wetness with my tongue. The wetness tastes of blood which I guess is where the shackle has broken the skin.

Cursing Debbie's madness I know that I must exercise my legs somehow. Moving closer to the hoop in the floor I squat down then stand up straight and do this twenty times. I move each arm in a circle twenty times and then squat down and stand up again.

With my new found sanity, even though I am starving hungry, I know that I must not let my body deteriorate like I have allowed my mind to do. I must keep fit as best I can. The last thirty hours or more reciting the times tables and working on math's problems has done wonders for my mind. I hope with the simple exercises that my body will recover as quickly; though a little food would certainly help.

Banishing this thought I return to squatting and standing picturing the numbers in my mind each time. I do not do many as I feel weakened due to the lack of food and water. The thought of drinking has me turning around and I flush the toilet and allow myself a little drink. The water helps refresh me and I wonder if there is going to be a health problem from continuously drinking out of the toilet.

I sit down and start to recite the times tables when the light suddenly flashes on. The light pierces my eyes and feels like red hot needles after the thirty or more hours spent in total darkness. I get to my feet and force my eyes open against the glare and have to hold my hand up between the light bulb and my eyes as I hear the key turn in the lock and the door opens wide.

Debbie stands in the doorway holding a steaming mug and stares at me. Squinting my eyes I can see that she looks gaunt, her hair is greasy and she wears the same blue T-shirt and jeans that she wore on her last visit. Her pale face and emaciated appearance makes her look ill; which I hope is due to understanding what she has done to me.

"Debbie," I say with a smile; "it is good to see you." Looking down at the steaming mug in her hand I ask politely; "Is that for me?"

Debbie takes several steps into the room holding the mug in front of her. Looking at the mug as if she has just become aware that she is holding it, says in a far away voice; "Yes, I have made you a nice cup of coffee," and she walks further into the room and stops at the chalked white line.

"I am really hungry as well as thirsty; I was beginning to think you had forgotten your old friend Patrick."

"Patrick?" she asks, seeming distracted.

I reply in my friendliest voice; "Yes, Patrick. You do remember me don't you? We used to work together at the clothes shop. We went to see your friend Sally on the Continent the other day."

Her eyes search my face and I am not so sure that she even recognizes me as she puts the mug of what looks like coffee exactly onto the chalked line. Straightening up she stares at me again as her face clouds over and the evil glint returns to her eyes.

I panic and almost shout; "I am Patrick, your friend Patrick. Phillip is not here, you split up with him years ago."

The mention of Phillip's name brings a red flush to her cheeks and I can see that a deep anger has replaced her confusion.

"You cannot fool me you bastard. I know who you are," she spits the words out and kicks the mug of coffee over. Staring into my eyes she suddenly turns away and runs to the door. Grabbing hold of it she takes a step forward and slams it hard behind her and I hear the key turn in the lock. The light is turned off and I am left in the total darkness and cursing my mistake.

Next time she makes an appearance I must not mention Phillip's name; and no way must I refer to him in any context.

Still cursing my mistake and the mistake of staying with her when I knew she was mad I sit back down and resume my times tables.

I can only guess that three or four hours pass when the light is turned back on. Time in the darkness has retained that same abstract quality making it difficult to understand how much time has passed. I was standing when the light came on and though it hurts my eyes I do my best to focus them onto the door.

The familiar sound of the key turning in the lock is followed by the door opening wide. Debbie still has that gaunt appearance and is still wearing the same clothes, but this time she is carrying a tray with a plate of food and steaming mug.

Not looking at me she walks into the room and puts the tray down onto the floor on the chalked line. I am too frightened to speak in case I antagonize her by saying the wrong thing and watch her as closely as my hurting eyes will allow.

As she straightens up our eyes meet and I see her pupils dilate as if she has stepped into the dark from a bright light. The mad glint is still there and I try my best smile and say 'Thank you'. Debbie merely nods her head in my direction and turns away and walks back out the door closing it quietly behind her and locks it.

I stretch out my foot and slide the tray towards me. Along with a steaming cup of coffee is a plate filled with a 'fry up' of bacon, sausages, mushrooms, baked beans and a fried slice of bread. The thought that I was not going to eat anything that she offered is pushed aside as my hunger takes over.

To avoid temptation after placing the tray on my knees I have to pick up the mug of coffee with both hands and pour it between my legs into the toilet. Returning the empty mug to the tray I pick up the plate and balance it on my left hand and grasping the fork in my fist I scoop the mushrooms between my legs and into the toilet. Not flushing the evidence away I load up the plastic fork with baked beans and put the food gratefully into my mouth. Holding a fork is difficult with no thumb and I have to clench it in my hand and make a fist to hold it. Once I have started, and with hardly chewing the food, I clear the plate in a few minutes.

I replace the tray back onto the line and flush the toilet and allow myself a decent drink of the flushing water. My stomach hurts with the amount of food I have put in it as I guess it has shrunk a fair bit due to the long empty hours. I can feel the food revitalizing my system and immediately feel tired but force myself to stay awake; even when the light is turned off sometime later. I wait with the patience of an oyster for Debbie to return and collect the tray, but the hours pass and the door remains firmly shut.

Now that I have got some food inside of me and after finally getting fed up waiting for her I return to my mathmatical problems. Adding up three sets of figures with a clearer mind is a lot easier and I feel triumphant after each problem is solved. The trick to remembering is each set of figures I come up with can be counted on my fingers. Four hundred and thirty one become four fingers counted out in the dark, then three tens created by opening both hands three times and imagining that I still have my thumbs and then use a finger to keep track. To remember the sequence becomes easier each time I do it.

Whether or not I am coming up with the right answers is still difficult to check as I do not have a calculator. By using the finger method I can repeat the sum and if I arrive at the same answer this convinces me that I am right. I vow to work on this to improve my memory and when I am not adding, subtracting, multiplying or subtracting I am doing my best to remember columns of figures.

My troubled mind has become relaxed and even the nightmares appear to have become a thing of the past. How much longer I can keep this positive attitude I do not know, but I know that it will be a long time before I run out of mathematical problems. I just hope that I do not become bored with it. My solution to the possible boredom is to make the math's harder and I reinforce this solution with the thoughts that if I do not keep my mind active I will go mad otherwise.

Debbie will not win. I will defeat her and once again walk in the sunshine. These few words have become a mantra to me and I will recite them a million times if need be, until I am free.

Chapter Fifteen

I can now feel that my fingernails have grown and I have got a healthy growth of beard on my face and know I have been here for a week or more. The darkness and silence cover me like a cold blanket and I also know, after all this time that I have to smell something horrible. My feet must stink inside my trainers as I have not taken them off all the time I have been here. The concrete is too cold for me to stand on without the small protection the soles of my trainers offer. Lifting up my right arm I bend my neck and smell my armpit. Yes, I do stink. The body odor smell makes me cough and I definitely could do with a shower or even better a bath.

Not much chance of that happening all the time I am chained up like this. Maybe if I ask Debbie for a bowl of water and some soap, being clean might help make me feel a bit better. I will have to be careful how I ask and choose my words carefully. That way I might even get warm water instead of cold; and not have it thrown over me.

I chant my mantra in my head; 'Debbie will not win. I will defeat her and once again walk in the sunshine.' I repeat it several times and the chant seems to make me stronger so I chant another ten times, counting the chants on my fingers and pretending that I still have two thumbs. The thought that Debbie will do me more harm suddenly fills my head and it feels dark and evil so I distract these thoughts by returning to math's problems. The hours quickly pass until the light is turned on and I hear the key turn in the lock.

Debbie looks clean and washed, her hair shines with an unnatural shine and she has changed her clothes. She looks quite smart wearing a matching top and skirt in a mid-gray color. Holding a tray in her hand I can see several sandwiches piled one on top of another and there are two small bottles of mineral water.

"Hello Phillip," she says in a pleasant voice as she walks towards me and puts the tray onto the chalked line; "I have to go out today so I have brought you some extra food; which is more than you ever did for me when you went out for the day. I will leave the light on for you and see you when I get back."

"Thank you Debbie, where are you going? I must say you look very smart and professional."

"Thank you for the compliment Phillip," she replies as the mad glint returns to her eyes; "Where I am going is none of your business."

Turning quickly she walks back to the open door and I think it wise to say nothing. As she holds the door open she turns and looks at me with triumph and walks out of the door and slams it shut behind her. The key turns in the lock and silence returns.

I look down at the tray of six white bread sandwiches that appear to have ham or baloney in them. The meat inside is a bright pink and they look freshly made and I slide the tray towards me with my foot. Picking up the tray I balance it on my knees and open the sandwich that is on the top. It looks innocent enough as there is just the sliced pink meat put between two slices of bread – no butter or margarine. Oh well, you cannot have everything I suppose. I hold the open sandwich to my nose and breathe in deeply; the ham smells fine and I put the piece of bread back on top and take a bite.

The sandwich tastes as good as it looks and I try not to wolf it down like some half-starved animal, though this is what I feel like. Picking up a bottle of the mineral water I see that the cap still has the factory seal unopened and with great difficulty, and having to use both hands, I put it in my mouth and grip the top firmly with my teeth and manage to twist the cap open. Taking a large swig I feel the cool water slide down my throat and it has to be the best water I have ever tasted. Drinking about half the bottle I replace the cap and belch deeply in satisfaction. Deciding to eat the other sandwiches later I put the tray down and look around the room.

The empty room is just the same as it was and I even manage to look at the light bulb for a short while without the light hurting my eyes. Turning around I look inside the toilet bowl and can see that it still looks unhealthy. Taking the dried blood encrusted handkerchief from my pocket I decide to give it a clean, especially around the rim as I have been drinking the flushing water.

Pushing the button to operate the flush I soak the handkerchief under the flowing water and wipe it around the rim. Wishing that I had not looked at it as it is covered in a brown slime from under the rim I wait for the cistern to fill and flush again. Soaking the handkerchief, and also my bandaged hand, I ring the handkerchief out and wipe the rim again. I do this at least ten times until I am convinced that the rim is as clean as I can get it. Washing out the handkerchief one final time and with great difficulty I do my best to wring it out. Even this small task is difficult with no thumbs and I wipe my face and am careful not to knock the scab off that has formed over the hole in my cheek. The wound feels as if it is healing well and whatever Debbie smeared over it has helped. If she had intended doing me more harm it has had the opposite effect.

I wash my hands several times under the flushing water and even under my arms, though the water feels ice cold. After a final soaking and wringing I spread the handkerchief out on the concrete to the far right of the toilet. The concrete should absorb the water and if I move it to several dry areas of concrete it may even be dry by the time Debbie comes back.

Removing my right trainer and sock I look at my foot and can see that it is filthy dirty. My ankle is red raw from where the shackle has rubbed up against it and I can see where the bleeding has been coming from. The outside of my ankle is still bleeding and I can also see why it is so painful as the shackle keeps rubbing on the wound and not giving it time to heal.

I cannot think of a solution other than to use my sock to cushion the shackle from my skin or to try and keep that leg still. My brain refuses to function over such a simple matter and the thought of not wearing my sock, and to use it as a cushion and put my bare foot in the trainer is not considered. I have always worn socks ever since I was able to crawl and not to wear one is as an alien thought as is not wearing underpants. In the end I decide to wash the wounded ankle as best as possible and to keep checking it to see (or feel) if it gets worse.

Washing the sock under the flushing water I use it to wash the blood off and to clean my foot as best as possible. Putting my foot on top of the trainer I remove my left trainer and sock and use the sock to dry my right foot. Putting my almost dry bare foot back inside my trainer feels awful and I am glad I made the decision not to go permanently sockless. I wash my foot using the wet sock and dry it with a now damp left sock. After washing both socks under the flushing water several times I spread them out on the concrete and put my trainers back on.

The feeling of accomplishment is amazing; even though I have not been able to wash my feet properly they feel clean for the first time in a week. My face and hands feel as clean and I have even been able to get rid of some of the smell from my armpits. The toilet rim looks clean too and I decide that I have done enough cleaning for one day.

A thought strikes me as to the anesthetic Debbie used on me when she removed my thumbs and with great difficulty I push my left sleeve up my arm and look closely. I cannot see any puncture wounds so pull the sleeve back down and push my right sleeve up.

Looking closely I can see just below the elbow on the inside of my arm a small bruise and a healing small hole. Debbie must have injected me with the anesthetic there and a cold shiver runs up my spine and fear once again fills my head. I hope that she has no further plans on using more anesthetic on me and tears fill my eyes.

I recite the mantra; 'Debbie will not win. I will defeat her and once again walk in the sunshine.'

I spend the next couple of hours reciting the times table and trying to solve difficult math's problems. The handkerchief and socks are drying well and I am optimistic that they will all be dry in a few hours. I keep moving them to drier patches of concrete and with luck Debbie might not even see the damp patches.

I eat another sandwich and drink the rest of the contents of the half consumed bottle of mineral water. I do not want to leave the other sandwiches for too long as the edges of the bread are already curling. There is also the thought that if I have not eaten them when Debbie returns she may well confiscate the uneaten ones so I keep them close and eat them about an hour later.

The light being on is at first a blessing but now I have done my chores I am finding it a distraction. When I close my eyes the light penetrates my eyelids and after covering my eyes with my hands for a long time my hands begin to ache. I turn my back on the bare bulb but it is so bright it still penetrates. I hated the darkness but wish that Debbie would return and turn the light off so that I can get back to my sums. The darkness helped me visualize the numbers which the light is preventing me from doing properly.

I soon get bored not being able to fill my head with numbers and the bad thoughts return. The pointed headed people keep just out of reach; I can see them at the edge of my vision when I close my eyes but keeping them open is tiring.

A headache forms, the first one I have had since being chained up and I wish for some painkillers or for the light bulb to fail. My thoughts start thinking about light bulbs and how finite they are and how they always blow when you do not want them to. Madness starts to take control and I slowly recite my times tables. Starting them easy at the two's but I only get to the fours when I start to make mistakes.

Chanting the Debbie mantra helps and afterwards I manage to get to the eights before making any mistakes. With this failure I feel my resolve weakening and wish for darkness. It is too cold for me to remove my shirt so I adopt the fetal position sitting on the toilet and bury me head in my arms. The darkness created by my arms is an enormous help and after reciting the Debbie mantra ten times I resume my recital of the times tables.

I am too scared to fall asleep under the bright light and examine the fear in my mind. I come to the conclusion that with the light on it underlines that I am alone and defenseless. The attacks made by Debbie with the sharpened cane and bowl of water would be much easier for her to carry out if she came in and saw that I was asleep.

Cramp starts to affect my right leg due to the awkward position I have adopted on the cold porcelain of the toilet. I try to rub the cramp away with my hands but end up sliding off the toilet onto the cold concrete of the floor. While I am down there on the floor I feel my socks, which are almost dry. Removing my trainers I struggle to put my socks on and pick up the handkerchief; which is still a bit damp. Folding it twice I hide it behind the toilet and then drink all of the remaining mineral water.

Six or eight hours must have passed since Debbie left and she could be back at any time. The waiting is getting on my nerves and the madness of an empty mind is eroding my sanity. In desperation I flush the toilet and with wet fingers try and write my sums onto the concrete in front of the toilet. The idea does not work very well as even though the concrete has been smoothed out it still feels rough under my fingertips and they soon start to get sore.

Trying to shorten my growing fingernails by rubbing them on the concrete floor is also a bad idea. They do get shorter but remain rough at the edges and if I scratch myself too hard they will easily pierce the skin and cause me more problems.

The waiting wears me down and I end up sitting down on the toilet rim and start to doze off. Every time I feel myself falling asleep I come to with a jerk and stare into the brightness until sleep starts to take over again. Several hours must have passed with me fighting the tiredness and sleep until I finally hear the key turning in the lock.

I quickly get to me feet and try to rub the tiredness from my eyes when the door opens wide. Debbie is still wearing the same gray clothes and looks tired after her long day. The mad glint is still in her eyes and she smiles cruelly at me;

"How has your day been then Phillip? It feels horrible to be locked up in here all day doesn't it? I am glad that you know what it feels like as you did it to me often enough."

"My name is Patrick, from the clothes shop," I say in a tired voice as that is exactly how I feel. Tired from the long day trying to stay awake; and tired from telling her that I am Patrick.

"How can you say that?" Debbie screams as her face flushes a deep red; "You do not even look like him. No, Patrick died years ago falling off the cliffs; and do not say he didn't as I remember the funeral."

I keep quiet as answering her back appears to antagonize her further. Maybe with the growth of beard on my face I do look more like Phillip and I remember that I was going to ask Debbie for a bowl of water and I could also do with a shave. The growth on my face, along with my long fingernails makes me feel dirty. Maybe if I shaved I would not look like the man called Phillip.

Debbie's face remains red with rage and I take the cowards way out and say nothing as I think asking for anything with her in a rage will only make her feel more powerful.

"Give me the tray back," she demands, taking several steps into the room.

I look down at the tray and see that it is several inches my side of the chalked line. Feeling defeated I push the tray over the line with my foot and sit back down onto the toilet rim.

"Don't you move," she orders as she walks over and picks up the tray; "and you can give me that other empty bottle."

I look at the tray and realize there is only one bottle. Looking down at the floor at my feet I see the other one lying on its side. Moving it with my foot I then kick it over gently towards her.

Bending over to pick it up she puts it onto the tray and looks at me with a challenging look in her eyes; "Well, aren't you going to ask me how my day went?"

"I would like to, but talking to me is not one of your greatest hobbies. How did your day go; I hope that you were successful?"

Debbie sneers at me; "You do not even know where I have been do you?"

"No," I reply in a humble voice; "You did not tell me where you were going when you left this morning."

A cold smile replaces the sneer; "And I am not going to. But yes, I did have a successful day thank you for asking. Are you hungry?" she asks in a sudden change of mood.

I do not feel hungry at all, sick would be a better description, but I know it will be a mistake to refuse her offer; "Yes I am hungry," I lie; "the sandwiches were nice but I ate them hours ago."

Debbie looks me in the eyes and I get the feeling that she knows I am lying and surprises me with her answer; "I feel too tired to cook. I have ordered a pizza; I will bring you some down when it gets delivered."

"Thank you," I say to her back as she turns and walks out of the door, closing it behind her. I do not hear the key turn in the lock as the quiet returns.

Time passes slowly while I wait for Debbie to return and I cast my mind back only a few minutes to her appearance and even though she got red-faced with anger I did notice a slight change in her for the better. She wanted me to show an interest in her and to where she had been and even wanted to talk a little. Admittedly she did not tell me where she had been but she does want to share her pizza with me.

My mind races as to what I might say to her on her next visit but my weakened condition does not come up with anything dynamic. Resigning myself to playing it by ear I shuffle in front of the toilet in agitation reciting the Debbie mantra in my head.

The door finally opens and Debbie walks in with the tray that has a plate covered in pizza and a steaming mug, of I assume coffee. Putting the tray down onto the chalked line she straightens up and looks me in the eyes with a questioning look and I hurriedly say;

"Thank you Debbie, that sure looks good and you got my favorite; pepperoni," and I give her my best smile and ask innocently; "Where is yours – aren't you going to join me?"

"Don't try your smarmy ways with me *mister*. I know your favorite pizza is the tropical one with pineapple and no, I will not be joining you," she says in an aggressive voice and quickly turns away and hurries out of the door and slamming it behind her she then locks it.

Throwing the coffee down the toilet I examine the pizza with suspicion. Picking a piece of pepperoni from the top I turn it over and then cautiously taste it. It tastes fine, a bit salty but that is normal and the rest of the pizza looks fine, and with no added ingredients that I can see. Wasting no time I force myself to eat it quickly and partly fill the mug with water from flushing the toilet. The water looks clear against the white of the mug and I drink several mug full's and put the tray onto the chalked white line.

Now I have some food inside of me my brain works more efficiently and I know that I must try and engage Debbie in some kind of conversation when she returns. My thoughts drift back to the shop as being the best time to talk to her about. My innocence in selling the rubber and PVC clothing would be a humorous way to start and it would also be a time long before Phillip came into her life.

The light is turned off and I sit on the cold porcelain of the toilet and patiently wait and rehearse my lines.

The cold awakes me several hours later and I quickly stand and put my arms around me in a vain attempt to get warm. I shuffle the eight steps and then back again and stamp my feet on the cold concrete floor.

Wow! It sure is cold and I wave my arms around hoping it will help. The cold penetrates into my body and I start to shiver and wish for more clothes to put on. I can only assume that it is the early hours of the morning when the night is at its coldest just before the dawn. I keep moving around to keep my circulation going which helps a little and I shiver for several more hours before I eventually warm up.

My stomach aches where I have wanted to go to the toilet and now I am warmer I drop my trousers and sit on the cold porcelain. The pizza has caused a bit of constipation or the cold porcelain is preventing me from emptying my bowels. I can only manage a few minutes more as I am getting cold again so I pull up my trousers and go back to moving around.

More hours pass until the light is turned on and the door is unlocked. Debbie stands in the doorway wearing a thick navy blue pullover, blue slacks and light blue trainers. Taking several steps towards me she looks at my obvious disheveled appearance;

"Have you been cold Phillip?" she asks in a sarcastic voice and laughs in a cruel way; "The amount of times you left me down here freezing my butt off; at last I can get my own back," she laughs again and walks forward and picks up the tray from the night before.

Now is my chance and I realize that I must not blow it and decide to ignore her cruel comments. Taking a deep breath I put on my best smile and say in my friendliest voice; "The pizza was good, thank you Debbie. Hey, do you remember my sandwiches when we worked at the shop together?" I laugh as best I can and try to keep my voice steady as I panic inside when I see her face screw up in an angry frown; "You used to laugh at my choice of sandwiches as I used to have them all neatly packed in my lunchbox." I laugh again, trying to keep the hysteria out of my voice; "There were two corned beef, and then two cheese and pickle with two strawberry jam sandwiches on the bottom." The last bit comes out in a rush and I open my mouth to say more but Debbie interrupts;

"I do not know where you heard that Phillip. Yes, Patrick always had his sandwiches in that order all the years he was there. And I did used to laugh at him." Debbie says the last sentence in almost a shout and she continues to shout; "You are not going to fool me you bastard. I probably told you that years ago and you are just twisting it around. *Bastard, you bastard*," she bellows and throws the tray at me. The tray hits me in the chest as the mug flies onto my head and I hear the plate crash to the floor as I fall back onto the toilet. The tray follows me down and I grab hold of it with both hands as the mug crashes to the floor somewhere to my left.

Debbie takes two quick steps towards me and I hold up the tray in front of my face as I hear her pick up the broken plate. She moves to my left and I keep the tray between my face and where I guess her to be.

"Give me that tray," she shouts a bit quieter than the previous shouting.

I lower the tray and see she is holding out her left hand, in her right hand are the remains of the plate and mug and I notice the red blood against the white of the crockery. With trepidation I stand up and hand her the tray and say in a calm concerned voice; "You have cut yourself."

"I know I have you bastard, *and it's all you fault*," she bellows and tries to regain her composure, but her face is bright red with anger; "I will make you suffer for that," she says a little calmer. Her blonde hair has fallen forward and she flicks her head back to get it out of her eyes. Suddenly she turns around and storms out the door leaving it open and hurries up the stairs.

The empty stairs seem to taunt me and I strain against my chains hoping to get free.

Debbie stomps back down the stairs and not looking at me grabs hold of the door and starts to close it.

"Debbie," I shout to a slamming door as the light is turned off.

I sit back down and feel the tears filling my eyes as the frustration puts butterflies in my stomach.

Well, that went well.

My chest hurts where the tray hit me and I have a headache and a bump on my head. I put my hand onto my head where the mug smashed into it. The bump feels very tender and I can almost feel it getting bigger as I feel around for blood and broken skin. The bump feels smooth and appears dry though I am now sweating. A line on my chest does feel a bit rough where the tray hit it and it is with relief that I can feel no blood.

I growl in frustration as I thought that my talking of times gone by would have penetrated her madness. At a total loss as to what to say to her next time I close my eyes and drift off to a troubled sleep.

"There's your food," Debbie says in a voice that is close to a growl.

Opening my eyes I see Debbie push the tray of food to the chalked line with her foot. The basement is in semi-darkness as she has not turned on the light but has left the door open that allows the light from the stairs to encroach on the darkness.

"Debbie," I say in surprise and open my mouth to say more but Debbie interrupts;

"Do not talk to me," she shouts and turns away quickly and hurries out of the door and slams it shut behind her. The familiar sound of the key turning in the lock now has a more ominous sound as the basement is returned to darkness.

I get to my feet and carefully reaching out with my right foot slide the tray towards me. Bending down I fumble around for the tray and knock over the mug of liquid. Searching the tray my fingers find the plate and I pick it up and carefully put it to one side. My fingers find the mug, which I note is cold, and also put that to one side near the plate. Picking up the tray I extend my arms and flick whatever liquid that remains on the tray away from me. Bending back down I put the tray back onto the floor and return the plate and mug. Picking up the tray and backing away slowly my left leg touches the cold porcelain of the toilet and I gingerly sit down and balance the tray on my knees.

Picking up the plate and having to use both hands as I cannot grip it having no thumbs, I bring it close to my nose; the food is also cold and smells of very strong cheese. My hunger overpowers my reluctance as memories of the horrid nightmares are dismissed and I pick up the cheese and take a small bite. The cheese is strong and tastes salty, making me think that it is a blue cheese, and I swallow it and take a larger bite. Searching the plate I find several slices of what I assume is soft bread and as I pick up a slice I notice that it feels slimy, rather than fresh.

Suddenly my stomach reacts to the cheese and my whole stomach contracts and I know that I am going to vomit. Quickly putting the tray in front of me on the floor I turn around and manage to get my head over the toilet bowl before I painfully throw up and regurgitate the cheese. A lot of it tries to exit through my nose and the stomach acid burns my nasal passages leaving an acrid smell in my nose that is more than the familiar smell of blue cheese.

There is a dank, stagnant smell that makes me heave again and I snort a strong breath through my nose to try to clear it. I am partly successful but the stagnant smell in my nose is even stronger and I retch painfully as my stomach is now empty of food. Falling painfully to my knees I retch again and again as a fit of coughing takes over. Tears stream from my eyes as I cough jerking my head downwards and I head butt the toilet bowl with my forehead. Stars explode inside my head and I fall to the floor coughing and gasping for breath.

I try to subdue the coughing and get to my knees as the stagnant smell in my nose is overpowering and I do my best to snort the horrible substance out of my nose and into the toilet. Crazy bright lights fill my head and I struggle to my feet as the smell of whatever it is I have regurgitated into the toilet covers my head like a thick gas. Searching for the button to flush the toilet my hands search the wall until I finally find it and push it as hard as I can.

Cupping my hand under the flushing water I get enough to put to my nose and quickly snort it in and then out again. Some of the cold water trickles down my throat making me cough more painfully. I position my head over the toilet as best I can and impatiently wait for the cistern to refill. The minutes stretch immeasurably and I cough and spit several times wishing for the pain, and the smell, to go away.

At last the cistern refills and I flush it again and this time use both hands to catch the precious water. I snort a little up my nose and some in my mouth and swirling the water around inside my mouth I spit it out and use the rest to wash my face. Clearing my nose I start to feel a slight resemblance to normality and wait for the cistern to fill up again. Pushing the button I cup my hands under the flow and tentatively take a sip and swallow. My stomach reacts violently and I bring up the water, losing what remains in my hands and then retch again painfully. The retching starts to spasm and I put my hands out against the wall and try to calm myself and hold the next retch inside me.

Wow! Do I feel ill.

My body and mind start to relax and I turn around and sit down onto the toilet as I try and gather my thoughts. The cheese is obviously not a blue cheese with edible mould and the bread could have been in a similar condition. Debbie had deliberately not turned on the light so that I would not see what condition the food was in.

The outside of my neck starts to hurt and I wonder what damage I had done while I was vomiting. Putting my hand up to the most painful part, which is at the right near my collarbone, I feel a wetness that is warm and put my fingers under my nose. It does smell like blood though it is difficult to tell as my nose is still sore and still retains a slight stagnant smell deep inside.

Bending down I explore the shackles around my ankles carefully. They feel sore where I must have put pressure against them when I was throwing up into the toilet but they feel dry and this is some small consolation.

Putting my hands up to the ring around my neck it definitely feels wet and sticky near my right collarbone. I wipe my fingers dry on my filthy jeans and explore the rest of my neck. It is sore near my left collarbone but feels dry as is the rest of my neck.

Getting to my feet I turn around and flush the toilet cupping my left hand under the flow. Using the water in my left hand I try to wash the right side of my neck but tip most of it over my chest. After several painful attempts I manage to wash a lot of the blood from my neck but start to get cold from the water and give it up as a bad job.

The light is suddenly turned on which hurts my eyes and I use my hand to cover the glare. I look down at the plate of food and can see that the cheese is a very dark yellow cheddar that is covered with blue and grey mould. The bread is as moldy and looks to be over a week old.

The door is unlocked and Debbie opens it wide and stands in the doorway. Seeing me and the condition I am in makes her laugh cruelly. Her shrill laugh grates my nerves and I feel a deep anger building within me. I clamp my jaw tightly and try to calm my rage. The voice of reason shouts inside my head not to provoke her and I stare at her angrily and think of a pleasant day at the beach so that she cannot see the anger reflected in my eyes.

Taking several steps towards me she continues to laugh staring into my eyes in an obvious challenge.

The voice inside my head shouts 'Careful, careful. Smile as best you can.' My mouth will not form into a smile as I feel the rage wash through me and I keep my mouth firmly shut so as not to tell her what I think of her. I break the gaze and stare humbly at the concrete floor.

"How do you like the moldy food then Phillip?" she asks in a cruel voice; "I can remember several times you expected me to eat moldy food. It is a bit different when you have to eat it isn't it? It made me feel good to hear you being sick so much, you have really made my day."

"You could hear me throwing up then?" I manage to ask, as I look into her eyes and can hear the anger in my voice.

Debbie's eyes lock onto mine and I can see the triumph in hers as she laughs again; "You have been a right bastard to me haven't you Phillip? Admit it."

"I cannot admit to something I have not done," I reply in a calmer voice but I see that this denial just provokes her and she takes several steps towards me;

"Don't lie to me," she screams as she suddenly shuts her mouth and then opens it as she spits at my face.

I try to doge my head out of the way but am not fast enough as her phlegm hits me in the right eye;

"You fucking *bitch*," I shout and wipe the phlegm out of my eye. Suddenly I feel a pain in my testicles as she kicks me hard and I step angrily towards her as the shackles bite hard into my ankles and I fall to the floor nearly strangling myself. Stars explode inside my head as she kicks me in the head several times and suddenly steps back.

I struggle to my feet and angrily shout at her; "Why are you doing this? I am not Phillip, I am *Patrick!*" I put as much emphasis into my name as I can and see her face turn red with rage;

"Patrick is dead. Dead, you hear?" she screams and steps forward again and aims another kick at my testicles.

I see the kick coming and turn quickly to the left and her foot kicks the top of my leg.

"You bitch. Stop it will you; why can't you see that I am not Phillip?"

Her mouth purses as she forms another spit and I turn my head quickly and feel the phlegm hit the back of my neck. Rage washes through me like a hot wave and I gather what saliva I have in my mouth with my tongue and spit back.

The look of surprise on her face as my phlegm hits her right on her nose is comical and I cannot stop the laugh that suddenly erupts; "What's the matter Debbie; don't you like it when you get your own medicine thrown back at you?" I take a step forward and make out I am going to kick her; "Unshackle me you bitch and I'll give your fanny a real good kicking," I shout as my anger envelops me. Suddenly I can take no more and I strain against my shackles and at the ring of steel around my neck; "Get these fucking chains off me. I am no lunatic ex boyfriend who tortured you. I am your friend Patrick. *Patrick!* But after this you can count me out as being one of your friends," I shout in desperation.

The anger fades from her face but the redness still remains. Her eyes stare into mine and I see her pupils dilate as an angry frown forms and her brow crinkles as the anger returns; "You are not Patrick. You are dead, that is what you are. *Dead!* You are going to be just like Patrick. *Dead*," she screams as her rage deepens and she kicks out again.

Her foot does not come anywhere near me and I laugh in her face; "You need to come closer if you want to kick me you stupid bitch. Come closer; *please* come closer," I plead and very eager to get my hands around her throat.

Suddenly Debbie takes several steps back and looks at the floor at my feet; "You have made a mess where you have been sick Phillip. I will go and get a bucket and a mop so that you can wash the floor. We do not want you to lay around in that mess; do we?" she asks, her voice calm as if the rage that overtook us both did not happen.

I am taken aback by her sudden change of mood; "I am sorry I shouted at you," I lie; "But what you are doing is not right."

Debbie looks at me with no expression on her face. Her eyes look dead and lifeless and she shrugs her shoulders; "I do not remember you shouting Phillip, but I can understand your being upset as it is not nice to eat food that is not fit for pigs; let alone humans."

'Keep her talking' the voice in my head says, sounding a lot calmer than what I feel; "There is no hurry to get the mop. Please stay and talk to me. If you are in the mood we could do some more mushrooms together," I ask, but I do not think my stomach would be able to keep them down. Also comes the realization that doing the magic mushrooms with her put me in this position in the first place. Apart from her mood swings we were getting along quite well until the mushrooms and then her overdosing on the ecstasy must have caused some kind of short circuit in her head. I had heard that taking psychedelic drugs can alter a person, but I never thought that they could cause madness and a total loss of reality.

"I do not think that is such a good idea Phillip as it was only a few weeks ago when I had some. It is better to wait at least a month or six weeks or they do not do anything," Debbie replies in a friendly voice and with a faint smile.

A few weeks? It somehow feels longer. "Whatever you say Debbie; do you have anything else that we could do together?" I ask, trying to match her tone of voice.

"No, I only have some sedatives and sleeping pills," she answers and suddenly laughs; "That would not be such a good time would it? It would be literally sleeping together with none of the action."

My brain suddenly races; "Action? I did not think that you thought of me that way," I reply trying to force a smile as I remember the awful smell that covered the bag of ecstasy tablets when she took them out of her vagina.

"I don't," Debbie snaps, sounding bitter; "I will go and get you that bucket and mop," she says as she turns around and hurries out of the door and leaving the door wide open runs up the stairs.

I sit back down onto the toilet bowl and think back over the past few minutes. I was lucky not to get seriously hurt with my outburst of anger, but I do feel better for it. My friendly approach does not appear to be working that well for me; in fact it seems to have the opposite effect. Maybe if I was to allow my anger to run its course next timewhen I feel it taking control and maybe, just maybe, I will be able to get through to her.

The voice of reason shouts in my mind that that thought is insanity talking and could make the situation much worse than it already is. Suddenly I laugh as the image of a drawing of two vultures sitting on a branch waiting patiently for something to die to feed their hunger fills my mind. One vulture turns and looks at the other vulture and says; 'To hell with patience, I am going to kill something.'

I have to admit to myself that is how I feel as my patience is running out and I am sick to death of being in this position. So what if I do antagonize her? It may provoke Debbie to do something drastic – maybe even kill me. Well, at least it would bring an end to this suffering. An insane laugh sounds in my head and I cannot help smiling at it. Feeling stronger with insanity running through my head I decide that aggression will probably be my best bet. As the decision is made I hear Debbie coming down the stairs and she appears in the doorway holding a mop and bucket. Our eyes meet and as if a switch has been turned on and my mouth opens of its own volition;

"You took your time getting them bitch," I say in an aggressive voice.

Debbie's eyes open wide and her mouth falls open in surprise and I maintain the attack;

"Put them there," I say as I indicate with my foot at the chalked line; "And you had better get me something decent to eat to replace that crap you just fed me. What were you thinking serving me that moldy food?" I continue in a loud voice.

"It is what you used to serve me," Debbie answers defensively.

"I never used to serve you with anything, bitch. As I keep telling you, you have the wrong man. Unshackle me at once," I shout.

Debbie takes several steps forward and stops a foot from the chalked line.

I can see the indecision in her mind and decide to push her further; "Put that bucket and mop down and get me out of these ridiculous chains," I shout keeping my voice angry.

Putting down the bucket and mop Debbie stands upright. Confusion seems to cover her face and for a brief moment I think she is going to unlock my chains. I can almost see her mind working as her eyes dart from side to side and then become still as she looks into mine; "I cannot unlock you as I do not have the keys on me," she says with a tremor to her voice and takes a step backwards.

"Go and get them then you fucking bitch," I demand, keeping my voice loud and annoyed.

"No, no I won't," Debbie replies; "When I think that you have suffered as much as I have, I might."

"Don't you think I have suffered enough? You have kept me chained up here for ages like I am some kind of wild animal and you have cut off my thumbs. Why did you do that to me?" I shout.

"Well you are, and I wanted to do something to make you remember me. You are still some kind of dirty bastard even with chains on."

"Unlock me or you will regret it," I shout even louder.

Debbie laughs and the mad glint returns to her eyes; "Clean up that mess you made and I might bring you some fresh food."

Debbie turns her back and walks out of the basement and slams the door shut behind her. I do not hear the key turn in the lock and assume that she has left the door unlocked.

I sit down on the toilet bowl rim stunned. My brain refuses to function as the last few minutes are replayed in my mind as if I am watching a video. The smell of disinfectant brings me back to earth and I stare at the bucket and imagine I can see the disinfectant odor coming out of the bucket in a cloud. The cloud drifts towards me surrounding me with its aroma and breathing becomes difficult.

I get to my feet and back away from it as if it is poisoning me as my senses return. The recent conversation with Debbie was definitely insane and I feel I came so close to freedom; if only she had the keys to my chains in her pocket it might have gone differently. It seems to be the answer; meet her insanity with an insanity of my own.

I step forward and with difficulty get my foot behind the bucket and pull it towards me. I can just reach the mop and pick it up having to use both hands and put it into the water. The disinfectant odor is almost overpowering and I contemplate throwing the bucket's contents down the toilet as the smell seems to get into the very pores of my skin. Deciding that it would be better to wash the vomit up and keep the germs at bay I start to mop the floor without wringing the mop out.

Debbie must have put half a bottle of disinfectant into the bucket as my eyes start to water and I decide after all to throw it down the toilet. I flush the toilet several times, each time putting the mop under the flow and use it to dilute the disinfectant that I had spread over the floor.

I recite the Debbie mantra as I clean; 'Debbie will not win I will defeat her and once again walk in the sunshine.'

After ten recitals the mantra has a distinctive hollow ring and suddenly I feel very alone. My previous prayers to my god now appear ridiculous and I fear that even He or She has deserted me. I not only feel alone I feel dirty and unwashed; which I am. I rub the growth of hair on my face with my filthy hands and long nails and wish for a bath. The wish turns to a dream and I imagine myself soaking in a hot bath with lavender perfume driving away the horrible body odor smell. The hair has gone from my face and my fingernails are short and clean.

The basement door suddenly opens waking me from my dream and Debbie walks in. Her eyes blaze with fury and I brace myself for the next onslaught;

"Think you are clever don't you Phillip? Well your silly mind games don't wash with me. How many times did you lock me up down here while you went out enjoying yourself with your mates?"

"I never locked you up anywhere." I answer in a calm voice.

"Give me the bucket and mop," she demands.

My earlier bravado deserts me and I meekly put the bucket and mop down onto the chalked line.

"Back away," Debbie orders.

I step back and feel the toilet bowl press up against the back of my legs as I feel the anger twist my stomach; "Let me go. My name is Patrick. Bring me something to shave off this beard and then you will see."

Stepping forward Debbie bends down and picks up the bucket and mop. As she stands upright she stares angrily into my eyes; "Trying your silly mind games again Phillip. I just told you they will not work."

"They are not mind games. Bring me a razor and you will see I am not Phillip," I reply, trying to keep the anger out of my voice.

Debbie continues staring at me and her eyes dart from side to side and I see the indecision return.

"Please Debbie, what can you lose by bringing me a safety razor? I can hardly use it as a weapon against you."

Debbie's brow crinkles in thought and with a deep breath she turns away and walks out of the basement, leaving the door wide open.

I watch her walking slowly up the stairs as if she is concentrating on my plea.

Several minutes pass and then Debbie's shadow blocks the light from the stairs as she returns – carrying a small safety razor. Stepping into the basement she throws the razor at me and warns; "If you are lying, you will not eat for a week." Slamming the door loudly she locks the door and silence returns.

I bend down and pick up the razor which landed on the concrete floor just inside the chalked line. Shaving foam would have helped but the cold water from the toilet will have to do.

It is very difficult trying to shave off the long growth of beard clasping the razor in my fist. I use plenty of water to soak my beard and wash away the cut hair and after what must be a good half hour my face feels smooth again. A little hair remains under my nose and I cut the skin removing it. Feeling cleaner I sit back down and await the return of my insane jailor.

Several hours pass before the door swings open and Debbie stares at me from the doorway. She looks confused and I stand up and face her defiantly;

"You see now don't you bitch?" I scream as a hot anger fills my body; "I am *Patrick*, your friend *Patrick*. You remember me don't you? We went across to the Continent to get your ecstasy tablets from your other friend Sally. Undo these chains," I demand, my voice sounding shrill and angry.

Debbie stares at me as the color drains from her face. Not saying a word she turns her back and slams the door shut and locks it.

'Well, another victory,' I say sarcastically to myself though in the back of my mind there seems to be a glimmer of hope. Her pale face appears in my mind and I get the feeling that I have managed to penetrate her madness.

With hope filling my mind I sit back down onto the cold porcelain and realize that she has left the light on. I stare at the door not taking my eyes off it as the hours pass when suddenly the light goes off and I welcome the darkness. More time passes and I start to visualize numbers in my head as I count and subtract and multiply.

The smell of food awakes me, the basement remains in darkness but somehow I know that a tray of food is before me. Feeling carefully with my foot it touches the tray which is a lot closer to me than normal. Scared of knocking the food over I remove my trainer and carefully extend my leg and then using my toes very carefully slide the tray towards me.

Picking up the tray I sit down and balance it on my knees. It feels heavier than normal and I can definitely smell oxtail soup. Feeling with my hands I can feel a plate containing sandwiches and also a large hot bowl. Moving my hands over it I can feel the steam coming off it and even feel the spoon that rests inside.

As my hands circle the bowl the back of my right hand detects more warmth and reaching out I can feel a hot mug. Picking it up with both hands the heat burns my fingers and penetrates my bandages. Raising it quickly to my nose I can smell real ground coffee, not the instant coffee that Debbie has been serving me. Returning it quickly to the tray I let my fingers cool down a little and return my hands to the bowl of soup.

Clasping the spoon in my right fist I take a sip of the oxtail soup, which tastes delightful. I can detect no other unusual flavors and taking my time eat the whole bowlful.

The coffee has cooled considerably and I take a tentative sip. The coffee tastes fine, a little bitter but that is to be expected and I take a large mouthful and return the mug to the tray. Focusing on the plate of sandwiches I pick one up and put it to my nose. It smells fine and could be ham or pork luncheon meat and I take a small bite. Chewing it slowly I am sure that it only tastes of pork and in my hunger I eat it quickly and then eat the rest and wash them down with the real coffee.

My stomach feels bloated after eating and I sit back and rest my head against the wall. My eyes suddenly feel heavy and I feel my eyelids closing as a soft feeling washes over me and I realize that I have been drugged again. I snap my eyes open in fear as the drug flows through my body as I feel the tray slipping forward and I hear a distant crash as it hits the floor and my eyes close again.

Chapter Sixteen

Crazy dreams fill my head as the pointed headed people point at me showing me their hands that have no thumbs. I open my eyes and can see that the basement door is open. A cramp in my left leg makes me straighten it and as I do I realize that my leg feels lighter and that I can straighten it to its full extent.

I bend down and feel my ankle – the shackle has been removed! I bring my right leg back and feel the ankle and realize that shackle has also been removed. Quickly putting my hands up to my neck I can feel it all as the steel collar has also been removed and I get to my feet.

The basement spins around me where I have stood up too quickly but I do not care and I take several steps forward towards the door; and hopefully freedom.

I am free! Walking across the basement is a struggle as my leg muscles protest and I walk through the doorway and start to slowly climb the stairs. My legs feel weird and I have to grab hold of the handrail to help me climb the stairs.

The door at the top of the stairs is also open and I step quietly through it. Seeing that the lounge door is slightly ajar I walk slowly across the passageway and put my head around the door and look inside. The lounge is in partial darkness as the curtains have been drawn but I can see that it is daylight outside.

Debbie sits in the armchair, her legs are brought up tightly against her as if she had tried to stifle pain in her stomach and instinctively I know that she is dead.

Opening the door wider I walk slowly in and walk over to her. Her face is grimaced as if she was in a lot of pain when she died and a feeling of release washes over me.

My nightmare is over; at last I am truly free!

Looking around the room I see on the coffee table about ten of the off white ecstasy tablets and several mugs of half drank coffee. My wallet lays open with a small pile of £20 notes lying on top of it. Somehow I know that I do not have to count them and that there is £180. Picking up the money with both hands I slide it between the fingers of my left hand and easing the back of the wallet open with the fingers of my right hand I slide the money in. Looking through my wallet I can see the money that was left in it when my nightmare started and also my credit cards, driving license and passport.

Putting my wallet awkwardly into my pocket I see my car keys on the table. Taking a final look at Debbie I pick up my keys and hurry out of the room. Walking quickly along the hallway I struggle to open the front door. Life without any thumbs is going to be very difficult I think to myself as I manage to open the door wide and step outside.

The day is cloudy and cold but I do not care as the day feels wonderful and I slam the door shut behind me and hurry along the path. My car is in the same place where I had parked it and is covered with dust where it looks like a dirty rain has fallen onto it.

As I step through the gate a lady walking along the path towards me and wearing a long grey overcoat and black wooly hat stares at me with disgust. Well I guess that I look a mess as I look down at my jeans and shirt. My jeans are covered in dried blood and excrement and my shirt has dried blood and food sticking to it. I try to brush my shirt with my hands as I walk quickly around to the drivers' door and push the key in the lock. Turning the key is difficult and I make a fist of my right hand and push the key between my fingers. Circling my fist with my left hand I grip tightly as I turn my fist to open the lock as a sharp pain envelops my hand and I know that I will have to go to a hospital and have my hands checked over.

The key turns and I open the door and get in. The lady walks past and still stares at me with disgust but I do not care. I manage to put the ignition key in the lock and put the key between my fingers as I make a fist again but I cannot turn the key. Frustration fills me and I grab my fist with my left hand and force my fingers together and manage to turn the key. The ignition lights come on and I pray that the engine will start as I turn the key further and the engine turns and fires up. I rev the engine up and let it warm as I struggle with my seatbelt. Using the heel of my hand I manage to secure the seatbelt and also using the heel of my hand release the handbrake and put the car in gear. My hands hurt like hell as I look in my rearview mirror and pull out onto the road.

More than anything I want to shower and change my clothes, I know that I should report to the police and go to the hospital but I would rather do that with some sort of cleanliness as I know that I smell something horrible.

Pointing the car in the direction of home I drive slowly along the road. I feel elated at my release but still feel groggy from the massive sedative that Debbie had given me. Several times on the way back home drivers behind me vent their frustration and anger by tooting their horns as I drive so slowly and it is about an hour and a half later before I arrive outside my apartment building and park the car.

Locking the car door is difficult as is unlocking my front door but by grasping my fist tightly around the keys I manage it and gratefully step inside.

As I walk into my lounge I can see that someone has been in here. Clothes litter the furniture and I recognize a T-shirt of Debbie's and an old pair of jeans. There are several items of underwear and three pairs of her knickers are on the back of a chair next to a set of clothes I had washed and put out to dry; an eternity ago now.

I go into the kitchen and see that there are the remains of a Chinese meal on one of my plates and it is going moldy; as are the remains of the food in the aluminum containers. The sink has several pairs of her knickers soaking and I pull the plug out to let the water drain away.

Looking around the apartment I can see that she has caused no damage and switch on the television remote control. The date and time shows as the television warms and I am shocked to see the date and to see that she had kept me a prisoner for twenty-nine days – the bitch!

Feeling very dirty and unclean I get a clean towel from the airing cupboard and go and have a shower. I must have stayed under the shower for more than forty-five minutes as I let the hot water wash away the weeks of accumulated dirt and blood. My neck hurts as does my ankles, especially the right one. The ankle is red and sore with a little blood seeping out and just above the heel my ankle looks infected as a little puss oozes out. The bandages on my hands become soaking wet and it is the pain in my hands that forces me to get out of the shower. Toweling myself dry is difficult with no thumbs and I throw the towel down in disgust and go into the lounge to put on clean clothes.

Making myself a cup of instant coffee I sit on an armchair and think back over the nightmare weeks that have just past. I know that I must report what has happened to the police as soon as possible as to leave it too long will only make it look bad on myself.

I quickly drink my coffee and after getting an empty plastic carrier bag from under the sink I put the empty Chinese food containers into the bag and also scrape the rotten food off the plate. Getting another plastic carrier bag I go into the lounge and put Debbie's jeans, T-shirt and underwear in it. Putting her underwear that was in the sink on top I try to tie a knot in the bag but only having fingers find it impossible to do.

Hiding my wallet under the sink and after looking around for any more of Debbie's clothes that may be lying around I put on my jacket. Picking up the carrier bags of Chinese food waste and her clothes I leave my apartment. Ensuring that I have my keys with me I slam the door shut and with my hands being so painful rely on the one lock to secure my door.

I decide to walk to the police station as it is only about a mile away on the other side of town. It feels so good to be free again and I walk along the seafront and throw the carrier bags into a public trash can on the way.

The day is still cloudy and there is a definite chill to the breeze that is blowing off the sea making me wish I had put a bigger coat on; but really do not care as it feels so good to be free again.

I walk slowly to the police station enjoying the day and the smell of the sea. There are a lot of people walking along the seafront with their dogs now that the summer restrictions have been lifted against dogs on the seafront. Reluctantly I turn away from the sea and walk through the town to the police station.

As I enter the police station the policewoman behind the counter looks at me suspiciously as I approach.

"Can I help you sir?" she asks politely.

"Yes please can I talk to an officer about a recent kidnapping, torture and a suicide?"

"Yes, you can talk to me. Who has been kidnapped and tortured; and who has committed suicide?" she asks curtly, all resemblance of politeness leaving her voice.

I look around at the empty foyer and return my attention to her; "Is there somewhere a little more private where I can talk please?"

"Here is fine sir; if anyone comes in we will take it from there. Now who has been kidnapped and you said something about a suicide?"

I look again around at the empty foyer to show my disagreement to be talking in such a public place but see that I have no choice; "I was drugged and kept a prisoner for twenty-nine days and tortured during that time." I hold up my hands and show her the grubby bandages; "As you can see I have had my thumbs cut off and I also suffered a lot of other torture."

Her face drops as it colors slightly; "Who is it that has committed suicide sir?" she asks failing to keep the horror out of her voice.

"That was my jailor. I was heavily drugged yesterday and when I woke up this morning I found that my chains were off. I was kept prisoner in her basement and when I went upstairs I found her dead in her lounge. Thankfully for me she had let me go before killing herself." I smile broadly in relief; as I am free!

A door at the side of the foyer opens and a police sergeant, a big man in his mid-fifties with gray hair and immaculate uniform looks at me; "You had better come in sir," he says in a friendly voice.

I smile at him as I walk towards him; "Thank you, it is such a relief to be free again."

He holds the door wider for me as I walk through; "Go into that room on your right please sir; I will be with you in a moment."

I walk into the room which has a large gray Formica topped desk and grey upright chairs; one in front and one behind the desk. I sit in the chair at the front of the desk and hear a whispered conversation as the sergeant talks to the policewoman but cannot hear their words. A minute later the sergeant walks in and shuts the door behind him. Walking behind the desk he puts a clipboard down containing several sheets of paper onto the desk and sits down on the chair.

"Now sir, can you tell me what has been happening to you and who it is that has committed suicide. Can we start with your name and address and do you have any identification on you?" he asks in the friendliest of tones.

I tell him my name and address and admit that I have no identification on me. He asks me my date of birth, employment and if I have any family. He dutifully writes it all down and then asks me my jailors name and I tell him as he asks for Debbie's address, her age and whether she has any family. I give him as much information as I can in which he gets to his feet and tells me that he will be back shortly.

The sergeant appears to be friendly and pleasant towards me but I am starting to get a bad feeling about this. After a minute or so after he left the door open a young police officer walks in and closes the door behind him. Standing by the doorway he stands and waits and the bad feeling I have magnifies.

Several minutes later the door opens again and the sergeant looks at the young police officer; "Thank you Tom, you can go and have your break now," he says in a friendly manner but I notice that he does not smile.

The young police officer walks out as the sergeant holds the door open; "Can you come with me please sir?" he asks.

I stand up and walk out of the room and he gestures with his arm for me to walk along the corridor. He keeps close beside me as we pass several doors and says; "The next door on your left please Patrick."

The door is already slightly ajar and as I push it open further I walk in to see another large table with a chair in front of it. Behind the table are two plain clothes officers in their mid-fifties who I assume are detectives. To their right is a small table against the wall with recording equipment on it.

"Please sit down Patrick," one of them says to me; "I am Detective Appleton and this is my colleague Detective Norton."

As I sit down Detective Norton nods his head in greeting as the door is shut behind me. The sergeant stands beside the door and I turn my attention back to Detective Appleton as he speaks; "By what Sergeant Marsh has been telling us you have had quite a time of it lately?"

"That is one way of putting it," I reply as alarm bells sound in my head.

Seeing my expression Detective Appleton smiles; "Nothing to worry about Patrick, we need to take a full statement off of you," he says as he stands up and walks over to the recording machine turns it on and looks at his watch and speaks aloud the time and the date and that I am to be interviewed. He speaks my full name and repeats that I am to be interviewed and in the presence of himself and Detective Norton and Sergeant Marsh.

Sitting back down he smiles again; "As I said Patrick, nothing to worry about. I know that this all looks a bit official and probably a bit scary to you but unfortunately we have to do things by the book."

I stare into his eyes and somehow know that he is lying to me. I smile back at him; "That is ok, I hope that you do not intend for this to take too long." I hold up my bandaged hands in front of me; "I should have gone to the hospital first as both of my hands are hurting and as you can see I have had my thumbs cut off."

He looks at my hands and then stares deeply into my eyes; "No, we do not intend to take a long time and we can see that you are in possible need of hospital treatment."

"I am in need, not 'possible' need," I say for the benefit of the recording device; "I would also like a drink of water if that is *possible* please." I put emphasis on the word 'possible' as I have suddenly become aware that I am being treated as a criminal; admittedly in a friendly way, but I do not like the looks of this.

Detective Appleton stares back into my eyes realizing my awareness and smiles again; "Of course Patrick, maybe you would prefer a cup of tea?"

"Coffee would be nice, but failing that water will be just fine," I reply, not returning his smile.

Detective Appleton looks towards the sergeant; "Could you arrange that please Bill? Patrick has obviously had a bad time, see if you can arrange a nice cup of coffee for the gentleman," he asks as he looks back at me;

"Milk and sugar?"

"Black please with two sugars, thank you as my mouth is really dry."

Detective Appleton looks up at Sergeant Marsh; "We will wait," he tells him.

I hear the door open and close behind me and in less than a minute the door opens again and Sergeant Marsh returns; "Coffee will be with us in a few minutes," he tells us as he returns to his position by the door.

Detective Appleton looks at me and smiles again; "Are you able to start telling us just what has been happening to you Patrick; or would you prefer to wait for your coffee?"

I do not smile back as I reply; "I can start now, the sooner we get this over with the sooner I can get to the hospital."

"Thank you Patrick," Detective Appleton says with his false smile on his lips; "The recorder is on, ready when you are."

I tell them of being drugged and finding myself chained up in the basement. The coffee arrives, carried on a tray by a young policewoman who puts the tray on the table. There are four mugs of coffee; one is black, with a large bowl of sugar and several spoons. I help myself to the black coffee and after awkwardly putting three sugars in stir it vigorously and take a small sip as I continue my narrative.

The police officers ask no questions until I finish with finding Debbie's body and getting out of her house as fast as I could.

The two detectives stare at me in shock for a few seconds when I finish and then Detective Appleton asks the inevitable question; "Why did you not go to the police as soon as you got out of your lady's house?"

"She was not 'my lady' as you put it. I had not washed or cleaned my teeth for twenty-nine days and felt really dirty and quite disgusting and I knew that I smelt something awful. I really had to have a shower, clean my teeth and put some clean clothes on before I came here," I reply, and knowing that they do not like my answer.

Detective Appleton pushes the point; "Do you not think it looks suspicious or even bad that you did not go straight to the nearest police station? You had escaped after all and your friend was dead."

"After twenty-nine days of not washing how would you feel? She was dead so it made no difference and she was certainly not my friend," I answer trying to keep the anger out of my voice.

He will not leave it alone as he asks; "Do you not think that any normal person after suffering such an ordeal would go straight to the nearest police station?"

"I nearly lost my sanity chained up in her basement and was also tortured for twenty nine days. Do you honestly think that I was 'normal' as you put it? I was just so glad to get out of there and needed some normality of familiar things around me like my television and my furniture and possessions. I returned to my apartment showered, cleaned my teeth, had a quick cup of coffee and came straight here. I was probably in my apartment for less than an hour before I came directly here."

Detective Appleton does not look convinced; neither does Detective Norton. Detective Appleton looks me in the eyes again; "You have to admit that it is unusual behavior?"

I laugh; "No I do not. I stank something horrible, my clothes were covered in rotten food, dried blood and even my jeans had shit on them. I am sure you *gentlemen*," I say as I look round at Sergeant Marsh and then look back at Detective Appleton; "would not appreciate me sitting here smelling of rotten food, blood, body odor, stale urine and shit?"

Detective Norton smiles coldly; "I do not think we would," he agrees as Detective Appleton fixes him with a withering stare.

"We will come back to that Patrick," Detective Appleton says.

"You come back to it as many times as you like mate and you will get the same reply each time," I say impatiently.

What is the matter with him?

They continue to question me for about two more hours when I lose my patience with them. Holding my bandaged hands up in front of me I tell them that I need to go to the hospital as my hands are hurting and that I will not answer any more of their foolish questions, until I have had some kind of medical treatment.

Detective Appleton's answer surprises me as he advises me that they have sent for a Doctor who should be here shortly. He turns off the recording device and asks me to 'come with him' as he walks across the room and stands in the open doorway, the door having been opened by Sergeant Marsh.

I stand up and follow him out of the door as he walks along the corridor. Detective Norton and Sergeant Marsh walk close behind me and I wonder what is going to happen next.

We turn the corner and at the end of the corridor I am led up to a large machine that has a large blank screen on it. Beyond the machine is a counter with several uniformed policeman behind it. As I approach the large machine one of the uniformed officers steps forward holding a long thin package in his hand.

He carefully opens the package which I see contains a cotton bud on a long stick; "Could you give us a DNA sample please sir? Take the item out of the packet and insert it into your mouth and press it up against your cheek and twirl it several times before removing it please."

I look at the package; "How am I going to do that then?" I ask holding up my bandaged hands; "I ain't got no thumbs mate as you can see, you will have to do it."

The uniformed officer looks perplexed and looks at Detective Appleton for guidance.

"He cannot do that Patrick as we need a DNA sample and his touching it may contaminate it. Do the best you can please."

I do not believe a word of it but reach out and put two fingers into the packet. Getting the stick between my fingers I pull it out and attempt to put it in my mouth. I miss, nearly putting the cotton bud end up my nose and it falls from my fingers onto the floor. I look Detective Appleton in the eyes; "Sorry officer, do you want me to pick it up?" I ask sarcastically as I am getting the right hump with these people.

"No, Officer Lloyd will get you another. Please handle the next one with a bit more care please."

"You want to try it with no thumbs Detective Appleton," I acerbically reply.

Officer Lloyd goes back behind the counter and gets another small packet. Coming back round he tears off the top and looks at me with some sympathy in his eyes; "Take your time sir, there is plenty of time," he says in a shocked voice.

"Thank you," I say as I once again put my fingers into the packet. I put them deeper in and push the stick up to the joint of my fingers. Gripping it as tight as I can I pull it out and open my mouth and put the end with the cotton bud in.

"Please rub it hard against the inside of your cheek please sir," Officer Lloyd asks politely.

I do as he asks and then pull out the cotton bud as he holds out the empty packet towards me. I push the cotton bud in as far as I can and he thanks me as he seals it shut.

"Please step forward and put your right hand on the glass Patrick," Detective Appleton asks in a strained voice.

I step forward as I put my hand on the glass.

"Please press your fingertips against the glass Patrick," he asks in a friendlier voice.

"Why are you doing this? You are treating me like a criminal, taking samples of my DNA and now you want my fingerprints." I ask in a soft voice.

"We need to eliminate you from our enquiries and to establish your true identity," Detective Appleton replies as the machine lights up and scans my fingertips; "and now your left hand," he orders and the machine lights up again. Appearing to be satisfied with the scans he steps away; "Follow me," he orders and I follow him back along the corridor and we walk down several steps which leads us to a long corridor that has a lot of closed cell doors.

"What the hell is this mate?" I roar; "You are not seriously going to put me in a cell?" I stare at him angrily.

He looks at me as I see a large shadowy figure coming up behind me. Turning to face him I see that it is a huge uniformed officer. He looks to be in his mid-thirties and is at least six feet six inches tall. Built like a weightlifter he looks more than eager to put his hands on me.

"Having a bit of trouble here?" he asks looking me up and down.

"You have to be the jailor." I say; "You look very keen to grab hold of me and throw me in a cell." I angrily say staring defiantly up into his eyes.

"No, no trouble Frank. I just want to put Patrick somewhere safe until the Doctor gets here," he answers in a calm voice.

Still staring at me 'Frank' smiles; "I have just the place for him," he says as he walks along the corridor and opens a cell door.

Detective Appleton looks at me; "There is nothing to worry about Patrick. Please wait in here until the Doctor arrives." Looking at his watch he says; "He is taking his time, I will go and telephone the hospital and find out what is happening. I will come back and let you know," he promises.

I look him in the eyes; "I do not believe you are doing this to me. I only just got out of being locked up and less than five hours later you are locking me up again. I can just as easily wait for the doctor in one of your offices as I am not going to run away."

"You will be safer here and I will get Frank to bring you another cup of coffee. Would you like anything to eat?"

"I wouldn't mind as I am really hungry," Looking at Frank who towers above us I look back at Detective Appleton; "I am going to be safe here with him am I? I would prefer it if you told him what has been happening to me and that I am a victim; in case he thinks I am some violent criminal or something."

"Yes, I will tell him. Please go inside and put your feet up while I go and see where the Doctor is," he replies in a friendly voice.

This is all becoming too much and my mind whirls in confusion, I feel unbalanced as if I am losing my mind. I feel scared, really scared as everything is getting out of control; and I feel too scared to do anything about it. That I am being held in custody is obvious and knowing I have little choice as Frank looks more than eager to get physical with me I walk into the cell and visibly cringe when the door is slammed shut behind me.

Chapter Seventeen

The cell is small, measuring about nine feet long and six feet wide. A small single cot with a very thin mattress and only one blanket is pushed against one wall. The single pillow looks to be as thin as the mattress and I sit down on the cot. Only a foot or so away from the top of the cot is a toilet with no seat. A small basin is next to the toilet and I notice that there is no towel.

Near the door there is a small table and hardback chair. The heavy steel door is painted in a dull gray color with a peephole and flap that is wide enough for a small tray. The walls are smoothly decorated in a speckled marble finish and I think to myself that I will not even be able to count the bricks to pass the time.

The ceiling is about nine feet above me with a light, about nine inches by four inches set into it. The light, coming from a single bulb, is very bright and is covered by a thick patterned glass with security wire embedded in it.

My situation, being locked up in this cell really scares me and I wonder why the police are treating me in this way. I can only assume that they must think I am responsible for Debbie's death. Detective Appleton certainly made an issue about me going home once I got away from Debbie's house. He did not appear to even consider my reasons; instead he seemed to think that it was an admission of guilt on my part.

The voice of madness echoes in my mind telling me that I am worrying unduly and the reason I am locked in this cell is so that they can have their dinner break. By being locked in this cell they will not have to worry where I am. They will obviously need to keep me for a few hours to check out my story and they are just following police policy and there is nothing for me to worry about. Debbie's death is definitely a suicide and the evidence of my imprisonment will be plain to see in her basement. My voice of madness sounds logical but I cannot suppress the fear and bad feelings that fill me.

The voice of reason echoes stronger in my mind making me realize that a part of me is losing it and that total madness is not too far away. How is it that I can believe I am in here because of a dinner break and police policy is mad thinking when it is evident that I am being kept prisoner and the charge looks like it is to be murder.

A half hour passes with no sign of coffee or food or Detective Appleton. I look at my bandaged hands and curse Debbie for what she has done to me. Maybe I will be able to have artificial thumbs fitted sometime in the future. It is very clever what doctors are able to achieve these days.

The door opening interrupts my thoughts and Frank the jailor stands in the doorway.

"Come with me please sir so that you can see the Doctor," he says in the politest of voices.

I make no comment as I get up from the cot and walk out of the door. As expected Frank holds my arm as we walk along the corridor and up the stairs. He leads me to a large room with many tables and chairs and I see the Doctor in a white coat and a nurse in a blue uniform standing beside a table.

On the table is a medical bag and Detectives Appleton and Norton stand close by. Sergeant Marsh stands by the doorway and there are three other plain clothed detectives, one with a large camera. Several uniformed police are also present and I feel badly outnumbered as Frank walks me over to the Doctor and he lets go of my arm.

The Doctor, a man in his early thirties with a very round face and black hair looks at me and smiles reassuringly; "I understand that someone has carried out an operation on you? Please sit here," he says indicating to a hard back chair; "and we will have a look at it for you."

Though friendly, the way the Doctor has spoken to me is as if he is doing me a great favor and that he would not be here if I had not insisted on it.

I sit on the chair indicated and not saying a word and hold out my bandage hands towards him. The Doctor puts on a pair of blue rubber gloves and I notice that the nurse already has a pair on.

Opening his case the Doctor takes out a roll of medical equipment and unrolls it. Taking a pair of scissors he approaches me and then turns towards the nurse; "Hold his hands please nurse, by the fingers please."

The nurse walks over to me and holds my fingertips as the Doctor starts to cut the bandage off my right hand. Everyone in the room looks on fascinated by what the Doctor is doing. As he starts to remove the bandage it sticks to my hand and I shout 'OW, that hurts."

The Doctor stops for a second; "I do need to remove this bandage," he says as he pulls again.

The pain is even more intense and I clamp my jaw shut but cannot help saying 'Bloody hell, sorry nurse that hurt.'

"That's ok," she replies as she looks down at my hand.

The sewn up wound is bleeding a little where the bandage had stuck to it and a part of it does not look a very good color.

"We will remove the other one before we have a closer look," the Doctor says as he starts to cut away the bandage on the left hand.

The bandage comes off easily and the sewn up wound looks slightly pink around where the stitches are, but everywhere else looks healthy.

"We need to take some photographs," says Detective Appleton as the Detective with the camera steps forward.

"Of course," replies the Doctor as he moves away from me, as does the nurse.

"Please put your hands on the table sir," the Detective asks; "With your palms facing upwards."

I do as he asks as he takes about ten photographs from different angles, some close-up; "That should be enough Tony," he says and he looks at Detective Appleton.

"Thanks Alan, please proceed Doctor," Detective Appleton says in a loud superior voice; and gracefully giving his permission for me to be treated.

The Doctor steps forward and looks at the nurse; "These will have to cleaned nurse," he says stating the obvious.

The nurse makes no reply as she goes to the medical bag and takes out cotton wool and antiseptic. Standing in front of me I can see the troubled look in her eyes. My hands are still resting on the table palm upwards from where they were photographed; "Please keep your hands where they are sir. This may sting a little so I will do your left hand first," she tells me in a strained voice.

The nurse washes my wounds and she was right as they do 'sting a little'. The right hand that is turning septic stings a lot but I clamp my jaw shut and bear the pain with no comment.

"That is good nurse," the Doctor compliments when the nurse has finished; "We will need to bandage these up again," he says as he turns and looks at Detective Appleton; "Do you want to take anymore photographs before we bandage his hands?" he asks him.

Detective Appleton nods his head towards Detective 'Alan' who steps forward and takes a photograph of each of my cleaned up hands.

The Doctor with the help of the nurse bandages my hands. The Doctor then starts to pack the equipment away.

"Don't you think that you better look at my other wounds before you go?" I mordantly ask the Doctor.

The Doctor looks at Detective Appleton and then looks at me; "Other wounds sir?" he asks as his face colors slightly.

"Yes, the one around my neck, which you must be able to see and my ankles need looking at too," I tell him in the same mordant voice.

The Doctor, who had removed his blue rubber gloves, reaches into his bag and pulls out a boxful of them. Pulling two out he puts them on and steps towards me; "Please raise your chin sir," he asks in a deadpan voice.

I raise my chin and he looks at my neck and walks around behind me and asks me to lower my chin. I do as he asks as he steps back round to the front of me.

"Yes, I see but it does not look too serious. Can you take your jacket and shirt off for me please?"

"I can, but I will need some help if you are in a hurry?" I reply, the sarcasm still remaining.

The nurse steps forward to help me.

"Yes please help him nurse," the Doctor says unnecessarily.

The nurse helps me remove my jacket and shirt and she is very gentle, which I really appreciate as my hands, especially the right hand, hurts like hell.

The Doctor steps forward again and has another look at my neck; "Please clean this nurse and bandage it when you have finished," he says as he removes his gloves.

The nurse gently cleans the wound around my neck, the antiseptic stings but it feels good and I make no comment. After putting some antiseptic cream on she gently bandages my neck. Her eyes look deeply troubled and I thank her for being so gentle and for caring. She makes no comment as she stands back and looks at me and then at the Doctor, aware that he has not finished his job. The Doctor looks all packed up and already to go and I look at him coldly;

"What about my ankles then?" I ask in that sarcastic voice; "Have you forgotten that I asked you to look at them a few minutes ago?"

"Ankles?" he asks appearing baffled.

"Yes, my ankles, I have been shackled to the floor this past month or haven't you been told that?"

"What is the matter with your ankles?" he asks, as an angry glint shows in his eyes.

The Doctor looks mad – how dare I question him?

"I just told you mate, sorry if I am keeping you from something important. Maybe if you had a look instead of asking damn fool questions you will be able to get home a bit quicker; or wherever it is that you want to go."

The Doctor's face colors a deep red as his anger takes over. Well if he did his job properly I would not criticize him, he appears so filled with his own self-importance and it is plain to see that I come a very poor second.

Pulling a hard backed chair towards me he tells me in an angry voice; "Put your foot on this."

I do as he orders putting my right foot on the chair. He roughly pulls my trouser leg up and just as roughly pulls my sock down as far as it can go.

"Looks infected to me mate," I tell him.

He looks at the nurse; "Help the gentleman remove his shoe and sock and also his trousers as well," he orders.

The nurse steps forward and gently removes my trainer and sock; "Can you put your left foot on the chair please sir? So that I can take your other shoe and sock off."

"Of course," I reply with a broad smile; "Anything to help."

The nurse allows herself a quick smile as she removes my other trainer and sock; "Could you stand please sir? Do you want me to help you remove your trousers?"

I get to my feet, my feet become instantly cold against the cold concrete floor; "Sorry to ask nurse, but if you just undo them I will be able to take them down thank you."

The nurse undoes the button and unzips the fly and then takes a step backwards.

I drop my trousers and step out of them as she picks them up and puts them on the table. I look at the Doctor who is putting another pair of blue rubber gloves on, having taken the others off. He looks at me angrily; "Please sit down sir and put your leg up on the chair."

I do as he asks putting my right foot on the chair as he looks at the nurse; "Please hand me the cotton wool and the antiseptic."

The nurse does not look happy but dutifully passes them over and I know what is coming.

Holding a piece of cotton wool in his hand the Doctor applies some antiseptic and starts to clean the wound – hard.

"Hey," I protest angrily; "What do you think you are doing mate? Let the nurse do it as she is a lot gentler than you are being. I know you want to hurt me for talking to you the way I did but if you did your job properly I wouldn't have had to."

The Doctor looks up at me and I can see that he is furious; "I am quite capable of cleaning a wound," he says as he brushes the wound hard again with the cotton wool.

I pull my foot away from him and fold my knee so that my foot is under my chair; "You like to hurt me too much, let the nurse do it as she cares about her patients."

"I care, now put your foot back up onto this chair," he orders angrily as a little spittle comes out of his mouth.

"No way," I angrily reply; "I will have you for assault the way you are carrying on."

"Help the Doctor, Patrick," orders Detective Appleton; "Put your foot back up onto the chair so that the Doctor can do his work."

I look at Detective Appleton and stare angrily into his eyes; "I just said no, you can see the way he is hurting me and you seem quite happy for him to do that. If he continues I will insist that you charge him with assault. Let the nurse do it and then this so called doctor can get out of here."

Detective Appleton stares back at me and I can see the indecision in his eyes as the nurse steps forward and takes the cotton wool from the Doctor's hand; "I will do it, I do not mind," she says in a soft voice.

The Doctor gets angrily to his feet and walks away to the far end of the room and sits down on a chair staring angrily at me.

"Thank you nurse, that Doctor friend of yours is a bit rough. Did you know that it was a nurse who did all of this to me? Had me chained up for a month while she tortured and starved me."

The nurse looks into my eyes and it looks like she is going to burst into tears; "No, I didn't know," she says as she glances over her shoulder at the Doctor, who still sits in the chair with a deep scowl across his face; "He is no friend of mine," she says in a quiet voice that only I can hear; "Right let me clean this up for you," she says a bit louder and starts to gently wash my wounded ankle with the antiseptic soaked cotton wool.

She gently cleans them and pays particular attention to the seeping wound on my right ankle. After putting some antiseptic cream on them she bandages them carefully and helps me put my trousers back on. Advising me not to put my socks on she puts my trainers on. My toenails are in bad need of cutting as are my fingernails and I ask her if she is able to cut them for me?

The nurse tells me that she is unable to as the hospital has special people for that job. She promises to make a note of it and will contact the right department for me. I thank her for helping me and apologize for upsetting the Doctor with her.

"He asked for it," she tells me with a warm smile as she turns towards the Doctor and tells him that she has finished.

"About time," he snaps and stares at me with a steely glint; "Is there anything else that you want me to look at before I go?"

I point to my cheek where Debbie pushed the bamboo through; "I take it that that is ok?"

The nurse steps forward and looks closely at my cheek; "There is a little red mark, but it looks fine," she says reassuringly.

I look into her eyes while pointing at my cheek; "Piece of bamboo, she pushed it all the way through."

The nurse looks like she is going to burst into tears again; "It is fine, it has healed ok."

"Thanks," I say with a smile; "and thanks so much for looking after me."

"You're welcome," she replies with a broad smile; "We need to give you an antibiotic injection, would you like me to do it?"

"Yes please nurse," I reply with a friendly smile and she picks up a small syringe from the table that I had not noticed.

Turning towards me she pulls up my right sleeve; "Little scratch," she says as she pushes the needle in and injects the clear fluid into my arm.

"Are we ready nurse?" the Doctor asks with deep sarcasm as he looks at Detective Appleton; "We have finished now but we will get someone to come by tomorrow."

"As long as it ain't you mate," I tell him which brings a smile to the nurses face.

The Doctor picks up his bag and walks out of the door followed by the nurse who turns back towards me and gives a little wave and says 'Goodbye'.

"You do like to upset people don't you?" demands Detective Appleton; "He was only trying to do his job."

I look at him and smile; "Not very well. I take it by his comment that it is your intent to keep me here?"

"While the investigation is being carried out," he replies in a firm voice.

"And how long is that going to take?" I ask trying to keep the anger out of my voice; and failing.

"We should be finished soon Patrick, there is nothing to worry about."

"You keep saying that and your attitude towards me is making me worry. By law you are only allowed to keep me here for a short while and then you will have to charge me with whatever it is that you think I have done to be able to keep me locked up. What happened to my coffee and food; is it your intent to starve me to death and finish what that mad woman started?" I ask indignantly.

Jailor Frank answers from the doorway; "The coffee and food had just arrived when Detective Appleton called down that you were wanted upstairs."

Detective Appleton looks at me with a superior look; "As you just heard your food and coffee is ready. Please go back downstairs with Frank and I will come and see you later," he promises.

"I still think you are well out of order keeping me locked up. I will have to insist on some kind of legal defense if you continue," I warn, though I admit that I am not sure of my rights and no one has advised otherwise.

"That is your privilege Patrick, please go with Frank and I promise you either Detective Norton or myself will come and see you after you have eaten."

I do not like this, do not like it at all and I can only assume that these people must think that I have killed Debbie. I have no choice and reluctantly walk across the room to Frank who steps outside and once again holding my arm he leads me back to the cells.

Chapter Eighteen

Frank leads me back to the cell and all of the time keeping a tight hold on my arm. He is definitely treating me as a prisoner and not as a victim. The police had to have gained entrance to Debbie's house by now and I can only assume that they have not liked what they have seen. After keeping me a prisoner and torturing me, especially cutting off my thumbs, in their eyes I would have had a good reason for killing her.

Frank brings me a fry up of two pieces of bacon, a fried slice of bread and a fried egg. The mug of coffee contains no milk and no sugar and of course, all of it is stone cold. I am so hungry and thirsty and I force it all down holding the plastic knife and fork in my fists and then lie down on the cot and stare moodily up at the ceiling.

I soon fall asleep as it has been a very long tiring day. I wake up sometime in the night as I feel cold and the one thin blanket does little to help keep the cold at bay. I do not manage to get back to sleep and after many hours the cell door opens and a different policeman brings me a mug of black coffee. I thank him and awkwardly pick up the mug and take a small sip. The liquid is barely warm and has no sugar and I ask the policeman if he is going to bring me anymore coffee and can it be hot next time; and can I have some sugar in it? He says that he will see what he can do and asks me if I want some breakfast and I refuse as I have no appetite.

I am kept waiting for several more hours when the cell door finally opens and the policeman stands in the doorway;

"Come with me please sir," he says in a polite voice, "They want to interview you upstairs."

I walk out the door as the policeman holds my arm and leads me upstairs to the same interview room where I spoke to the Detectives yesterday.

Detective Appleton and Detective Norton sit behind the table and there is a uniformed officer sitting at the table where the recording equipment is. As I sit down the recording equipment is turned on and Detective Appleton says the time and date and who he is interviewing and he names Detective Norton and Officer Michael Lloyd as being present;

"Good morning Patrick, I hope that you slept well and are able to answer our questions this morning?" Detective Appleton asks with a hint of sarcasm to his voice.

"No, I did not sleep well as it is cold in that cell as was the food and coffee that was served to me yesterday and the coffee was stone cold this morning and with no sugar," I reply in a firm voice.

Detective Appleton makes no comment as he opens a desk drawer and reaches in and puts a plastic bag on the table. In the plastic bag is another bag of ecstasy tablets that Debbie must have got from Sally and I look at it with no expression.

"What can you tell me about these Patrick?" Detective Appleton asks in a cold voice.

I lean forward and do not touch the bag but look at it closely; "They look like some of the tablets that are similar to the ones that were on Debbie's coffee table," I answer.

Detective Appleton and Detective Norton stare at me for what must be a full minute and I stare back at them.

"Can you tell me why these were found in your apartment?" Detective Appleton asks.

I stare at him in absolute disbelief and look back at the bag of tablets on the table as several minutes pass. They had obviously searched my apartment and I quickly arrive at the conclusion that Debbie must have put them there – the bitch!

"In my apartment – you cannot be serious; what are they?"

"As you well know they are ecstasy tablets. Now, do you want to tell me where you got them from and why you have so many?" he asks angrily.

"I don't know anything of the kind. You say that you found them in my apartment well I say that you are lying; as I have never seen them before and I do not have anything to do with drugs."

"They were discovered in your apartment hidden on top of the wardrobe in your bedroom. I say that you are the one who is lying as they have your fingerprints all over the bag."

"What!!" I exclaim; "How can they be? I have never seen them before," I lie angrily.

You bitch Debbie, you have stitched me right up!

"Do not lie to us Patrick. They have your fingerprints all over the bag. Now, where did you get them?" he demands.

"I've told you I do not know anything about them. I know that Debbie used my apartment when I was kept prisoner by her and she must have put them there. As for my fingerprints being on the bag she must have put it in my hand after she had drugged me. I give you my word they are nothing to do with me."

Detective Appleton opens a folder that is in front of him and I see that it contains a lot of paperwork. On top of the folder is a copy of fingerprints that I assume are mine.

Looking slowly through the folder Detective Appleton looks up at me; "This is not the first time that you have been in trouble with the police is it? Would you like to tell us about that?" he asks, but demands.

I look at the folder aware what he is referring to and feel the anger rise within me as that incident happened more than fifteen years ago. So much for crimes being 'spent' after eleven years; and supposedly forgotten.

I stare back at him and know that I am in a lot of trouble as I gesture towards the folder; "Doesn't it tell you about it in there?"

He stares back at me and then glances briefly at the folder and stares into my eyes; "Yes it does, but maybe you would like to tell me your side of it?"

I feel that there is no point as he has the look that whatever I tell him he will not believe it anyway; but once again it appears I have little choice; "I was walking home from a night out at the Pub when I got attacked by three youths. I was drunk, but not that drunk and I fought like a cornered rat. I pushed one of the youths away from me as hard as I could and he fell against some spiked railings. The railings had only just been put up and they had not even been painted. The railings were quite sharp and he ripped a big gash in his arm as he fell against them. One of the spikes went through his chest and punctured a lung. There was a police car driving past at the time and the two officers inside it got out and broke the fight up.

When it went to court the three youths said that it was me who attacked them. The only bruising I had was mainly on my fists where I managed to smack two of them in the face. Due to not having any real injuries and the three youths' testimony that it was me that attacked them, the judge had no choice but to sentence me for three years for causing actual bodily harm.

The youth who had fallen against the railings ended up with blood poisoning. His lung repaired itself but when he attended court he was bandaged up and everything went against me; a bit like is happening now."

Detective Appleton stares at me and I know he has not believed a word I have said. Detective Norton looks a bit more sympathetic, but it does not help.

I gesture towards the folder again; "It must say what the judge's summing up was in there. He admitted at the time that he thought that the youths' were not being entirely truthful but the evidence was against me."

Detective Appleton looks down at the folder and then back up at me; "Yes it does have the judge's summing up."

"Does it also have in there that about ten months later the three youths' attacked someone else? They all got done for robbery and causing grievous bodily harm and they all got sentenced to three years each. That done me a big favor as it brought my court case into question and I got released after doing fourteen months, though I was closely monitored until the three years were up."

Detective Appleton looks down at the folder again; "Yes it does say something about that in here," he admits as he takes out a charge sheet from the folder and stares coldly at me; "It is my duty to charge you Patrick Rant with the crime of possessing one hundred and fifty tablets containing ecstasy and a barbiturate with the intention of distributing same. What do you have to say about this charge?"

"That you are making a mistake. As I said to you before I know nothing about them and can only assume that Debbie Dulok put them there."

"Well you will have your opportunity to say that in court but as of now I am charging you. As you know you have the right to a Lawyer and if you do not have one, one will be appointed for you. In the meantime you will be kept in custody while we carry out our investigations and I am of the belief that you will be charged with a more serious offence."

I take the news calmly as in the back of my mind I knew that this was going to happen. I stare at the Detective with tears in my eyes; "You are making a mistake, I know nothing about those tablets," I protest as I indicate towards the bag of ecstasy tablets; "I did not kill Debbie Dulok as I said to you before she was already dead when I got out of her basement. She had drugged me and for some reason set me free; I did not escape as I had been trying to get out of those shackles for weeks."

"You cannot deny that in your mind that you had good reason to murder her?" Detective Norton says in an accusing voice.

"I did not kill her, she committed suicide and her body was cold when I found it," I exclaim in frustration.

"And the contents of her stomach contained twenty-five ecstasy tablets containing the same ingredients as what was found in your apartment; with your fingerprints on them," he continues in a loud accusing voice showing his anger.

"You are wrong, you are wrong," I say as the helplessness I feel turns to anger.

I hear the door to the interview room open behind me; "Take him downstairs Frank until he regains his composure and we will continue this in a few hours," Detective Appleton says as I hear the recording machine being turned off.

Frank gets hold of my right arm up and pulls me upright; "Come with me sir, please do not resist."

I am shocked to my core and fear what is to me a now obvious future drives away the anger and I am far too shocked to resist. The vision of me getting old in a prison cell fills my mind and I allow myself to be led out of the room.

Chapter Nineteen

I sit on the cot in a total daze as waves of sadness and despair flow through me. Debbie has done a good job in 'stitching' me up and I curse myself for not looking around my apartment for anything else that she may have done. Admittedly I would not have looked on top of the wardrobe anyway and I try to pull myself together for anything else that may occur.

I hear the cell door open and see a tall figure, who must be Frank the jailor, come in but I do not look up at him. He slams the door shut after he walks out which makes me jump and I look around to see a white mug on the little table. I am not thirsty but if it is a mug of coffee the sugar that should be inside of it will help my state of mind.

I stand up and walk over to the little table and see and smell that it is a mug of black coffee. I take a sip of the warm liquid and can taste the sugar present. I continue to stand as I hold it with both hands and drink it all down and then walk over to the toilet. Struggling to undo my zip I curse Debbie for removing my thumbs but eventually manage it and urinate.

Sitting back down on the cot I curse her out loud and hear the little spy hole in the door open. Aware that it is probably Frank who is watching me I fall silent and stare at the floor. He continues watching me for several more minutes and I hear the spy hole close. Several hours pass by until Frank opens the door and comes in carrying a tray;

"I do not usually do this, wait on my charges but under the circumstance I thought that you may prefer to be on your own."

Surprised at his compassion I thank him and ask him what he has brought me;

"I have brought you a good meal of mashed potatoes, mixed vegetables and a small beef steak all covered in rich gravy," he smiles; "and a nice hot mug of coffee with two sugars. Eat it before it gets cold and I will come back for the empty plate in a while."

"Thank you Frank, I really appreciate you looking after me like this and please accept my apologies for being so rude to you yesterday."

He nods his head and smiles; "I understand sir as this all must be a shock to you."

"Yes you are right there, thanks again," I say as I stand up and walk over to the table and sit down on the hard backed chair.

Frank walks out of the cell and slams the door shut behind him as I pick up the coffee (again using both hands) and take a sip. The coffee is sweet and hot which is a pleasant surprise. Putting the mug back down I pick up the plastic knife and fork and clench them in my fists and eat the food that is offered. The steak is a bit tough and difficult to cut so I stab it as best I can with the fork and take a bite out of it. I eat slowly and manage to eat it all and wash it down with the remains of the coffee.

Frank soon comes back and is pleased that I have eaten all of my meal. He advises me to sit and rest as he tells me I will be called back upstairs shortly. After thanking him I go and sit on the cot and worry what is next in store for me.

About twenty minutes later Frank opens the cell door and tells me I am to go back upstairs. I stand up, walk out of the cell as he grasps my arm and leads me upstairs. I make no comment about him holding onto my arm even though I feel it is unnecessary as I am in no position to run away. He leads me back to the interview room where Detectives Appleton and Norton await me. The same uniformed officer sits by the recording equipment and there is also another plain clothes Detective sitting next to him. I sit down on the chair and Frank goes and stands by the doorway. He shuts the door and I look at Detective Appleton as I hear the recording equipment being turned on.

Detective Appleton talks out loud for the benefit of the recorder stating the time and date and who he is interviewing and also who is present. I make no comment and break his gaze and stare down at the table.

"I need you to explain your motives again Patrick as to why you did not immediately go to the local police station when you left Debbie Dulok's house yesterday morning," he says in a loud official voice.

I know it is pointless to argue and to say that I have already explained why, so I do my best to repeat what I said yesterday.

"You did not think that your behavior would look suspicious by going straight home?" the Detective sitting beside the uniformed Officer asks, who Detective Appleton said was called Detective Marchant.

I look over at him; "I didn't really think about anything except to get home and have a shower as I stunk something horrible after being chained up for twenty-nine days."

"What were your other reasons for going home rather than to the local police station?" he asks annoyingly.

"I had no other reasons apart from making sure my apartment was secure."

He stares at me and then looks over at Detective Appleton who says in that same official loud voice; "We have had a further analysis on those tablets that we found hidden in your apartment," he says as he opens the folder in front of him; "The exact analysis gives the percentage of ecstasy as 39%, barbiturate 41% amphetamine 11% and an unknown substance at 9%. Do you know what this other substance may be?"

"As I told you yesterday I know nothing about them, even though the bag supposedly had my fingerprints on it," I reply as my mind races. This unknown substance may have been what was responsible for Debbie's breakdown and following insane behavior.

"No *supposedly* about it Mister Rant," he says triumphantly.

"Where did you get these tablets from?" Detective Marchant asks.

I turn and look at him; "I do not know anything about them apart from the strong possibility that Debbie Dulok planted them in my apartment after putting my fingerprints on them."

"How could she have done that?" Detective Marchant asks.

"I believe that she did that after she had drugged me sometime during my captivity, it is the only explanation I can think of. I know nothing about them other than what Detective Appleton has told me. I do not do drugs and never have, and I certainly am not a drug dealer even though I have been charged with that offence," I reply angrily and try to calm myself down.

"Yes we have that to do," says Detective Appleton as he looks over at Frank who still stands by the door; "Please ask Doctor Huxley to come in will you Frank?"

Frank nods his head in acknowledgement and goes out the door to return almost immediately accompanied by the Doctor who treated and abused me yesterday.

"What is he doing here?" I demand.

"It is necessary for us to take a blood sample from you Patrick before too much time passes," Detective Appleton tells me.

"Well he is not going to do it. He abused me yesterday and you were witnesses to it, except you were not here," I say as I turn to Detective Marchant.

"What is this Tony?" demands Detective Marchant as he looks at Detective Appleton.

"I did not abuse you," protests Doctor Huxley; "I was trying to clean your wounds and you refused to let me."

"You weren't being very gentle about it were you? That is why the nurse had to take over," I reply as this Doctor scares the hell out of me and I look at Detective Appleton; "If he lays a hand on me I am going to insist that you charge him with assault. You saw him do it yesterday and you let him do it; and as far as I am concerned this business is getting out of hand. I am going to insist that you appoint a Lawyer on my behalf before this goes any further."

Detective Marchant sees my fear and he looks at Detective Appleton; "You had better explain what is going on here. Did this man abuse Mister Rant yesterday?"

Detective Appleton's face colors as he looks at me; "Doctor Huxley is the stations' appointed physician and he would not abuse anyone."

"He did yesterday and I insist that you get another Doctor to carry out the test as any results he comes up with will be false," I reply in the calmest voice I can muster.

"That is quite an accusation," Detective Appleton answers as Detective Marchant interrupts him; "I asked you for an explanation Mister," he says angrily staring Detective Appleton in the eyes.

Detective Appleton is at a loss to reply as I realize that Detective Marchant is his senior. He looks at Frank who still stands by the door; "Take Mister Rant out for a cup of coffee please and take him to Interview Room 2 which is not being used. I will call you," he says as Frank walks towards me and I get to my feet and walk towards the door as Frank reaches for my arm.

I sidestep quickly; "There is no need to keep holding me all the time," I tell him as I step quickly outside the door and wait for him to catch up. He shuts the door behind him and walks along the corridor; "I will follow you Frank, anyway you are a lot bigger than me. Do you work out?"

He turns and smiles; "Follow me Patrick, is it coffee you would like?" he asks in a friendly voice.

"Yes please, if that is ok?"

"It is with me," he answers.

I follow him along the corridor and he opens a door and we enter a small room with several tables and a coffee machine; "Black with sugar isn't it?"

"Yes please Frank, do you want me to sit down while you operate the machine?"

"No I do not think that will be necessary," he says as he walks up to the machine and presses a button. An empty cup drops down into a holder and the machine whirrs as it dispenses the coffee. Taking the cup out Frank hands it to me; "Be careful, that will be hot," he warns; "Follow me please," he orders in that same friendly voice.

I take the coffee from him with both hands and which is in a thick cardboard cup and follow him back out into the corridor. Returning the way we came he opens a door and turns and looks at me; "In here please Patrick," he orders as I walk past him and into the room. Interview Room 2 is a duplicate of the other room with the same desk, chairs and recording equipment. I sit down on the chair and look up at Frank; "Aren't you going to have a cup of coffee?" I ask innocently.

I can tell by his expression that he wants a cup as well, though he makes no reply.

"If you do want one I will not go anywhere I give you my word," and I laugh; "and as you are my jailor you are in a position to cause me a lot of problems if I lie to you."

Frank looks at me and nods his head; "I will trust you Patrick," he says as he turns and walks out of the door.

Frank soon returns carrying a cardboard cup and his expression does not change when he sees that I am sitting in the same position. Sitting opposite me he puts his cup on the table which I can see and smell is Tomato soup.

"What do you do for work Patrick?" he asks.

"I am an air conditioning and central heating engineer" I reply;" as I look up at the ventilation grill on the wall which I recognize as I have installed thousands; "Same air conditioning system as you have installed here. I have not worked in a police station before but I have worked in a lot of council offices, commercial buildings and factories," I answer as I look down at my bandaged hands; "That is, I was, with no thumbs I will have to look for some other kind of employment."

Frank nods his head in agreement and looks at me sizing me up; "How is it that a big strapping lad like yourself allows a woman to chain you up then?"

"She put a powerful sleeping drug in my coffee and I woke up in her basement with a large hoop of metal around my neck and my ankles were shackled and chained to the floor."

"Didn't you suspect that she was going to do something like that to you?"

"No, she was all friendly the day before and the days previously as we went shopping and walking together," I reply thinking it best not to mention the magic mushroom picking, the trip to the Continent and that mad glint in her eye.

"You were staying with her then; were you lovers?"

"No, we weren't lovers. I used to work with her over twenty years ago and we had kept in touch, but just as good friends."

"Things are not looking good for you, you know that Patrick? The discovery of all those ecstasy tablets in your apartment does not bode well for you."

"Yes I know, that Debbie must have put them in there when she had me chained up," I answer with a wry grin as a thought strikes me; "Was it just my fingerprints on that bag or were there any of my thumb prints on it?" I ask in sudden realization and also to wondering just what did she do with my thumbs once she had cut them off?

"I do not know anything about that," Frank replies as he stares at me.

"She must have put my hand around the bag when she had me drugged and I bet it was after she cut my thumbs off. I do not take drugs Frank; the blood test will prove that though it will show that I have some kind of sedative or sleeping drug in my system as she had drugged me the day before yesterday."

"You will have to ask Detective Appleton about that as he has all the details."

"Have you been down to the house and seen the basement where she kept me chained up?"

Frank shakes his head; "No, I haven't, the three Detectives you have just seen have been there along with the local police. My job is looking after our inmates."

"Do you like your job Frank as it must get a bit rough at times?"

"Yes, I like it. The money and benefits are good; mind you we do get some characters in here from time to time. The drunks are the worse as it is my job to clean up after them."

"I bet there are not many who get violent with you as you look like you are well able to take care of yourself?"

Frank smiles; "You would be surprised, there are a lot who don't think size matters, in fact it seems to provoke some of them. You had that attitude when you first came in." he says as his smile grows wider.

"I was just so upset about being locked up again. The past weeks have been an absolute nightmare and the way things are looking to me with Detective Appleton's and this Detective Marchant's accusations. I really get the feeling that they think I killed that crazy woman."

"I agree it does not look good for you as you did have a strong motive. I would not dismiss Detective Marchant so easily he is a stickler for detail and he has been in the job a long time."

"Is he the superior Detective? I got the impression he was the senior man in there."

"Yes he is and he is good at his job. As you could see he was not happy about that business with Doctor Huxley and I think you are onto something about your fingerprints being on that bag; even though they were found in your apartment."

I make no reply as my mind races. Frank appears to believe me and he appears also to be a friend and I badly need a friend at the moment, especially in this place.

We talk of other things, the way of the world and we both agree that the behavior of the people in this world is getting worse rather than better. About an hour passes before the Interview Room door is opened and Detective Marchant walks in.

"Everything alright Frank?" he asks.

"Yes fine thanks Mick," he replies as he looks at me; "We have been having quite a chat."

"I will talk to you later," he says and looks at me; "There is another Doctor waiting for you as you requested and your Lawyer is here. Do you want to talk to him after the blood test?"

"Thank you Detective, that Huxley fella really frightened me. I will talk to my Lawyer later if that's ok? But I would like him present if you want to continue questioning me."

"That is why he is here. Shall we go then?"

"I need the little boy's room first if you don't mind?"

Detective Marchant looks at Frank; "Go with him please Frank and I will meet you in there."

Chapter Twenty

On entering the Interview Room I see Detectives Appleton and Norton sitting behind the desk. Detective Marchant sits next to a different uniformed officer by the recording equipment. A gray haired Doctor in a white coat stands beside them and sitting on a hardback chair beside him is a young man in his early twenties wearing a new black suit. The white shirt he wears has a collar that is far too large and his gaily colored floral pattern tie looks right out of place. Sergeant Marsh stands beside the door and Detective Marchant asks me to sit down.

As I sit down Detective Marchant gets up and walks behind the desk; "This is Doctor Bellar from the local hospital and he will take a blood sample from you and look at your injuries."

I make no reply as Doctor Bellar steps forward and puts his medical bag onto the desk. Opening the bag he takes out an individually wrapped syringe and several small containers for my blood. He also takes out a small packet containing an antiseptic wipe. He puts on a pair of blue rubber gloves and then turns and looks at me; "As the Detective has just advised you I need to take a blood sample. Are you able to roll up your sleeve sir?"

"I can manage," I gruffly reply as I push my right sleeve up above the elbow.

"That is fine, thank you," he tells me as he takes the syringe out and connects the small glass container. Wiping the inside of my arm just below my elbow he says; "A small scratch," and pushes the needle into my arm.

I watch the glass container fill with blood which he removes and then he fits another container. Putting a cap on the full one he puts it onto the table as the second glass container fills with blood and he repeats the procedure filling a third. Pulling the syringe out he places a cotton wool ball onto the hole; "Press down please sir," he says as he turns and rummages through his bag again. Pulling out a small packet containing a square plaster he tears open the packet and after getting me to remove the cotton wool ball, sticks the plaster on.

"That is good thank you; now I need to look at your injuries sir," he tells me; "I will start at the top by looking at your neck first," he laughs; "You have been in the wars haven't you sir?"

"Yeah, you could put it like that," I agree thinking that the last thing I want is a bloody comedian.

He removes the bandage from around my neck and appears happy in what he sees. He applies some antiseptic cream and puts a new bandage on.

"Now let me look at your hands, you choose which one you want me to examine first," he says with a big beaming smile and I can see that this is a man who enjoys his work.

I make no comment as I hold up my right hand and he carefully unwinds the bandage and on seeing that I have no thumb says; "My, my, I read the report and could not believe it," he says as he bends down and looks closer; "This is excellent work. There is a small infection but apart from that the work is first class. Who did this to you?"

"I am glad you like it," I reply with deep sarcasm; "A nurse did it, she cut my other thumb off as well," I tell him as I raise my bandaged left hand.

"That is on a need to know basis Doctor," Detective Appleton says in a loud commanding voice.

Doctor Bellar looks across the table at him; "Of course, of course," he says as he looks back at my hand.

"I don't mind you knowing who did it, it was a nurse called Debbie Dulok. Maybe you know her?" I ask as I see his expression change and I get the strong feeling that he did know her.

"Can't say that I do," he lies; "A nurse you say? She has done an excellent job by using the skin of the thumb to seal the wound. Excellent work, is it painful?"

"Yes it is, as you can see it is infected but it does feel and look a bit better than it did yesterday."

He rummages in his medical bad and pulls out a light brown A4 folder. Opening it he looks through it and returns it to the bag; "I see that you were given an antibiotic injection yesterday. I think it best if we put you on a course of them, I will write out a prescription and maybe one of these nice officers can arrange to have it collected from the chemist?"

I make no comment as he returns his attention back to my hand and after repeating; 'Excellent,' several times he applies some antiseptic cream and using a new bandage carefully binds it up.

Removing the bandage from my left hand the Doctor is even more delighted; "This has been done very expertly and I can see that it is healing nicely. I will apply a little cream just to be sure, as the skin is a little red where the stitches are," he tells me with a big beaming smile.

"Do you know if there are any artificial thumbs available? As you probably realize life is difficult with no thumbs."

"Oh yes, I am sure that there are," he reassures me as he bends down for a closer look. Holding my hand he runs his thumb over the little stump that protrudes as Debbie cut my thumbs off at the second joint; "Is that painful?" he asks.

"A little; feels more weird than painful."

"Yes I am sure that it can be attached to what remains of your thumb. I have not had any personal involvement but you will have to go through your General Practitioner. I would make an appointment as soon as you can," he advises.

"I think that will be a bit difficult as these gentlemen have a prior claim on me."

"Yes, yes of course," he answers and not taking his eyes off my hand; "I will apply a little cream and put a fresh bandage on for you."

After bandaging my hand he refers to his notes; "I understand that you have some ankle injuries?"

"Yes, where I was shackled and chained to the floor. The right ankle was a bit infected yesterday. Do you want to have a look?"

"Oh yes," he answers as he looks around. Walking across the room he picks up a hard backed chair and puts it in front of me; "Are you able to remove your shoe?" he asks appearing delighted at being able to do some more work.

"Yes, no problem," I reply as I take my right trainer off using my left foot and put my foot on the chair.

Pushing my trouser leg up to the knee he unwinds the bandage and looks at my sore red ankle; "Oh yes, I can see where it is infected. Do not worry sir; even though it looks sore and must be a little painful there is nothing to worry about."

Now; where had I heard that before?

The Doctor examines my ankle closely; "Shackled you say; how long was you shackled for?"

"Twenty-nine days."

"Twenty-nine days; had you done something wrong?" he asks appearing fascinated.

"You do not need to know that Doctor," Detective Appleton tells him in that same loud voice.

"I need to know all the facts sir and how this gentleman's injuries were caused to give a correct diagnosis and treatment," he tells Detective Appleton firmly as he stares into his eyes.

Detective Appleton makes no reply as the Doctor returns his attention to my ankle; "I will need to clean that first," he tells me as he reaches into his bag and takes out another antiseptic wipe.

He takes his time cleaning my ankle and after applying more antiseptic cream he bandages it up and then treats my left ankle.

"Have you anymore injuries sir?" he asks.

"Not physical, my mind is still a bit disturbed after being tortured for so long," I answer with a thin smile.

"Tortured!" he exclaims; "What did that involve?"

Detective Appleton twists in his chair but keeps silent as I tell the Doctor how Debbie hurt me and of the rotten food she sometimes served me.

The Doctor looks very troubled and concerned as I relate my story; "Are you alright now sir? That sounds horrific. Do you feel that you have need of any treatment? Would you like to see a psychiatrist?"

"No, I am ok thanks. I know what happened to me and I know why and even what caused her breakdown. She is dead now so I have nothing else to fear except for what these gentlemen have in mind for me," I reply with a broader smile.

"Dead you say? Well if you do feel that you need to talk we have excellent staff who are very experienced in dealing with trauma."

"Trauma sounds too gentle a word; horror would be a better description."

"Yes, yes of course. Well if you do feel that you need some help please contact your local GP," he tells me appearing disappointed that his work is complete. He puts the chair back against the wall and after putting everything in his bag he closes it with a snap and turns and looks at Detective Marchant; "I have finished here, I will write out the prescription and leave it at the desk for you before I go," he tells him and turns back to face me; "Please take care of yourself and do not forget what I said. You have had a very bad time and you tell me your mental condition is kind of ok but there are many people who you can talk to."

"Thank you Doctor and thank you for caring I really appreciate it," I tell him with a broad smile though my stomach twists in fear; is that his way of telling me I am to be accused of being insane?

He nods his head and looks around the room as he walks to the door. Sergeant Marsh opens the door for him and with a 'Bye everyone' he walks out of the door and Sergeant Marsh closes it after him.

"Right, now maybe we can get on," says Detective Appleton in a loud impatient voice

"Sorry to keep you waiting," I say with deep sarcasm; "At least he did not abuse me like that Doctor did yesterday; and you let him do it," I continue in an angry voice.

"Abuse; what is this about abuse?" asks the young man in the black suit.

"This is Christopher Osborne your appointed Lawyer," Detective Marchant says; "Do you feel that you have to talk to him before we begin questioning you?"

I look at the young Lawyer who, being so young, gives me little confidence in his abilities; "Good morning Christopher. There was a right naughty Doctor here yesterday who was very rough in his treatment of me and the nurse had to take over."

"Doctor Huxley is a very competent physician who did not hurt you intentionally," Detective Appleton interrupts in a loud angry voice.

I turn and face him; "Don't lie; you saw that he was hurting me and you let him do it."

"Doctor Huxley is a qualified Doctor and he would not intentionally hurt his patients," he replies in that same angry voice.

"He hurt me and being a qualified Doctor does not make him a saint. I know of several people who have been abused in hospitals by Doctors. Doctors have been known to do such things even to kill their patients. There was that Doctor a few years ago who murdered over two hundred of his patients. What was his name, Shipley?"

"Shipman," Christopher Osborne corrects.

"That was an isolated incident," Detective Appleton shouts.

"Isolated; what are you talking about? Last year there was a nurse who killed six of her patients and it is quite common to read in the papers of old people being abused in these so called care homes. So it is not so unusual," I reply feeling the anger in my face which I feel sure has turned red.

"Enough, enough," shouts Detective Marchant as he looks at me; "Before we start is there anything you would like; do you need to use the toilet?" he asks.

"I wouldn't mind using the little boy's room first and my mouth is really dry. Is it possible to have a black coffee with two sugars, if not I will need some water," I answer as I turn towards him showing him a grateful smile.

Looking over at Sergeant Marsh he says; "Take Mister Rant to the toilets will you please Bill? And please take him to get a cup of coffee as I think things need to be a lot calmer before we start interviewing him."

Sergeant Marsh looks at me; "When you are ready sir."

I am still furious with Detective Appleton and his stupid remarks and I remain seated for a few more seconds before standing up and walk slowly out of the door.

Sergeant Marsh holds tightly onto my arm as he leads me along the corridor.

"There is no need for you to keep a hold of me you know, I am not going to run away," I tell him.

"Sorry sir, it is procedure," he replies but does loosen his grip.

We return to the interview room about fifteen minutes later and I resume my seat in front of the table and in front of Detectives Appleton and Norton.

Detective Marchant says in a loud voice as the recording equipment is turned on the time, the date and that I am being interviewed and the names of everyone present.

"You did not answer earlier if you wanted to talk to me first?" asks Christopher Osborne.

I look over at him and smile my thanks; "No, we will talk later but please remain and advise me what to say if you think the questions are unfair or things are getting out of control or a bit heated," I reply as I turn and stare Detective Appleton in the eyes.

Detective Appleton stares back at me in a superior way and I know he has got some unpleasant surprises for me as he asks, but demands; "Where did you get the ecstasy tablets from that were hidden in your apartment; and that had your fingerprints all over the bag?"

"I have already told you that I do not know where those came from. As for the fingerprints I have already told you that I think Debbie Dulok put them on the bag. You claim to have found my fingerprints on the bag, were there any thumb prints? As you well know I was chained up for twenty-nine days and the bitch cut off my thumbs," I impatiently ask as this Detective geezer is giving me the right hump.

"So you claim. How are we to know that you are not lying about the length of time that you were held captive? You could have easily been released and then murdered her in a fit of rage as you had the motive and concocted this crazy story. As for the fingerprints I will have to check that out as to whether there were any thumb prints or any other unknown prints come to that," he answers in his smugly superior sort of way.

"You're crazy," I yell; "I did not murder her, she was already dead when I got out of her basement. An autopsy should tell you the time of death," I continue angrily as I nearly choke with anger.

"Calm down Mister Rant, the Detective is only doing his job," Christopher Osborne advises.

I look over at him; "He wants to do it in a different manner, it is madness to say I murdered her as it is to say that I am some kind of drug dealer."

"I have an autopsy report here," says Detective Appleton as he opens the folder in front of him and picks up a piece of paper; "It does give the time of death as approximately 10 p.m. the night before you claim to have escaped the confines of the basement. It also says that her body has suffered much bruising. The contents of her stomach contain ecstasy tablets and the opinion is that she was made to swallow 25 of these tablets that have the same chemical signature as was found in your apartment. The contents of her stomach also contained a large quantity of poisonous toadstool namely the Death Cap toadstool. A jar of these poisonous toadstools was found in Debbie Dulok's kitchen and they had your fingerprints on them," he says in a triumphant voice; "Would you care to explain this?"

I feel the blood drain from my face as I am totally shocked by what he has just accused me of. I stare back at him in total confusion and make no reply.

"Take your time," he says with a triumphant smile; "We have got all day if need be."

I continue staring at him as I try to gather my thoughts and control the rage that is beginning to fill my whole body. You bitch, you fucking bitch, I angrily think as I start to feel a little calmer;

"I think that I had better speak to my Lawyer before this insanity continues," I say in a shaky voice.

"Of course you can, that is to be expected," Detective Appleton says with a smarmy smile as he puts the autopsy report of Debbie back into the folder and takes out another piece of paper; "Before you go off and have your little chat I had better mention that two young girls died several days ago. They died from taking ecstasy tablets that on analysis and their autopsy reports were shown to have the same chemical signature as the ecstasy tablets found hidden in your apartment."

"Hey!" I shout; "What the bloody hell are you doing now? I know nothing about them and I am no drug dealer."

"So you say," Detective Appleton smiles at me in an infuriating way and I really want to punch him on the nose.

Chapter Twenty-One

We are directed to use Interview Room 2 and I sit down at the familiar table as my Lawyer Christopher Osborne sits opposite me. He looks very unsure and totally out of his depth and he does not help when he says; "Things are not looking good for you Mister Rant. What is it that you think I can do for you?" he asks in a nervous voice appearing to also believe that I am guilty of drug dealing and now murder!

I look him in the eyes; "In the first place I want you to believe that all of this is a load of bollocks. In the first place I am no drug dealer and I do not even do drugs and never have. In the second place I need you to believe that I am no murderer. Debbie Dulok was already dead when I found her; she had committed suicide and took those ecstasy tablets and poisonous mushrooms herself without any encouragement from me. She had given me a strong sleeping drug the night before I got out of there and there was no way that I could have done that."

Christopher Osborne has a folder with him which he opens and reads several lines of the first page, of what looks like a considerable report and he looks across the table at me; "You cannot deny that you had a very strong motive for killing her and the evidence, with her body being covered in bruises, does point to the fact that she was forced to swallow these tablets and poisonous mushrooms."

I look down at the folder; "What evidence? And it appears that you have a lot more evidence and suppositions than I know about. The only way I can see that we can go forward with this is to tell you the whole story of what recently occurred and my relationship with Debbie Dulok. If that is alright with you?" I ask and stare into his eyes.

Christopher Osborne stares back and then shrugs his shoulders; "It is what I am being paid for. Maybe you can start at the beginning and tell me when you first met," he says as he looks down at the folder; "this Debbie Dulok."

I take a deep breath and tell him of the shop and of selling the rubber clothing to mainly those with a rubber fetish as he writes in a small notepad. I talk of the passing years and of the accidental meeting in Wales. I also talk of her ambitions and divorce and friendship that had lasted nearly all of my adult life. He stops me at this point saying that he needs to use the toilet and that he would also like something to drink.

I stop talking as he gets up and opens the Interview Room door and I see Sergeant Marsh standing outside. He tells the Sergeant that he needs the toilet and a drink and Sergeant Marsh steps inside, closing the door behind him. He says nothing as he stares down at me and I look away and look down at the desk.

My so called Lawyer returns after about twenty minutes carrying two cardboard cups. He puts one in front of me that I see contains black coffee. I thank him as Sergeant Marsh goes out of the door and he makes a point of closing it firmly behind him.

I look at my Lawyer; "You were quite a while. I assume that you went somewhere else other than the toilet and the coffee machine?"

He looks at me, his look appears friendlier; "Yes, I have been talking to Detective Marchant who introduced me to Frank Miles, the officer who has been looking after you?"

"Yes that's right and I get the feeling that Frank is my only friend in this horrible place."

"Not only officer Miles, Detective Marchant felt that he should express some doubts to me that he had. Now where were you?" he says looking down at his notes; "Oh yes, Miss Dulok's divorce."

I continue talking of our rather distant friendship during that difficult time and how our friendship became renewed. I was not sure that I was getting everything in the right order but I continued to talk and told him of my move to my new apartment and of Debbie's telephone call. I had to stop myself then as I badly needed to pee.

After being escorted to the toilets by Sergeant Marsh and brought back (and he held my arm each time) I resumed my narrative.

I tell him of my time with Debbie but do not mention the magic mushroom picking or of taking them. I also keep quiet about Debbie's use of ecstasy and of her buying the tablets from Sally and of the mad glint in her eyes. I do make a point of saying about the fingerprints on the bag of ecstasy tablets found in my apartment and that there are probably no thumb prints. I also hope that that is the case with the poisonous toadstools.

After many hours the door to the Interview Room opens and Detective Marchant walks in; "Have you gentlemen finished your conversation?" he asks.

"Very nearly, Patrick has been telling me a fascinating, though at times very gruesome story. I have to admit that I do believe him and that I think Detective Appleton is being a bit zealous; and I do believe he is wrong and is doing this to further his career," Christopher boldly tells him.

"He has to follow procedure," is Detective Marchant's reply; "It is time for a lot of us to go home and I need Mister Rant to come back to the Interview Room."

"Yes, of course, if you can give us just a couple of more minutes and we will be along," my Lawyer assures him.

"Please do not be too long otherwise these people will have to be paid overtime," Detective Marchant says as he walks out of the door.

Christopher Osborne looks me in the eyes; "As you heard Patrick I do believe you, though I do think you are not being entirely truthful with me about everything. It may surprise you that I think I know what they are but I am sure you have your reasons. Stick to your story and I am sure that I will be able to get you out of this. I am going to have a long talk with my superior this evening and we will resume this tomorrow," he tells me as he holds out his hand for me to shake.

I am surprised but instinctively hold his hand and we shake hands, though gently; "Thank you Christopher, I really appreciate it."

"Let us go and see what the Detective wants," he says as he lets go of my hand and picking up his notebook and folder walks across the room and opens the door.

Sergeant Marsh is waiting outside; "The Detective would like a word with you first please Mister Osborne, they are in Interview Room 1. I will accompany Mister Rant and bring him along in a few minutes."

My Lawyer walks past him and then along the corridor as Sergeant Marsh walks into the room; "We will give them a couple of minute's sir," he tells me as he looks at his watch and I turn around and go back and sit down on the hard chair.

The Sergeant looks at his watch after a few minutes; "I think they have been given long enough, come with me please sir," he asks politely, but it is an order.

I follow him out of the room and after grabbing hold of my arm he walks me along the corridor and into Interview Room 1. All three Detectives are present as are the uniformed officer and my Lawyer and I walk over to the chair to sit down.

"There will not be time for you to sit down," Detective Appleton says in a cruel voice and I look towards my Lawyer for guidance as I sit down. He looks pale and once again unsure of himself and I get a sick feeling in my stomach and look back at Detective Appleton.

Holding a piece of paper he looks at me with a satisfied gleam in his eyes as he waits for me to stand up, which I reluctantly do.

"Mister Patrick Rant I hereby charge you with the murder of Debbie Dulok. You have the right to reply but anything that you say and may rely on in court may be taken down and used against you in a court of law."

The shock hits me first and then anger fills my body and mind; "You are fucking mad mate, I ain't killed anyone and you know it."

Detective Appleton stares at me and I know that I want to get my hands around his neck and strangle the life out of him. Someone grabs hold of my arm tightly and I hear Sergeant Marsh's voice in my ear; "Calm down Patrick do not make us use force against you."

I turn and look at him and can tell by his eyes that he regrets what is happening and that he does not want to use force against me. I feel my body slump in submission as Detective Appleton continues;

"You will be taken to a more secure location shortly," he tells me as he smiles broadly and I have a really strong desire to hit him in his smarmy face; and hit him hard.

"I would like to talk to my client before you take him away," says my Lawyer in a strong commanding voice.

Detective Appleton stares at him and I get the strong feeling he is going to refuse him when Detective Marchant interjects;

"Yes, of course Mister Osborne. We will wait outside," he says as he stares at Detective Appleton.

They all walk out of the room, Detective Appleton is the last to leave and cannot resist gloating by saying; "Do not make any attempt to escape Mister Rant, you are on the first floor here and there are police officers guarding the building inside and out."

I ignore him as he walks out of the room and shuts the door loudly behind him.

"I am so sorry Patrick; I swear to you that I did not know that was coming. Try not to worry; I will have a long talk with my senior colleague this evening. They have told me where they are taking you and I am afraid to tell you that you will be appearing in court tomorrow. I will be there but I do not think we will get much opportunity to talk. You will be more formally charged in court tomorrow with murder and possession of those ecstasy tablets with intent to supply. The charges will be read to you and all you will have to do is confirm who you are and your address. Please, please, do not say anything else as it will go against you and I promise I will see you sometime in the afternoon."

Christopher Osborne holds his hand out which I take a hold of with my mind in a constant whirl as he gently shakes my hand; "It may appear serious but there is nothing to worry about," he says as he lets go of my hand.

Now, where have I heard that before?

My Lawyer walks out of the door as Detectives Appleton and Marchant walk in. I can see Detective Norton and Sergeant Marsh in the corridor as they say 'Goodbye' to my Lawyer.

Detective Appleton walks towards me holding a pair of handcuffs in his right hand; "Hold your hands out," he orders in a harsh voice and I do as he tells me.

As he starts to put the handcuffs on Detective Marchant warns him; "Be careful of his hands and make sure that you do not put them on too tightly."

Detective Appleton looks around at him; "I need to secure him and he is my prisoner after all, as it has also been my case," he says in an aggressive voice.

"Make sure that you do not do them too tight, and as it for being your case; it may only be for a short time," he warns angrily.

"What do you mean by that?" Detective Appleton protests; "I have followed procedure to the letter," he says as he puts the cuffs around my wrists and cannot help himself by doing the right wrist far too tight.

"Hey, the right one is too tight, what do you think you are doing? Hey that hurts," I say in a loud voice.

Detective Marchant walks over and examines the handcuffs on my wrists; "I told you not to do them too tight. This man is badly injured whatever you think of him. Wait there as I will have to go and get a key from the Duty Officer," he angrily says as he walks out of the door.

"They are going to lock you up for a very long time," Detective Appleton taunts; "Thought that you could get one over on us didn't you?"

I stare into his eyes and I guess that he can see the hatred that is contained in them as he breaks the gaze and looks away and he takes several steps back.

My right hand is beginning to hurt a lot and it is a good five minutes before Detective Marchant returns with a handcuff key. It is five minutes of feeling a complete hatred for Detective Appleton and he must feel my hate as he makes no attempt to look at or approach me in that time.

Detective Marchant walks over and unlocks my right wrist and looks at the fingers of my right hand; "I am sorry about my colleague Mister Rant, he takes his job far too seriously at times and can also be a bit misguided," he tells me as he turns and stares at Detective Appleton who refuses to meet his gaze.

Turning his attention back to me he says in a kindly voice; "I will have to leave that one off for the time being. Do you give me your word not to attempt to escape?" he asks; but I notice he still holds tightly onto the handcuff.

"Of course you have my word, just keep that lunatic away from me," I say looking over at Detective Appleton with hate filled eyes.

"There is no need to be abusive Patrick," he says trying not to laugh; "We will now escort you to the van where you will be taken to a more secure location."

"Are you coming with me? I would not like to be left alone with *him*."

"Yes I will be coming with you. Now shall we go?" He says as he leads me out of the room by the handcuffs.

I am led out of the building to a waiting police van and ushered inside. I notice that we do not descend any steps making Detective Appleton's statement about me being on the first floor an outright lie.

Inside the van are two uniformed police officers and as Detective Marchant gets in behind me he hands the handcuff key to one of them; "Take that back to the Duty Officer for me please Tim, I will make sure our guest is comfortable."

The uniformed officer takes the key from his hand with a nod of acknowledgement and gets out of the van as Detective Appleton climbs in. I sit near the front of the vehicle and letting go of the handcuffs Detective Marchant sits beside me as Detective Appleton sits down near the back doors with a surly expression on his face.

"Comfortable Patrick?" Detective Marchant asks.

"Not really, I would rather be sitting at home in my comfortable armchair watching the television," I reply in a shaky voice.

"That will not happen for a long, long time," Detective Appleton cannot avoid saying.

"We will have less of that thank you Detective Appleton," Detective Marchant says in a loud voice and turns his attention back to me;

"It will only be a half hour drive, traffic permitting, and then we will get you bedded down for the night," he says in a friendly voice.

I make no comment as Tim the uniformed officer returns and climbing in slams the door shut behind him. Detective Marchant bangs on the side of the van with his clenched fist and shouts; "Take it away driver."

The engine starts up and the van drives away to my secure location; wherever that may be.

Good to Detective Marchant's word a half hour later the van stops and the engine is turned off. The driver gets out and walks around to the back and opens the doors wide.

Tim the uniformed officer gets out and Detective Appleton gets out behind him as the other uniformed officer stands up and gets out of the van.

"Give me your right hand," orders Detective Marchant; "I will have to put this back on," he says; "or Appleton will tell on me."

I hold out my hand quickly as he snaps the cuff around my right wrist; "After you Patrick, stand still when you get outside the van."

"Whatever you say sir; and thank you for your kindness," I say as I get out of the van and stand and wait.

Detective Marchant gets out and grabs hold of my right arm; "Come with me please sir," he says in a loud voice as we walk towards a large steel faced door at the back of a large building.

As we enter I see that it is another police station and Detective Marchant leads me to a counter with a very tall skinny Sergeant standing behind it. He looks to be in his sixties as his thin face is heavily lined and his hair and close cropped beard and mustache are almost white.

"Who do we have here Mick?" the Sergeant asks, though I get the feeling he already knows and Detective Marchant looks over at Detective Appleton who stands sulking close by.

"Tony will give you the details, if you will be good enough to book him in as I need to use the toilet," he says as he lets go of my arm and walks away along a dark corridor.

The Sergeant looks at Detective Appleton; "What is this gentleman's name please Tony?"

Detective Appleton makes no reply as he hands the Sergeant a folder.

The Sergeant opens the folder and looks at me; "Could you tell me your name please sir?" he asks.

"Yes, it is Patrick Rant," I reply in a deadpan voice.

"Thank you sir, I don't think we need you to keep them on," he says looking down at the handcuffs I am wearing; "Please put your hands onto the counter sir," he asks/demands.

I put my hands up onto the counter and the Sergeant looks at the bandages; "Are you alright sir; have you been in some kind of accident?"

"Had my thumbs removed," I answer in a surly voice.

The Sergeant looks at me with a troubled expression and then looks away as he opens a drawer beneath the counter. Taking a small key out, he then unlocks the handcuffs and removes them and puts them in the drawer along with the key.

Movement along the corridor attracts his attention and he sees Detective Marchant walking towards us and then looks back at me. Seeing that I still have my hands on the counter he says; "You can put your hands down now, thank you sir."

I put my hands down and watch Detective Marchant approach and he looks at the Sergeant; "Ok Ron, have you booked our guest in?"

Ron the Sergeant writes quickly into a large open book on the counter; "He is now," he says as he takes a hold of the folder Detective Appleton had passed to him.

"We will take him down then," Detective Marchant says as he looks at me; "Come with us please Mister Rant," he says formally and I follow him along the darkened corridor with Detective Appleton following closely behind.

The corridor ends in a long flight of steel stairs that go downwards and I follow the Detective down to the bottom where there is a more brightly lit corridor. A young uniformed policeman stands behind a small counter and looks at us approach.

"We have another guest for you Stan. He will be staying the night and I hope that you will make him comfortable?" asks Detective Marchant.

"Yes I can do that. All our guests are made comfortable," he replies with a broad smile. He looks to be in his mid-twenties and has short black hair on top of a very round face. I can tell by his build under the tight uniform that his muscles are large and firm and I make a vow not to upset him.

"We will leave him with you then," says Detective Marchant as he turns and looks at me; "Stan will look after you and I think it is cauliflower cheese for tea tonight. Try and get some sleep and I will see you tomorrow."

I thank him as Stan the jailor comes out from behind the counter and I can see that he is a hugely built policeman who looks like he probably works out in the gym regularly.

Detectives Marchant and Appleton turn away and walk back up the stairs as Stan looks at me; "Follow me please sir," he says as he looks at the bandage around my neck and at the bandages on my hands; "Have you been in some kind of accident sir?" he asks showing real concern; "Is there anything for me to worry about sir?"

"I wouldn't call it an accident, I have been locked up the past month by a lunatic woman who cut off my thumbs and tortured me," I reply trying to keep the emotion out of my voice as I am close to tears and feel like sobbing my heart out.

"Oh dear sir; Why are you here then?" he asks.

"That damn fool of a Detective Appleton thinks I murdered her."

"Did you sir?" the jailor asks innocently.

"No, I promise you that I did not and please stop calling me sir. My name is Patrick Rant, Pat to my friends."

"Very well sir... Pat. Please follow me," he says leading the way along the brightly lit corridor. Stopping outside a large metal gray door with a peephole, metal flap and the number seven painted on it in black paint he asks/orders; "Step inside please Patrick. The Detective was right, it is cauliflower cheese tonight. I will call you when it is ready."

I walk past him into the cell which is a lot larger than the one previous, it being about eleven feet long. The toilet is in the same place as is the sink, cot and small table and hard backed chair. I sit down on the cot and stare at the gray painted wall in front of me and I notice that there are bricks underneath the paint.

"Are you alright si... Patrick?" Stan the jailor asks.

"Not really I have to admit that this is all too much. I think that I am going to have a very long cry, please do not worry about me."

"It is my job to look after the inmates, if you feel the need to talk please call me. My name is Stanley or Stan to my friends."

"Thank you Stan I will probably take you up on that later."

"Take it easy please Patrick, tea will be ready in about an hour," he tells me as he closes the door quietly and I hear the key turn in the lock.

Chapter Twenty-Two

I sit on the cot and stare at the painted brick wall in front of me. Looking at the bricks I start to count the rows from the bottom up, get halfway through and decide that I do not care how many bricks make up a cell.

I have a lot more to think about than bricks and my mind replays the awful time in the police station. Detective Appleton's sneering face appears and I feel my anger build. A thought does cross my mind and I wonder just what I would have done if I had found that Debbie was alive when I got out of the confines of her basement? I know that I would have caused her some kind of harm, even killed her, and as has been said to me many times I did have a good reason.

The flap in the door opens and a tray is placed on it and I am surprised that an hour has passed already; "Here is your food Patrick," Stan's voice tells me and I stand up and walk over to the door.

The smell of cauliflower cheese drifts up my nose and I see on the same plate a portion of baked beans. There is a small bowl of rice pudding, a mug of what looks like tea with milk and a small translucent cup with two green capsules in it.

"There is the medicine from your Doctor," Stan says; "I need you to take them in front of me please."

I say nothing as I pick up the capsules and put them in my mouth and picking up the mug with both hands and which is tea, I wash them down with the smallest amount of liquid. Putting the mug back down onto the tray I look at Stan; "I cannot really drink tea with milk as I have irritable bowel syndrome. I will have to throw that away, is the water from the tap drinkable?" I ask politely.

"I am sorry, I did not know. Yes the tap water is ok to drink," he answers and not offering to replace the tea with anything else; "The memo that came down with your medicine said the tablets may make you feel sick and it is advisable to eat as much as possible."

I look him in the eyes and take hold of the tray; "Thank you Stan," is all I can say as I step back and go and sit down at the little table.

The cauliflower cheese tastes good though it is barely warm as are the baked beans. I manage to force it down though I am not the least bit hungry. After tipping the tea down the toilet I struggle turning the tap on the little sink and have to use both hands. I only manage a couple of spoonfuls of the rice pudding as already I feel sick. The feeling grows and I hurry over to the toilet and retch painfully over it without bringing anything up. I sit back down onto the cot after several minutes and stare at the brick wall.

The flap in the door opens and Stan asks for my tray and I get up and place it on the flap.

"I see that you have managed to eat most of it," he says; "I am sorry, I should have asked if you needed any help. I take it that you can eat ok?"

"Yes, it is a bit of a struggle holding a knife and fork but I can manage. Can I keep hold of the mug as I am still a bit thirsty?"

"Not that one," he replies; "I will bring you another one," he says as he takes the tray and closes the flap.

Several minutes later the flap in the door is opened and a plastic cup is placed on it; "There is you cup Patrick," Stan tells me and I walk over to the door and pick up the cup using both hands. He makes no comment as he shuts the flap and I walk across the cell and put the cup on the sink and then go and sit back down and worry about my future.

I do not sleep well as my mind refuses to turn off. One of the other 'guests' further along the corridor keeps banging on his cell door demanding to be let out which does not help. The cell is a little warmer than the one in the other police station but it does not assist either to help in getting me to sleep.

The door flap opens very early in the morning and I guess the time to be about 6 a.m. and a white mug is placed on the shelf; "Here is your tea sir," says a strange voice and I walk over to the door and look through the open flap.

A much younger uniformed police officer stands the other side of the door; "I cannot drink tea with milk as I have irritable bowel syndrome," I tell him and trying to keep the anger out of my voice as this is a bad start to the day. I like my morning coffee; "You might as well take it away as I am unable to drink it," I tell him.

He makes no reply as he takes hold of the tea and returns it to a trolley. He then shuts the flap in my face and I try not to say out loud what I think of him.

About an hour later the flap opens again and a tray is placed on it. I get up and see that it is breakfast of two rashers of bacon, a fried slice of bread and a fried egg. A mug of tea stands behind the cup and I look angrily at the young police officer; "I cannot drink tea," I tell him as I pick up the tray and go and sit at the little table as the flap is slammed shut.

The breakfast is stone cold and once again I am not in the least bit hungry but force it down as I know I have a difficult day ahead of me.

I am not kept waiting long when the cell door opens and Detective Appleton walks in with a smarmy look on his face. I am glad to see Detective Marchant walk in behind him and I notice that Detective Marchant does not look at all happy.

"I have to put these on you," says Detective Appleton as he holds up a pair of handcuffs.

I stand up and extend my bandaged hands; "Don't do them so tight this time," I say and trying to keep the hatred I feel for him out of my voice.

He looks at me sharply and I guess he does know how I feel about him. He puts the cuffs around my wrists and does not do them too tightly. They are fixed firmly around my wrists but they do not hurt.

"Come with us," orders Detective Appleton as Detective Marchant walks out of the cell door.

I step out of the corridor as Detective Appleton grabs a hold of my arm firmly. A bit too firmly as his grip is tight and it hurts.

"Hey, leave it out will you?" I protest; "You are really hurting my arm. If I end up with bruises I am going to have you for assault," I threaten angrily as this geezer does really piss me off.

"Loosen you grip Detective Appleton," commands Detective Marchant.

"This is a proven murderer and I certainly do not want him to escape," replies Detective Appleton defensively as he loosens his grip; a little.

I stare angrily into his eyes; "I ain't a murderer and you know it. Hoping to get a promotion out of this are you because you think I am easy? Well you are wrong and time will prove it."

"That is enough you two," says Detective Marchant; "You calm down Mister Rant as you will get your opportunity to have your say in court."

I turn and look him in the eyes; "Not today I won't will I?"

Detective Marchant makes no reply and we continue walking along the brightly lit corridor. The young uniformed police officer sits behind the counter with his head down as if he is reading something. I can see that he does not want to get involved and I follow Detective Marchant up the metal stairs with Detective Appleton holding firmly onto my arm.

I am taken to a waiting police van with the back doors already open. Detective Marchant stops by the doors and looks at me; "Get in please Mister Rant," he tells me as he looks at Detective Appleton; "Let him go Tony, he is not going anywhere except with us."

Detective Appleton reluctantly lets go of my arm as I climb in but he follows me closely. I sit down near the front of the van and Detective Appleton sits down beside me and so close our bodies are touching and I move forward a little to put some distance between us. He stares at me with a haughty expression but says nothing as Detective Marchant climbs in and sits opposite us.

We sit quietly until another young uniformed officer joins us in the back and slams the doors shut behind him. I hear the drivers' door open and the door is slammed shut as Detective Appleton shouts jubilantly; "Take it away."

The engine starts up and we drive slowly away from the police station.

It is only a short drive before the van stops and the engine is turned off and I get out of the van and look at the back of a very modern looking building and I am led inside. As we enter the building I see by the signs that it is the courthouse but am given little opportunity to examine it closely as I am ushered downstairs and put into a cell. Detective Appleton removes the handcuffs and quickly leaves the cell as the door slams shut behind him.

I remember my Lawyer's words and him saying that I will be charged today and for me to say nothing except to confirm my name and address. I sit down on a hard bench as there is no cot, chair or toilet and I guess that I am not to be held here very long.

I am still kept waiting for more than an hour when the cell door opens and Detective Appleton walks in carrying a pair of handcuffs; "Put these on," he commands as he reaches out towards my right hand as I extend it towards him. He puts the handcuffs on, once again firmly, and pushes me out of the door. A uniformed officer stands waiting and I am escorted up the stairs and into a large court.

An elderly looking judge sits behind a large mahogany desk that is fronted with panels of mahogany. I am led by Detective Appleton to a small enclosed area which can only be described as the witness stand. The court has about ten people sitting on chairs and I recognize Detectives Marchant, Norton, Sergeant Marsh and my Lawyer Christopher Osborne.

I notice that Christopher Osborne does not meet my gaze and I look around at the other people who are complete strangers to me.

The judge wastes no time as he asks me my name and address which I say in a loud firm voice. My Lawyer looks up at me as I speak and he faintly shakes his head as the judge picks up a piece of paper;

"Patrick Rant; I charge you with the murder of Debbie Dulok and for the possession of one hundred and fifty tablets containing ecstasy, amphetamine and a barbiturate with the intention to distribute."

He continues reading and then says in a loud voice; "Court will be set for the 6th of February next and due to the seriousness of these crimes no bail will be granted. Take him down," he orders as a man sitting at the desk in front of him wearing a pale gray suit and receding hairline says in a loud voice; "Next case."

The uniformed officer takes hold of my arm and pulls me out of the witness stand and I am taken downstairs and returned to the same cell. My handcuffs are removed as I enter the cell and the officer says nothing as he walks out and slams the door shut behind him.

About twenty minutes later the cell door opens and the uniformed officer walks in carrying the now familiar handcuffs. I stand up and hold my hands out towards him as he puts the handcuffs loosely around my wrists. Looking at the bandages around my hands he asks in a voice with no emotion; "Are you in pain?"

"A little," I reply trying to match his tone of voice.

"Come with me," he orders as he grabs hold of my arm and walks me out of the cell.

I am taken to the rear of the building and led to a large blue police van. This van is of a different construction to the other one, it being of a square construction and has two small windows at the side. The windows are fitted with an opaque glass and are covered with a strong wire meshing.

I am pushed into the back of the van and as I enter I see two long metal benches along each side. There is a uniformed police officer sitting beside another handcuffed prisoner. I am led/pushed along the inside of the van and I sit down opposite the other prisoner.

"What happened to your hands mate?" the prisoner asks me.

"No talking," says the uniformed officer.

I look at the other prisoner who has dark slicked back hair and a long dark skinned face. He looks like a traveler aged in his early twenties and aware that I may be doing time with him I answer gruffly; "Had my thumbs removed."

"No talking," repeats the officer in a louder voice.

The traveler ignores him; "Did that hurt mate?"

"I said no talking," repeats the officer even louder.

I look at the officer and then back at the traveler; "Not much," I reply as I look down at the metal floor of the van.

"There are only these two," says the officer who escorted me into the van to his mate and he slams the back doors shut and bangs on the side of the van with his fist. The engine starts and we are driven away.

The journey takes about an hour and a half and I wish that I had used the toilet as I really need to pee. By the time the van stops I am in a lot of pain and really hope that I do not embarrass myself by peeing down my leg.

The back doors are opened and we are led out of the van and across a small courtyard through a very secure looking steel door. I do not get much opportunity to look around but I see that the courtyard is surrounded by a high brick wall that must be twenty feet high with coiled barbed or razor wire on top.

We are marched through the door and along a short corridor into a large room. A high metal counter faces me with three prison officers standing behind it. Before them is a queue of seven prisoners who all stand in a line.

I look at the officer who still holds onto my arm; "I really need the toilet mate and wish you had given me the opportunity to go before we left the court."

He looks at me with an unfriendly gaze; "You need to be booked in first," he says in a voice that matches his gaze.

It looks like I am to be treated as guilty before I am proved innocent and my anger rises;

"I have irritable bowel syndrome mate and it is on my medical record," I say loudly so that all can hear; "You did not even ask me if I needed the toilet before you pushed me into the back of that van."

He stares at me and repeats in a bored voice; "You need to be booked in first."

My anger gets the better of me; "Is it your intention to humiliate me by making me piss in my trousers?" I ask in an even louder voice.

"What is going on over there; is that prisoner giving you trouble officer?" asks the eldest looking prison officer from behind the counter.

"He insists that he wants to use the toilet sir and says that he has irritable bowel syndrome," he answers in an angry voice.

"Well you had better remove the handcuffs and take him to the toilet then. I do not want my nice clean floor covered in that man's urine," he orders, much to the delight of the other prisoners as one says; "You tell 'em mate."

"Quiet!" roars the officer from behind the desk.

My handcuffs are removed not too gently and looking at me with an angry glare the officer says; "This way," and walks across the room.

He leads me through a thick gray painted metal door to the end of a short corridor that has a doorway with no door.

"You can use that one in there," he grudgingly tells me as he stands to one side to allow me to pass.

I walk past him and see two toilet cubicles inside with no doors.

I struggle undoing my zip and look around at him; "I am really sorry to be such a nuisance to you mate. I really hate this IBS and have suffered with it for years and it really restricts my social life," I tell him as I manage to undo my fly. I turn towards the stainless steel toilet and it is with relief that I manage to urinate. There is no handle to pull to flush the toilet and I see a recessed panel that is covered with a small darkened piece of glass. Realizing that it is an automatic flush I struggle with the zip of my fly and after managing to close my fly I step back as the toilet flushes.

I smile at the officer; "Thank you, sorry to make a fuss I was in a lot of pain," I say as I walk past him along the corridor. I push the steel door open and walk into the room;

"Go and stand over there against that wall," he tells me pointing at the wall opposite.

A bit dismayed that I am not to join the queue of prisoners as the traveler has and stands at the back of the queue. I make no comment and do as I am told.

I am kept waiting for over an hour and a half as each prisoner is booked in, made to strip naked and issued with blue prison clothes. They are each instructed to sit on a hard bench as some of them make ribald comments about the sizes and shapes of the other prisoners' penises.

The officer who escorted me from the court stands dutifully near me as the prisoners are booked in and allows me to use the toilet two more times while we wait. The other prisoners are then escorted out of the room.

Finally it is my turn and the elder prison officer asks me my name (which I am sure he already knows). I tell him my name and he looks through a folder as he looks at me in an unfriendly manner; "According to your file you have not been behaving yourself, have you?" he demands.

I stare back at him confidentially; "I have done nothing wrong and you should not believe everything you read."

My confidence and reply shocks him as his eyes widen; "According to this report you have murdered your girlfriend and a large quantity of drugs were found in your apartment," he says in a loud stern voice.

I continue staring into his eyes; "In the first place she was not my girlfriend," I tell him as I hold up my hands; "A girlfriend would hardly imprison me, torture me and cut off my thumbs. In the second place I have not murdered anyone as she was already dead when I found her and in the third place I know nothing about any drugs."

He stares into my eyes and looks back down at the folder; "This large quantity of illegal drugs was discovered by the police in your apartment; are you saying they are lying?"

"Drugs were discovered by the police in my apartment so I have been told. But I never put them there and as I just said I know nothing about them other than what the police have told me," I say in a firm voice and stare back at him defiantly.

He stares back at me focusing on my eyes and I meet his stare without wavering. A long minute passes as we continue to stare at each other and I see that he is trying to break me down. I have done nothing wrong and certainly have nothing to be ashamed of. The 'battle' continues and I refuse to break the gaze and after another thirty seconds or so he finally looks away and returns his attention back to the folder in front of him. At first he does nothing except look at the folder and then he picks up a ballpoint pen and writes something down and then looks up at me;

"It is necessary for you to remove your clothes and you will be issued with prison clothing. Will you need any help to get undressed as you have no thumbs which I imagine would make life difficult?" he asks in a friendlier manner.

"I only need some help to undo the button on my trousers. My shirt has 'poppers' instead of buttons and my trainers are loose, but I will be a bit slow and may take a long time; if that is alright with you?" I ask and try to keep the anger from my voice.

He looks at the officer beside me; "Time is one of the things that you will find you will have here. Help him with his trousers please," he says in a gruff voice.

The officer steps forward and I say hurriedly; "Only the button on my trousers."

He makes no comment as he undoes the button and stands back as I slowly remove my clothes. I soon stand naked and very aware that there will be no privacy for me in this horrible place. Blue prison clothing is put onto the counter and I struggle into the shirt and trousers as the officer steps forward and does up the button on my trousers and starts to button my shirt;

"Please only do a few of them up as buttons are very difficult for me."

He makes no comment as he fastens three buttons and then steps back. I struggle putting the pair of socks on and the officer helps me again as he does help with the prison shoes which fit loosely.

"Thank you for your help, sorry to be a nuisance," I say to him in my politest voice.

"You are not a nuisance," he replies and I notice that I am not called 'sir' anymore. I look at the officer behind the counter who then looks down at my folder;

"I see that you are to go to the prison hospital after you have been booked in;" he says as he looks at the young prison officer to his right; "Take him over there and stay with him. After the Doctor has finished with him take him to Block C."

"Yes sir," replies the officer and does not smile.

The elder prison officer looks back at me; "It will be necessary for you to be kept in solitary for a while as you made the midday news. Your case made headline news and sorry to tell you they named the road and the town that you live in. There are many prisoners here who have also committed murder, rape and violent crimes. There are also a lot of drugs here which we try to prevent. You claim that you know nothing about any drugs and if I find that you have been lying to me and I catch you under the influence of any drugs it will not go well for you," he warns me in a very firm voice as he looks at the young officer next to him; "Take him across Andy," he says, effectively dismissing me but I stand my ground and stare at him.

He feels my eyes on him and looks at me; "Is there anything else *Mister Rant?*"

"Yes there is; one is that you used the phrase 'have also committed murder' and I am not a murderer. The other thing is that I have not lied to you; I have never taken drugs and most definitely have not taken ecstasy which I know can kill you. You will never find me under the influence of drugs or anything else come to that unless it is forced into me which I cannot see happening," I say with great determination and stare into his eyes.

He only stares back for a few seconds and then looks away with a faint smile on his lips; "Time will tell Mister Rant; and time is what you will have here."

"Until my court case, which is in February; unless I am released before that," I tell him in a firm voice.

He makes no reply as he looks back at the young officer; "Take him across please," he asks; but orders.

The hospital wing is across the other side of the prison and Andy the prison officer (or shall I call him prison warder?) takes me the long way round. We walk around the main prison building and I am taken across several yards that are surrounded by a twenty foot high wall with a roll of razor wire on top. I am also taken past the recreational field and two football pitches. After walking along several long deserted corridors we finally arrive at the hospital.

Taking me into a large empty waiting room Andy tells me to take a seat as he approaches a large counter that is enclosed by glass paneling. Telling the hospital orderly, who wears a white coat, of my arrival he comes and sits down next to me. We do not speak and after about twenty minutes the orderly shouts across for Andy to take me into the Doctor.

The Doctors' office is a mass of gray steel cabinets and the Doctor tells me to sit down as he looks up at Andy; "This is going to take a little while, have you been instructed to wait?"

Andy replies that he has and the Doctor tells him he will call him when he has finished his examination. Andy walks out and closes the door quietly behind him.

The Doctor looks at me over the top of his black rimmed glasses and then looks down at a folder on his desk. He takes his time reading through it and finally looks up at me;

"According to this you have had a rough time recently. Please tell me in your own words what has been happening and then I will have a look at you."

I tell him of my imprisonment and torture and about the removal of my thumbs and he makes no comment. He finally stands up and with a curt 'come with me' I follow him out of a side door into his surgery. Telling me to sit down at a large white table he puts on a pair of blue rubber gloves and first removes the bandage on my right hand.

His examination of my injuries is quite thorough and after a half hour I am the reluctant owner of new bandages. We go back into his office and he asks of my medical history. I tell him of my irritable bowel syndrome, bad back, collapsed lung and also of the mild heart attack I had last year.

He makes no comment and writes nothing down and I assume that all that I have just told him is already written down.

He looks at me over his black rimmed glasses; "I see that you have been prescribed a course of antibiotics. Do you have them with you?"

"No I do not; two were issued to me last night at the police station."

"I have not been issued any for you and it looks like I will have to make a telephone call and find out where they are. Have the warder take you to where you are going to stay while you are with us and I will probably call on you in a few hours; "Do you know what the time was yesterday when you were given the antibiotics?"

"No, other than they were given to me with my evening meal."

He looks at his watch and sighs with exasperation; "Very well. I will call on you later," he tells me and returns his attention to my folder.

I stand up; "Thank you for changing my bandages," I say as I walk out of the door and he makes no response.

Andy stands up as I walk into the waiting room; "All done then?" he asks and already knowing the answer and I nod my head and do reply 'yes'.

"I will take you to where you are going to spend the night and probably the next few weeks. Follow me," he orders.

I follow him out of the door and along several corridors. Prisoners lounge around and sit at tables when I am taken through a large room that has the appearance of a large cathedral except for the open cells that line the walls. I do not make any eye contact with anyone and keep looking straight ahead. There are two floors above us lined with cells and a big anti suicide net circles each floor.

Leading me into a long corridor we then go down several flights of stairs until we reach a long brightly lit corridor that is lined with cell doors each side. There must be twenty or thirty doors on each side and Andy takes me along the corridor until we reach a cell with the door wide open.

Stopping and turning to look at me he indicates with his hand that I should enter the cell; "You will stay here tonight, they may move you somewhere else tomorrow but make yourself comfortable and I will go and report that you are here."

I make no reply as I enter the dismal looking cell and look down at the uncomfortable looking cot that is against one wall. Laid out as the previous cells the toilet is in the same place, as is the sink and small table and chair. Andy slams the door shut and I sit down on the cot and it feels like I am going to have some kind of mental breakdown and 'pins and needles' fill my head as welcoming darkness fills my head and I pass out.

Chapter Twenty-Three

I was kept in solitary confinement for three weeks and during that time I was interrogated five times by an aggressive Detective Appleton. Detective Norton was present and each time he said nothing during the interrogations.

Detective Marchant was also present as was my Lawyer Christopher Osborne. They did not take part in the interrogations apart from occasionally correcting Detective Appleton when needed.

Detective Appleton did become more aggressive towards me during these interrogations and many times was allowed to continue with his aggressive behavior. I stayed with the same story which I repeated over and over again and questioned his evidence and often asked if there were more fingerprints on the bag of ecstasy tablets and jar of poisonous mushrooms. Each time there was no answer and even my Lawyer made no comment which filled me with despair. He denied knowledge of other fingerprints or any DNA found on the bag of ecstasy tablets discovered in my apartment, but I did get the feeling that he was lying.

This did fill me with some hope but he refused to see me other than this one time and after three weeks I was 'released' into the general population of the prison.

Put in the same cell as a convicted drug dealer and two other prisoners who were in for violent crimes, I much preferred life in solitary confinement. Their disgusting habits of constantly picking their noses and of constant farting made life very difficult and unbearable at times. Their conversations left a lot to be desired as they had two main subjects; sex and football.

Being locked up and kept away from the fairer sex and my recent experiences with Debbie, had made me not think of sex and I had little or no desire for it anyway.

I have not been a great one for football, especially professional football as I think that most games appear fixed. I did try to get into watching football many years ago but after watching a top player pass the ball to the opposition and at times lose the ball within seconds of getting in control of it I gave up.

Reading in the cell was impossible as the only reading possible was the tabloids. My cellmates would only read the headlines (if they were not about politics) and would go straight to the cartoons and then onto the sports pages. The prison did have a library and a prisoner would bring round a trolley of books but as I said, reading, especially a book, was impossible in the cell. The library times were very restricted as was much of life as the prison I was in was a high security one.

Excuse me reader for not going into great detail about my life in this horrible prison as I hated every second of my time there. I will relate a few serious events that did occur but will not mention any names in case life takes a serious turn again and I find myself incarcerated in the same place.

The first serious event occurred only a few days after my release from solitary confinement.

I was lying on my bunk in my cell enjoying one of those rare occasions when I had the cell to myself. My cell was situated on the first floor and one of the 'hard nuts' of our wing occupied one of the cells further along the landing. He was one of two brothers who had been incarcerated for robbing a post office. They had forced their way into this village post office and they had been both armed with sawn-off shotguns. One of the brothers had shot the legs of the postmaster's wife, forcing the postmaster to hand over the money.

I had been warned by one of my cellmates to stay away from both brothers as the other brother was also kept in a cell on the ground floor. I had heeded his advice as the two brothers' main objective in life was to be bullies and to 'control' all other inmates on our block and in the prison generally.

As I was laying on my bunk the light became diffused from the landing outside by two figures that stood in the doorway. It was both of the brothers and they entered my cell and I could see by their faces that they were going to give me a good hiding and very possibly cause me some permanent damage. The larger and older of the two brothers walked quickly over to me and pinned me down by pushing down on my shoulders. He smiled cruelly at me when I felt a sudden pain in my testicles as the other brother had punched me there; and hard. He then sat on my legs and even though I tried hard I could not move.

I was very scared as neither of them said anything and I was trying to brace myself against more pain when a loud voice with a Polish accent shouted at them to let me go.

The brother sitting on my legs told him that I needed to be taught a lesson and that I needed to know who was really in charge around here.

The loud Polish voice continued; "Patrick is a very good friend of mine and if you do not let him go *now* you are going to have to answer to *me*."

They immediately let me go and stood up and the brother who had spoken said; "We did not know that he was a good friend of yours. We thought that he was just a woman killer."

"Well he is not," the huge Polish man said to them; "Walk away," he orders in his thick Polish accent.

The two brothers walked quickly out of my cell and I got a good look at my rescuer. I had seen him before and he had to be the biggest man on our wing. He appeared to be the leader of about ten other Polish prisoners in a gang and who all look very fierce with their shaven heads and tribal tattoos.

The Polish man says to me; "It would be best in the future that you do not stay on your own in your cell as you may have noticed no one else does," and without giving me any opportunity to reply he quickly walked away along the landing.

Getting to my feet I quickly walked out of my cell to see the huge Polish man walking down the stairs. I hurried along the landing and followed him down. When I got to the bottom of the stairs I looked around and could see that he had rejoined his gang at a table with his back to me. I walked quickly over to the table as two other Polish prisoners stood up and stepping forward barred my way.

I looked the biggest one in the eyes; "I really need to talk to your friend there," I said as I looked down at my rescuer.

Many long seconds passed with my rescuer looking straight forward and not even acknowledging my presence as I stood there feeling very conspicuous and uncomfortable.

Suddenly he said something in Polish and the two prisoners moved out of the way and I walked past them and stood in front of him. He still sat there looking straight ahead and apparently right through me. I stayed where I was until he looked up at me with a questioning look in his eyes.

"I do not know you but you obviously know me. I want to thank you for what you just did as those two animals would have hurt me real bad, probably even killed me," I say to him in as firm a voice as I can.

A faint smile forms on his lips but he makes no answer so I continue;

"As far as I am concerned I owe you my life and if there is anything that I can do for you and it is in my power to do it I will. You just say the word and I mean that now or even several years down the line if we ever get out of here," I tell him with all sincerity.

He still continues looking at me with that faint smile on his lips and barely nods his head towards me; and still says nothing.

"I owe you and I will never forget what you just did and I hope you never do," I continue a little nervously as he is still staring at me and saying nothing and I feel fear growing inside me.

With a friendly nod in his direction and a grateful smile at his 'gang' I walk away and go and sit at a partly empty table where two prisoners are playing draughts and another prisoner is reading a newspaper.

After that event I made sure that I was never in my cell on my own and always kept close to other prisoners that did not look too dangerous; and there weren't many of those.

During my stay at the high security prison the large Polish man never did ask me to do him any favors and I still wonder at his behavior.

Another event or incident that occurred happened a few weeks later;

I was outside in the yard walking around as part of our exercise period when I was approached by a prisoner I had never seen before. He fell in step with me as I walked around the yard and on our third circuit together he looked at me;

"I know who you are," he said in an accent that I recognized to be Dutch; "We used to have a mutual friend in my country and who is dead now."

I immediately knew that he was talking about Sally and I looked at him with a certain amount of fear.

"I hear that you have kept your mouth shut. I know that a lot of them got arrested and we know that you have kept quiet about her and whatever else you know," he continued in his thick Dutch accent.

I took a close look at him; He was about the same height as me with long fair hair that was tied back in a pony tail and we could also have been the same age. I had never seen him before in my life or anyone resembling him and I have to ask; "How do you know that?"

He stared back at me with cold gray eyes; "We all know and just make sure that you continue keeping quiet," he said in a low spoken voice so that those around us could not hear.

"You did not answer my question mate?" I ask in a quavering voice.

He smiled at me and raised his eyebrows and walked away.

That was the only time I saw him as I never saw him again.

What he said frightened the hell out of me. As far as I was concerned the only people who knew about my visit to Sally was Debbie. Was his knowledge about me derived somehow from the police and from what country?

But it did not make any sense unless he or the 'we' he referred to must think that I know a lot more than I do. Was Debbie a bigger player in dealing or importing and if that was the case, and he was a part of a big drug distribution network, it would be in their interest to silence me permanently and then no more worries. It would be an easy thing to arrange especially in here where pain and even death were enjoyable to a lot who surrounded me. Drug trafficking can involve billions of pounds each year and 'customers' do die, another death would hardly upset things.

I could only assume that 'they' thought that killing me, or attempting to, may attract unwanted attention. The matter has remained a total mystery to me and made me very unsure of the police and of the people around me in general.

Drugs were rife in the prison and many times our landing would be enveloped in the sickly smell of marijuana. The wardens appeared to have little control and I often wondered why more serious steps were not taken against this problem. The violence in the prison was reduced during these times and I could only assume that the drug taking was at least tolerated as the place did become a lot less violent.

The drug dealer, or should I say ex drug dealer in our cell would suffer badly during these times. The marijuana smell would drift into our cell and trigger his addiction cravings. He would become very morose and even aggressive towards us when we used to try and distract him.

He would pace up and down the cell and sometimes this would continue all night and we found that it was best to leave him alone. His constant pacing would prevent us from getting any sleep especially when he would keep punching the walls to try and relieve his frustration. He had served two years of a nine year sentence and I guessed that he had seen the error of his ways as during the time I was there I never knew him to take anything or be under the influence.

To see him pacing the cell and struggling with his addiction was a sad thing to see and I was glad that I did not have a similar addiction.

The only thing that I craved was freedom and for my name to be cleared of these terrible accusations made against me.

The day before Christmas and Detectives Appleton and Norton pay me a visit.

I was taken into a small room by two warders and you can imagine my dismay when the two Detectives walked in. The warders left me alone with them and I admit I was very scared as there was no sign of the stabilizing influence of Detective Marchant.

Detective Appleton was even more aggressive than he usually was and I guessed by his attitude that things were not going well for him. Detective Norton took his usual stance of sitting quietly and saying nothing as Detective Appleton repeated the same questions he had asked me maybe a hundred times before.

He made an issue out of my fingerprints being on the bag of ecstasy tablets. He kept repeating himself and how they had been found in my apartment.

At first I argued with him and protested my innocence but this seemed to inflame him more. I soon gave up arguing and just sat there staring at him and saying nothing. After about half an hour he suddenly lost the energy and just stared back at me with an angry look in his eyes. Just as suddenly he stood up and walked out of the room and a few seconds later Detective Norton followed him out.

I was escorted back to the cell and it being a recreation hour the warders walked away and I went downstairs. Sitting at a 'safe' table I thought over what had just happened and could only arrive at the conclusion that the investigation had turned against this extremely unpleasant Detective and that one day, maybe soon, I would be able to get out of this lunatic asylum and be free.

It did make a happier Christmas day and helped to keep away the deep depression that affected many of the other prisoners. Christmas is meant to be a time of spending with loved ones and family. I had no family apart from a sister somewhere who I had not seen for about eighteen years, but I did enjoy a Christmas sitting in front of the television. I would sometimes treat myself to a bottle of Tequila and sometimes vodka and get very drunk and fall asleep in front of the late night film.

Chapter Twenty-Four

The following month dragged by with violence amongst the inmates becoming more common. Every day there was a fight somewhere in the prison and two prison warders got badly beaten. One of the warders had to be taken to the local hospital and everyone was locked up in their cells for three days.

The culprits were never found but the warders had to know who had beaten them up. Life being a prison warder was very difficult especially when they had families on the outside and this also made them vulnerable.

The first of February arrived and I was taken to the small room where the two Detectives had questioned me. I was made to sit and wait and expecting the worse I was delighted when my Lawyer Christopher Osborne walked in. We shook hands and he was all smiles and told me that my case, which was coming up in six days time needed to be talked over with him.

At first he got me to repeat my sad tale of captivity and torture which I think he did to see if my story had changed. The story was exactly the same and when I finished he opened his folder and looked at me with a broad smile.

He told me of the difficulties he had encountered when trying to review the evidence against me. Detective Appleton had been most uncooperative and Christopher told me he had had to go over his head. Debbie's fingerprints and DNA had been taken before she had been cremated and her thumb print and the fingerprint of her right hand little finger was found on the bag containing the ecstasy tablets. Her thumb print and two of her fingerprints were also found on the lid of the jar of poisonous mushrooms.

To me all of this was fantastic news and Christopher's final good news was that Debbie's body had been examined by independent Doctors. It was their opinion that the bruising on her body had been caused by a fall, possibly down a flight of stairs, and was not considered as being caused by being restrained.

We talked for several hours but Christopher did warn me that though the evidence left good reason for doubt that I would still be tried by a jury. It could very easily all go against me and that I was not to get my hopes up too high. The court case would still be long and difficult and as my hands and wounds had healed and I wore no bandages I would not appear so vulnerable. The court and jury would still have to decide if I was telling the truth and if they thought I was lying I could very easily spend the next ten years or longer in jail.

I was escorted back to my wing and I sat down at a table with hope filling my heart. There was as usual a lot of noise around me and I ignored it all until a very large figure sat down opposite me.

It was my Polish rescuer and he looked at me with a smile, which was very expressive for him.

"It appears that you will be a free man very soon," he said in his strong Polish accent.

I looked at him in complete surprise and could not hide what I felt as I had only been sitting at the table for about five minutes when he came over; "How do you know that?" I asked in a squeaky voice.

He just looked back at me without saying anything.

"You do know that your intervention with those two brothers has kept all the other lunatics off of me?" I tell him with a grateful smile.

He still makes no reply but a faint smile does form.

"I owe you my life, I still mean it when I say if you ever need any help all you have to do is say and not ask," I tell him and tell him my address.

"It will be many, many years before I am released," he replies and I don't think that he paid much attention to my address. Suddenly he extends his hand towards me and very surprised I grasp it as firmly as I can; "Good luck to you Patrick just make sure you don't come back here," and with those final words he lets go of my hand and walks away.

I sit there in total confusion as to how had he known about my Lawyer visiting and of the evidence and so soon? I had not spoken to any of the warders on the way back or anyone else.

I hardly slept while I impatiently wait for my court case. The 6th of February arrives and I am escorted out of the prison and taken in that large blue van to the court. I am not given the opportunity to change out of my prison issue clothes, a fact I feel sure will go against me.

I am kept in a cell for a short time and my Lawyer, Christopher Osborn pays me a brief visit. He is full of enthusiasm and appears confident that I will win the case but he does not say it directly.

I am taken into the court which has three judges sitting at the bench. The judge sitting in the middle is the elderly judge who had sent me to prison, granting me no bail. The jury consists of six women and six men and a lot of them look bored.

Detectives Appleton, Norton and Marchant are present as is Sergeant Marsh and two other uniformed officers who I recognize. I am made to sit in the front row next to my Lawyer and another elderly gentleman wearing a dark blue pinstripe suit. As I sit down Christopher introduces the blue pinstripe as Albert Higgins, the senior member of his firm. I shake hands and look at the judges. A man wearing a gray wig and black clothes get to his feet and he reads out the charges of murder and drug possession with the intent to supply.

Detective Appleton is called to the stand first and not being able to hide his delight he tells of my first visit to the local police station. He makes a big issue of my delay in visiting the station and of not visiting the local police station in the town where Debbie lived. His 'evidence' is portrayed as if I was well aware of my actions and that he could only arrive at the conclusion that I murdered Debbie and also that I was a drug dealer and that he had no option other than to charge me with these very serious offences.

Silence falls on the court when he finishes giving his evidence and conclusions and my Lawyer gets to his feet to 'ask some questions' as he politely puts it.

I can only describe Christopher Osborne's next hour and a half as he cross examines Detective Appleton's 'evidence' as admiral.

At first he talks of my imprisonment and torture by Debbie and insists that the police photographs of my injuries, especially of the removal of my thumbs be shown to the court and jury. He talks of my state of mind and of getting away from the basement and of finding Debbie dead. He also tells of my physical, dirty condition and can find no objection to me returning to my apartment to wash and change.

He then questions Detective Appleton about the bag of ecstasy tablets found hidden in my apartment. He also says in a very loud voice that mine were not the only fingerprints on the bag and that the bag also did not have any of my thumb prints. He also mentions the blood test taken at the police station stating that the result was negative of any illegal drugs in my system; especially ecstasy.

My previous conviction is not mentioned but he states that a full set of my fingerprints and thumb prints were on police record. He makes a point of telling the court and jury of my explanation of how my fingerprints were found to be on the bag. He also says in a louder voice that there was no trace of thumb prints and how it would be difficult for me to pick up a bag with no thumbs; especially as I would have been in so much pain. He also makes the point that when I was charged for this offense that it was stated, by Detective Appleton, that there was only my fingerprints and no others on the bag; which was now proved to be false.

My Lawyer, Christopher, then talks of the accusation made against me of murdering Debbie Dulok. He makes Detective Appleton look to be a vindictive policeman who has made a case to further his own ambitions in the police force.

I am amazed by him as he questions the so-called evidence against me and my Lawyer says in a louder voice of the opposition that Detective Appleton made each time he wanted to review the evidence against me.

He talks as Detective Appleton's anger rises until a recess is called for lunch.

The afternoon that follows is one of my Lawyer contradicting all of the evidence against me. The Doctors are called who examined Debbie's dead body and also of the 'supposed' forcing of the ecstasy tablets into her by me is refuted. The judge tells everyone that court will resume again tomorrow at 10 a.m. and we are all told to stand as the judges make their exit.

The court is cleared and I am escorted back downstairs and put in a cell. About ten minutes later a large policeman opens the cell door carrying a pair of handcuffs. He tells me to hold out my hands and I am handcuffed and escorted by him and another uniformed policeman. I am taken upstairs and put in the large blue police van. I am taken across town and taken to the second police station where I was imprisoned before and taken down to the cells. Put in a cell and this time I have to put my hands through the flap of the door for my handcuffs to be removed.

I stand over the toilet trying to urinate as my IBS has kicked in badly by this time. It feels like I really want to pee but I only manage a few drips. The feeling remains however and I stand over the toilet for what must be half an hour before the flap in the door opens.

"Here is your food and a nice cup of coffee," says a familiar voice and I put my penis back into my trousers and without zipping up my fly walk over to the door.

"Hello Andy, thank you for the coffee; and thank you for remembering," I say as I take hold of the tray and go and sit at the little table as the flap is gently closed.

It is cauliflower cheese and baked beans again with also a bowl of rice pudding. The coffee smells good and using both hands I take a mouthful of the fairly warm coffee and eat all of the food in front of me.

I am awoken early in the morning with a large mug of black coffee with sugar and about an hour later am served with a breakfast of two slices of lightly fried bacon, a fried slice of bread and a fried egg. The breakfast, true to form, is stone cold and I curse the lack of imagination of the police force without offering a variety for breakfast. The black coffee that comes with it is slightly warm and tastes bitter as I think it only contains one spoonful of sugar this time. I force everything down and shortly afterwards have to put my hands through the flap. I am handcuffed taken upstairs, put in the blue van and taken to court.

A very long day follows that involves a testimony from Doctor Bellar on my condition at the police station. The photographs of my hands, my neck and ankles are shown again and discussed in more detail. Doctor Bellar also confirms that the blood test carried out on me showed it to be negative of any illegal substances. The tests did show a faint trace of a strong sedative he admits but he does not name what kind of sedative it was and is not asked by anyone to give any details.

Detective Appleton is made to take the stand again and my Lawyer questions him on his opinion of my physical condition. Detective Appleton is of the opinion that apart from my obvious injuries, my health, including my mental health, is good.

My Lawyer tears his opinions apart and Detectives Norton and Marchant are also called to the stand and questioned about my health. They contradict Detective Appleton's opinions and both say that they thought my health, especially my state of mind, was poor at the time and Detective Marchant expresses the opinion that under the circumstances of my recent torture and imprisonment it was to be expected.

Doctor Bellar is called to the stand again and agrees with Detectives Norton and Marchant and states that it will be a long time before my mental health returns to normal.

The elderly judge sums up the evidence at the end of the day and tells the jury that he has doubts as to the evidence against me. He says that he believes the charge of possession with intent to supply the ecstasy tablets is questionable and that there is the possibility that Debbie did plant them in my apartment.

He also states Debbie's time of death as being the evening before I got out of the confines of her basement. He talks of the bruising and several photographs of Debbie's body are produced. They clearly show the bruises on her arms and legs, back and abdomen. He tells the jury to seriously consider his words and the evidence and with a bash of his gavel says that court will reconvene tomorrow at 10 a.m.

I am escorted directly to the blue police van which is parked at the back of the court by the same policemen as yesterday. The handcuffs are shown to me and I instinctively extend my hands;

"I do not think we need to use these do we Mister Rant," the policeman says with a smile.

I smile back; "Thank you; it would be the height of stupidity for me to do a runner now," I answer as I feel my smile broaden.

"Don't tell anyone. Anyway we think that you have suffered enough."

The next day court begins at exactly 10 a.m.

I am made to stand as the elderly judge looks at the jury; "Has the jury come to a full decision?" he asks in a very formal manner.

A middle aged man wearing a white shirt and very loud patterned sports jacket stands up and I assume that he is the appointed foreman. Holding a piece of paper in front of him he looks at it and then back at the judge; "Yes, we have your honor," he replies.

The judge looks at me and then back at the foreman; "For the charge of possession with intent to supply 150 ecstasy tablets how do you find the defendant?"

In a loud clear voice the foreman replies; "Not guilty your honor."

I hold onto the desk in front of me as I feel a sensation of 'pins and needles' flood into my head.

"For the charge of murdering Debbie Dulok, how do you find the defendant?"

The foreman looks over at me; "Not guilty your honor."

I feel myself fall forward as tears fill my eyes as Christopher claps me on the shoulder and grabs a hold of my hand and shakes it vigorously; "Well done Patrick," he says with enthusiasm as he laughs.

"Mister Patrick Rant you have been found not guilty of the crimes made against you and you are free to go." The judge says in a very loud voice above the hubbub of the people in the court.

The tears flow freely now as my Lawyer continues to shake my hand.

"Let me congratulate him," says his boss as he grabs hold of my left hand and shakes it firmly.

The court starts to empty and Detective Marchant comes over to me; "Congratulations Patrick, you are a free man now. I hope that the medical profession can sort you out with some artificial thumbs very soon," he says and as Christopher is still shaking my right he extends his left hand. I take his hand and we shake hands firmly.

"I have not told Patrick fully of your help yet Mick," my Lawyer says to Detective Marchant.

"Don't make a big thing of it Mister Osborne, I was just doing my job," he answers with a broad smile.

"I am going to make a big thing of it," my Lawyer replies; "If it wasn't for your help I think the outcome would have been a lot different."

"I don't think so," laughs Detective Marchant as he lets go of my hand; "It appears that Mister Osborne is not going to keep quiet. By way of thanks Patrick, make sure that I never see you again in an official capacity."

I laugh and try and wipe the tears away; "On that you can put money on," I assure him with a big smile and start to laugh.

"You have a lot of living to catch up on and some compensation coming to you which I am sure Mister Osborne will help you with," says Detective Marchant as he walks away.

The policeman who accompanied me in the van stands in front of us and looks at me; "Would you be good enough to come with me sir?" he asks politely and I look at him in alarm.

"Nothing to worry about sir," he says as my heart sinks and he smiles broadly; "We need to get you out of those prison clothes."

I feel the relief flood through me as more tears flow down my cheeks.

"Come with me please sir," he says and keeping the smile on his face.

Christopher finally lets go of my hand; "Go with him Patrick, I need to have a quick word with Albert. I will be right behind you," he promises.

I step out from behind the desk and nearly fall over as the officer says; "Let me help you sir," and he puts his arm around my shoulders and holds me up.

We walk across the court as the jury is filing out and the foreman looks at me with a broad smile.

"Thank you all so much for believing me," I say to him as the tears flow even faster down my cheeks.

"It was an easy decision to make; enjoy the rest of your life sir," he says with a broader smile that shows his tobacco stained teeth.

"Thank you, thank you all," I reply as I look past him at the rest of the jury who have stopped and they all smile back at me.

"Come on sir," says the uniformed officer as he still has his arm around my shoulders; "We need to change those clothes."

I let him help me out of the court and we walk along a corridor a short way and he opens a paneled door. Inside on the table are my clothes and trainers.

"Get changed sir, the quicker you change the quicker you can go home," he tells me.

"You do not know how good that sounds," I say as I walk across the room.

Christopher insists that he drives me home and I raise no objection as the alternative is to get a taxi which would cost me quite a bit. After I had changed out of my prison issue clothes the police officer handed me my apartment and car keys. He also handed me my mobile telephone and wallet containing my driving license, credit cards and passport. There was also £270 in my wallet which included the £180 that Debbie had left for me. I know that I had left my wallet in my apartment but made no comment apart from to say 'Thank you' and to put it in my pocket.

Christopher told me of how Detective Marchant had helped him while he was gathering the evidence for me on the drive back home. By what Christopher told me, Detective Marchant helped a lot as Detective Appleton did his best to prevent him from obtaining anything. I vowed to myself that I would keep my word and avoid all trouble; whatever kind. I am not a gay boy but I know that for many years I will not even attempt any liaison with the fairer sex.

My car was still parked in the road where I had left it all those months ago. It was covered in dirt and both of the wing mirrors had been broken and the wiper blades had been stolen. Sticking on the windscreen was a notice from the council saying that the vehicle excise duty (the car tax) had expired and the vehicle would be towed away, and in only five days time. This did puzzle me as I thought that the tax would have been automatically taken out of my bank account when the old tax expired.

I asked Christopher to come up to my apartment with me in case the police had caused any damage when they searched the place. He watched me struggle with my door keys and gently pushed me aside and unlocked the door for me. On the mat just inside there was a pile of envelopes, several in red. The red envelopes were soon explained as the electricity supply had been cut off as had the telephone been disconnected.

My apartment was in a bit of a mess where the police had searched it and they had put very little back where it belonged. The back of the television had been removed much to my dismay but it did not make a lot of inconvenience as I had no electricity supply to power it anyway. I asked Christopher to open my envelopes before he went and thanked him again and again for helping me.

Christopher slit all the envelopes open for me using a kitchen knife and holding out his hand wished me luck. Reaching into his pocket he gave me his business card with the telephone number and address of his law firm on it.

"I will be looking into compensation for you Patrick and if you ever do need a Lawyer in the future, please call me."

I took his hand and we shook hands firmly and I promised him that I would. I also promised to write to him every now and then to let him know how I was getting on. I also assured him that he would be on my Christmas card list for many, many years to come.

When Christopher left I thought that the first thing I should do was look through my mail and get the electric and telephone reconnected. Due to the location of my apartment and the sea views and its desirability I had had to pay six months in advance. Even though I had no electric I did have a roof over my head.

There were several demands from the electricity company for me to pay the bill and several advising that the supply would be cut. It was a similar scenario with the telephone company and there was also a letter from my bank saying my account had been suspended.

Putting on a larger coat I locked up securely (using both hands to turn the keys) and hurried down to the bank. After queuing for about half an hour I got served at the counter. Passing my letter from them through the grill along with my driving license, passport and credit cards the lady quickly reinstalled my account as if it was a daily occurrence for her and she even gave me a current statement, but no explanation and I did not ask. My money was all there which was a huge relief and having a 'pay as you go' mobile phone I got her to put £20 credit onto it.

The next hour involved telephoning the electricity and telephone companies from the foyer in the bank. They were happy to accept my payment against my credit card but it took ages and by the time I had finished I was down to 5 pence credit on my phone. I put another £10 on it and made my way home.

I telephoned the scrap yard as soon as I got home for them to take my car away. The car had been identified by the locals that it was my car and was a 'one of a kind' as I had had to paint the roof a bright red as a lot of the paint had peeled off over a year ago. The rest of the car was dark red and I thought that the paint was the same color when I bought it but when I applied it, it was very different. Walking back from the bank I could not fail to notice the looks of hatred that many people gave me, especially the women. That they had recognized me was no surprise as my picture had made the television news and the papers had also showed my picture and named the town and road that I lived in. I hoped that my recent acquittal and innocence would be as widely reported.

The scrap yard told me that they would come and collect my car tomorrow providing that I had sufficient proof of ownership which I assured them I did. They would only give me £50 for it saying that scrap metal prices had plummeted recently. I did not argue with them even though I was disappointed as the car was easily worth twenty times that but I had no choice really. If I spent good money on it to be repaired the chance of it being vandalized was quite high and time was against me. I vowed to buy another car soon; maybe after my new thumbs were fitted.

I ignored the mess the police had made in my apartment and spent the rest of the day walking along the seafront. It being early February it was very cold with ice on the ground in many places but I did not care. I hardly felt the cold with my big coat on with the hood up and with a wooly hat and a scarf wrapped around my face I felt quite warm. As the other beach walkers could not see my face I was not recognized which was a relief and I decided it would probably be best for me to grow a beard.

The man from the scrap yard turned up in a big tow truck at 7.30 a.m. the next morning and after giving me a check for £50 he loaded my car up and drove away; which was a relief as that was one thing less for me to worry about.

The telephone company telephoned me two hours later to tell me my telephone was reconnected and which I already knew; as I had to answer the ringing phone in my apartment. The engineer from the electricity company came shortly afterwards and reconnected my electricity. I had to go to the supermarket as I had little in the cupboards and I met with a lot of hostility getting my shopping as a lot of women recognized me and stared at me with disgust and hatred. I decided to buy a laptop and do my shopping online in future.

The months have passed and after sorting out my affairs and having to claim welfare; and having to give up the apartment, I have moved far inland across the other side of the county. This sadly, I had to do as the local paper when published that following week after me getting home, did report on my court case. But it had been on page five and there had only been a small paragraph so not many people got to see it, and I never did make the local news on the television this time. My beard did help but as most of the locals knew where I lived and the animosity I felt each time I went to the town or along the seafront was too much to bear.

I called in at the prison just after I moved as I had bought another second-hand car and to tell my Polish friend of my new address. Driving is hard without thumbs but over the past few months my grip has improved by using just my fingers.

It was very difficult getting into the prison, it being a high security one and I did not know the name of my Polish rescuer and could only describe him. The prison warder did recognize me and after disappearing for about ten minutes he came back and told me that my friend had been moved to another prison. He would not tell me what prison and as I was not a relative, the information had to be kept confidential. I let it go; life is full of surprises and not all of them are unpleasant; maybe in the years to come our paths may cross again.

My sister contacted me through social media a few months ago and I found that she is living in a lovely village in Scotland. It was difficult to believe that eighteen years have passed since we had seen each other. I did manage to visit her and she listened with shock to my horrific story but it did me good to see her well and happy, and with two dogs of course. After spending several days with her I said my goodbyes and as I walked out of her front gate and turned and waved goodbye I knew that I would never see her again; well not on this world, hopefully on the next.

I am to visit a hospital in London next month to have artificial thumbs fitted which will be a blessing, as life is sure difficult without any thumbs. My future looks hopeful and with new thumbs I may even be able to get off welfare some day.

The End

The Author

Gary L Beer was born in Kent, England and is of English and Welsh descent. After raising a family Gary went to university and achieved a BSc in Pharmaceutical Chemistry following this with a Masters Degree in Chemistry, studying nano-particle science at the very cutting edge of technology. Able to turn his hand to most things in life he has worked as a Carpenter, Car Mechanic, Panel beater, Chemist and a Teacher. Gary still enjoys writing novels and has many more publications planned for the future.

Gary has written many popular novels;

Journey Thru America My Quest For Peace
Journey Thru America The Way Home
Journey Thru America The Complete Journey
A Good Find
SUZY
Grailem
Starship Stinedern
Albraise A Traveller's Tale
Belief of the Reborn
Alashaine
A Glistening Planet

Printed in Great Britain
by Amazon